Behind His Lens

R.S. GREY

Published: R.S. Grey 2013
authorrsgrey@gmail.com
Editing: Editing by C. Marie
Cover Design: R.S. Grey
All rights reserved.
ISBN: 1494808587
ISBN-13: 987-1494808587

R.S. Grey

This book is dedicated to all my readers.
Enjoy this book with some chocolate—it's mandatory!

Chapter One

Jude

"BULLEIT NEAT, PLEASE."

I offer a half smile to the young bartender glancing up at me. A rosy tinge dots her cheeks as her eyes scour down my body like I'm a brand new Maserati with a cherry-red bow. The girl looks like she's been on her feet for the past ten hours; she's probably nearing the end of her shift. I notice this, not out of empathy, but for a more self-serving purpose. After all, I've never been with a bartender who wasn't more than willing to display her keen talents in the bedroom.

"Anything else, sir?" she drawls seductively, looking back over her shoulder as she reaches up on her toes to grab the bottle of bourbon. Her brown eyes linger on me a beat too long, as if she's hoping I'll ask for her number instead of another drink. I let my dimpled smile spread an inch wider, and just like that, I know I could take her home if I wanted. Girls are easy and that's the way I like it.

"That'll be it." I toss down a hefty tip as waves of laughter overtake the guy next to me at the bar. Bennett, my best friend and lifelong wingman, is taking a swig of his IPA, apparently entertained by the spectacle.

Pulling my glass of bourbon toward my mouth, I lean back against the bar, waiting for the bartender to walk out of earshot.

"Sorry, man, I guess some guys just have all the luck," I mock before tipping back a sip of the dry, smoky liquor. It warms my stomach like sunshine.

"Yeah right, asshole. She'll come back around and I bet she'll only have eyes for me," he goads.

This is exactly how our friendship works. Bennett and I each have our own style. He's uptown; I'm downtown. He's a fancy accounting exec and always wears a suit to the bars right after work. His dark blond hair is always slicked back with pretentious hair gel, but women eat it up. I, on the other hand, prefer brown leather boots to loafers, and I always have an afternoon's worth of stubble to run my hand across. Nevertheless, women usually go for one or the other, which is why our setup is flawless. We never leave a bar alone.

"Is that girl you met the other night meeting you here?" Bennett asks, scanning the dark club for any prospects.

Natasha. I should be excited to see her again, but it is what it is. She's hot and wanted to meet up; I didn't feel like saying no. It'll make tonight a lot easier, and after a long day, that's exactly what I need. Don't get me wrong— she knows exactly what the score is. My M.O. has been the same for four years. I meet women that want exactly what I can offer: sex with no strings attached and no hope of any kind of relationship.

Ever. Seeing Natasha for a second time is pushing it, but she made it clear that she knew what the arrangement is.

As if my thoughts have conjured her on the spot, I peer over just in time to see Natasha saunter through the club's front door. In the smoky room, it takes her a second to find me by the bar, but once she does, her seductive smile amplifies tenfold. I ignore the emptiness in my stomach. I don't feel a thing for her, but she's hot and one part of my body doesn't seem to mind watching her head over. She's wearing a skintight red dress and heels. Her brown hair falls straight to the top of her shoulders and her dark brown eyes gleam with excitement as she steps closer.

"Hey sexy," she coos once she's standing in front of me. Her gaze drifts down my body and I have to fight the urge to roll my eyes. Any concern I had about meeting up with her again is completely vaporized. We both only care about one thing.

I arrogantly drag my gaze down her body, not bothering with any pleasantries as I rub a finger across my jaw.

"This is my friend, Bennett," I finally offer, trying to feign politeness as I gesture toward him.

She flits her eyes in his direction for the briefest moment. "Nice to meet you."

Bennett lifts his beer in greeting, but by then, Natasha is already turned away, locked onto her prey—me. She looks like she's about to straddle me on the bar, and I can't help but let those images take root.

"Are you ready?" she asks, leaning forward to whisper in my ear. I bristle as her cheap perfume overwhelms my senses, but I ignore the sensation.

My dick doesn't care how she smells. With a sturdy hand I brush her curvy figure aside.

"Let me finish my drink first. Do you want something?"

This is as close as I get to dating. I'll buy her one drink and then we'll leave so we can finish the night off. I have to get up early for a shoot and I don't want her thinking she can sleep over.

She pushes her arms under her pronounced cleavage, making sure it's visible to everyone at the bar, and leans closer.

"A beer would be great," she sighs, while running her fingers down the buttons of my shirt. The act feels much too intimate and I instinctively pull her hand away with a laugh. Easy tiger.

When the bartender approaches, I order Natasha an import and watch as she brings the bottle slowly to her lips. She really is hot. She has exotic features and dark, sultry eyes. Too bad I'm not interested in getting to know the person behind them.

As the club's music grows louder, her free hand shifts to my thigh and Bennett clears his throat as she runs her hands up and down suggestively. I have to fight back a laugh. We could probably just head to the restroom here and make it a lot quicker. I brush the hair away from her shoulder and lean in to whisper those exact words. I know she's game, and honestly, it's easier. I don't even have to worry about getting her to leave my apartment afterward.

God, I'm an asshole. I chug the rest of my bourbon in a silent toast to that thought and slam it on the bar, making eye contact with the cute bartender and flashing her one more languid grin. Natasha giggles like a slutty schoolgirl behind me, drawing my attention away. I nod a goodbye to Bennett. He knows exactly what I'm planning, but he's not one to judge.

Putting my hand on the small of Natasha's back, I lead

her through the crowd, trying to decide if I want to take her in a dark corner or in one of the bathrooms. I pat the back of my jeans to confirm that my wallet and condoms are still tucked away safely; I'd never fuck around without one.

"I've been thinking about this all day," Natasha oozes sensually as we wind through the club with my hand gripping her ass.

I bite my tongue instead of commenting because to be honest, I hadn't thought of her until Bennett brought her up. She's a means to an end, and I thought we were clear about that fact.

I brush her words aside and am about to lean in to whisper some bullshit about fucking her against the wall, but the sentiment stalls on the tip of my tongue when I see *her*.

She's across the dim room on the dance floor. The crowd has parted so she's barely visible between a thin gap of dancing bodies. A few seconds later, the dancers move and she's hidden away again like a distant mirage. When the thump of the dubstep song fades into a pop remix, the crowd dwindles and I'm left with a perfect vantage. My jaw hits the floor as I watch her persuade the world around her to bend toward her presence. My eyes scan up and down her body, caught in her allure. She's wearing a flowy white dress, and I can't tell if it's that or the light blonde hair spilling down her back that makes me think she's a fucking angel.

There are bodies all around her, shuffling and dancing. Every guy that spies her tries to get closer, but her friend doesn't seem to allow it. She's like a queen among peasants.

Would her friend let me get close?

I doubt it.

The two girls dance together, smiling and getting lost in the moment, oblivious to the club-goers around them. Her friend is pretty too, exactly the type of girl Bennett would lose it over, with dark hair and a dark complexion. Has he seen her yet? This could work out perfectly.

No, it couldn't.

I've already found a girl for the night. I'm not in the habit of exerting unnecessary effort, especially when girls are just so compliant.

I become vaguely aware of Natasha rubbing my thigh and whispering in my ear, but it's nothing more than a faint buzzing. I would rather watch the angel move on the dance floor. She's completely unaware that she has the attention of every single person around her. She lifts her arms in the air, as if reaching for the wild hues strobing above her head. Then she runs the fingers of her right arm down to her left elbow, swaying to the beat of the song. I've never seen someone move so erotically, and I can feel my dick stir in my pants just from watching the innocent act. What the fuck? What the fuck am I doing?

I shake the thoughts from my head, but I can't tear my concentration away from her. I don't want this hazy dream to end.

"Baby, kiss me." Natasha shoves her glossy pink lips directly in front of me, forcing the rest of the club into hazy submission behind her. With a gruff sigh, I reluctantly oblige. This is who I am.

Wrapping my hands around her neck, I lean back against the wall and drag her in front of me. She sidles between my legs, skimming the top of my jeans with her fingers and pushing her greedy tongue into my mouth. I kiss her hard, willing every other thought out of my mind, but it doesn't help. Her mouth feels wrong.

I pull away harshly, breaking our kiss, but Natasha takes it as an invitation to string kisses down my neck. Good. It means I can gaze over her head toward the dance floor. The angel is still there, laughing with her friend and drawing me in further. Somehow the club's spotlights only seem to cast their gentle glow around her, and I can't help but want to shatter the bulbs so no one else can see her.

The thought makes me clench my eyes closed as I remind myself of reality. I don't want a girl like that. She doesn't look like the fast and easy type, and I have no business thinking about her. Get it together.

Natasha's prying finger dips between the buttons of my shirt and it hits me like a semi-truck—I have a gorgeous girl ready to let me fuck her in the back of a club and I couldn't care less. Since when?

I've got to leave. I don't want Natasha anymore and I don't trust myself to move closer to the blonde angel. She doesn't belong to me and it's better if I leave now.

"I'm leaving," I bark, grabbing my wallet and pulling out a fifty for Natasha's cab fare. It's the least I can do considering I'm leaving her hanging.

"Jude! What the hell?" I shove the bill into her hand, ignoring her confused expression. Not my problem.

"I'll see you around," I mutter flatly over my shoulder as I push through the crowd toward the front door, never once looking back.

"Jude!" Natasha calls behind me, but I keep walking.

I'll text Bennett later. He's probably already found a girl anyway. He doesn't need to know about the blonde. I plan on forgetting her myself just as soon as I get home. I usually run in the mornings, but tonight I'll take on the city's abandoned asphalt until I can't fucking move if it means I'll go back to the way I felt thirty minutes ago—

before I saw her.

As I stumble out onto the curb, I inhale a mouthful of crisp night air, trying to cleanse my senses. After a few more clarifying breaths, I realize that seeing that girl, that angel, was probably the closest I'll ever come to finding love at first sight. A twisting sensation pierces my gut at the thought.

Good thing I lost my heart four years ago...or I'd be a fool for leaving without getting her name and number.

Chapter two

Charley

"HOW'S IT GOING my sweet, hung-over friend?" I sing into the phone, knowing Naomi will kill me for calling her before her alarm. It serves her right for dragging me to the club last night. I'll admit it was fun, but I would be much more rested for the photo shoot I'm heading to if I hadn't agreed to go dancing with her.

She's so convincing though. Naomi is like a little minx that can get anyone around her to do exactly as she asks. The worst part is she isn't even obnoxious about it. I don't know how she does it, but she's exactly what I need. If we were living in a sitcom, she would be the sassy gay best friend. At every moment she tries her damnedest to get me out of my shell, even though I put up a tough fight most of the time.

"Uggh. Tell me you are not calling me at this hour—or

if you are, at least tell me you're outside my door with a Bloody Mary and a Cronut." She sounds like she's battling a drunken haze; I can't help but smile.

"Yes, Naomi, because after we go clubbing, I love nothing more than to wake up and stand in a three-hour line for a Cronut at five AM," I quip, knowing she can keep up.

"They're so good though," she hums dreamily into the phone.

"I know, such a genius idea," I relent. "I'm on my way over to MILK Studios and I wanted to check in."

"How very generous of you, my dear," she drawls sarcastically, making me smile.

"Also, I left a pumpkin spice latte outside your door."

Naomi lives a few apartment buildings down from me and there's a Starbucks in between, so I usually grab her something if I'm planning on walking by.

She squeals. "God you're the best. This is why I keep you around."

"Also for the free swag I pass on. Don't forget that."

"Never. Did you have fun last night?"

I mull over her question, twisting my head in both directions before I cross the street at a rapid pace. Even at six AM, Manhattan is already in full force. Taxis are weaving in and out of traffic as brave bikers attempt to traverse the busy roads.

"Actually I did, but that was probably because you literally stared daggers at anyone who approached us."

"Sometimes girls just wanna dance!" she sings loudly into the phone—so loud the small Asian man in the business suit crossing by offers me a snide glare. I try to shoot him an apologetic nod, but he's already looking down at his phone.

"All right crazy. Some of us have to look our best in

about…" I glance down at my watch with the thin cream band. "Five minutes ago! Crap!"

"Knock 'em dead, sister. Make sure you sneak pictures of the male models for me, though. I can't get through a day at the accounting firm unless there are booty pictures being delivered every hour, on the hour."

I toss my head back and laugh at the idea. Naomi works for a prestigious accounting firm in the financial district. Knowing her outside of work makes it nearly impossible to imagine her having a straight-laced corporate job, but she loves it. While she works a nine-to-five, my days rarely fit into standard working hours.

"I have no clue when this shoot will wrap, but I'll call you when I get off."

"Sounds good," she mumbles into the phone as I hear her open her front door to grab her latte.

As soon as I click off the call, I pull open the heavy glass door to the studios and rush inside the sleek building. I've been here so many times over the past two years, I know the layout like the back of my hand. I dart across the lobby and press the elevator call button, willing the glossy metal doors to magically open immediately. But, of course, the old monster barely clanks to life and I'm left teetering between waiting and darting toward one of the hidden staircases.

As I'm waiting for the elevator with antsy feet, a few other crew members funnel in through the glass door. I sigh, twisting around to offer them a simple smile—at least I won't be the only late one. I usually strive to be on time. In fact, being late is a major pet peeve of mine—just *one* of the engrained etiquette rules from my Upper West Side upbringing. But honestly, nothing tells someone they don't matter to you quite like showing up late for a meeting or date.

My body shuffles back and forth as I watch the numbers illuminate above the elevator doors. I'm silently praying to the speedy-elevator gods (they exist) when two girls come to stand next to me. I subtly slide my gaze toward them. From their wild pink and purple hair, I know right away they're part of the hair crew. Why is it that people who do hair for a living always seem to have the wackiest styles themselves? Maybe they get bored with the same old same old every day.

"You're Charley Whitlock, right?" the girl with pink hair asks shyly. When she speaks, I realize she's probably close to my age, if not younger. She's got bright pink eye shadow caked over her eyelids and solid black gages piercing her dainty ears. Total rocker chick. I wish I could pull off the look half as well.

"Oh, um, yes." I smile and take a sip of my coffee just as the elevator doors open and we step inside.

I don't get recognized very much, and honestly, it makes me more uncomfortable than anything else. That's not why I became a model; it's just a troubling side effect that comes along with it. I never had to worry about it in the past, but lately my jobs have picked up drastically. I'm doing more editorials and inserts than ever before. My agent, Janet, is obviously thrilled and keeps pushing me to do more and more, but soon I'll have to tell her I want to cut back. I model for the money and that's it. Modeling isn't my passion, not like painting is.

I stumbled into modeling my senior year of college and everything happened in a flash. At the time, I'd been looking for a way to make ends meet, knowing I wanted to paint full time. Modeling honestly seemed like the perfect fit until I realized my quiet life might soon be threatened.

I shrug off the uneasy feeling and remind myself that the girl only recognized me because she's in the fashion industry, and she's obviously working on the shoot. To most people I'm still a nobody.

That reassuring thought settles the nerves that have bloomed in my stomach right as the elevator dings, alerting us that we're on level three. The moment the doors slide open, the photo shoot unravels before me like a three-ring circus. Loud music pounds from a stereo system, pumping a heavy beat through the entire room. People are darting around in every direction. Stylists are picking accessories and shoes while tossing away the rejects into a messy pile. Their assistants are steaming the wrinkles out of dozens of couture gowns that hang like pieces of art in need of worship. Photographers are already checking the lighting and marks for the planned shots.

Even though the scene is a complete mess, it makes me smile. No one thinks about the manpower that goes into one single photograph in a magazine. You see the flawlessly airbrushed model and subconsciously want to buy whatever she's wearing, but no one considers the assistant that had to hold the diffuser for three hours to block unwanted shadows. I like seeing the behind-the-scenes of production; it makes the end result all the more amazing.

"Where the hell is our model?" A deep voice suddenly snaps from behind the digital monitors set up for the director and head photographer. The gruff voice takes me by surprise and I have to swallow my nerves before answering.

"I'm sorry I'm late! I lost track of time," I chirp lamely. Deep Voice doesn't even have the decency to raise his head above the monitors.

"Charley, we need you in hair and makeup, please," chimes the art director, Mrs. Hart, as she rounds the table away from the cranky photographer. Mrs. Hart is one of the best directors in the industry and I can't believe I'm getting to work with her—not to mention, at just shy of fifty, she still looks flawless. Everything about her oozes style. I've looked up to her for some time. I'll have to stay focused and make up for my tardiness. First impressions are important, and she probably already has a negative opinion of me now. I don't want her to think I'm taking this shoot for granted—it's paying my rent for five months, and in New York, that's no small feat.

"Hello, Mrs. Hart." I smile brightly. "It's such an honor to work with you. I'm so sorry for being late." I shake her hand hurriedly and keep talking as I walk toward the corner where the makeup crew is set up. Vanity mirrors hang in front of black swivel chairs.

Mrs. Hart replies with a genuine smile before turning to the inspiration boards where Polaroids of each outfit are being pinned by her assistants. I breathe a sigh of relief. At least she doesn't seem to mind that I was a teensy bit late. Now I'll just have to work on the *photographer*.

I drop my bag out of everyone's way, up against one of the black tables, and then gaze upon a sight that never seems to get old. It's the only part of modeling I don't have to pretend to enjoy. Lying on the surface of the table is every kind of cosmetic imaginable. Creamy blushes, silky mascaras, and bright lipsticks are lined up in perfect rows, ready for the taking. As a painter, I love gazing upon the rows of makeup as if they're the tools for creating the perfect masterpiece: unyielding beauty, flawless enough to conceal the demons lying beneath the surface.

I thumb a bright red lipstick that looks like a sparkling

ruby and try to commit the name to memory. *Nars - Heat Wave.* How fitting. I may have to pick up a tube on my way home later.

A throat clears softly behind me and I look up to see the pink-haired girl prepping her curling iron and smiling over at me.

"I think we'll all try to work on you at once, Charley, if that's all right?" she asks timidly. Her demureness is strange to behold in an industry where everyone seems to take what they want, when they want it. I'm usually the shyest on set, but I think she may have me beat today.

"That sounds great, Miss...?" I reply, sitting down in the black chair in front of her.

"Oh! You can call me Joanie!" she answers swiftly as she unravels a shiny black smock. Before she can slip it around me, I peel off my old college sweatshirt. The razorback tank top hidden underneath should provide me with enough warmth now that I'm inside the studio, and they'd kill me if I ruined my hair later on.

I sigh happily into the seat and meet Joanie's eyes in the large mirror before me.

"Have at it," I joke with a shrug, knowing my body is about to go through one major transformation.

In a matter of minutes, I have five different women pulling and plucking me. A small, wiry-haired woman is buffing my nails before applying a simple cream polish. Joanie is curling and tweezing my hair into a modern up-do that pulls my long blonde hair off my neck.

Most of the time I have to keep my eyes closed so the other women can work on my makeup, but every now and then I chance a peek at myself in the mirror. I know I'm pretty, or I wouldn't be hired for jobs, but it amazes me that with the help of five well-trained women, I can end up looking sort of…unreal. I realize it's just the makeup, but sometimes I let myself imagine that the radiance shining through is coming from me instead.

"How are we doing over there? Are we almost ready for wardrobe?" Mrs. Hart asks as her designer heels clap across the stained concrete floor, heading in my direction.

"Just a few last minute touches," Joanie offers sweetly. I find myself wishing I could have her with me on every photo shoot. Despite her pink rocker hair, she has quite a calming presence.

"Oh, simply gorgeous! You have the most exquisite bone structure, Charley," Mrs. Hart oozes as she pats my arm over the black smock. I feel my cheeks glow bright, even under the blush. It's not every day that a woman as influential as her notices me.

I keep my eyes closed and soak in her compliment. "Thank you, Mrs. Hart," I chirp.

"I think we ought to add a red lip though, ladies. She's wearing a cream gown for the first few shots and we want her lips to stand out."

"Oh definitely," Joanie agrees, and I hear her reaching over to grab one of the tubes off the table. I hope it's the ruby red.

Jude

Assistants bust their asses around me, shifting the lights and fixing the draping so the model can step onto the set in a moment. It's times like these that I hate my job. Models are not the easiest people to work with, especially when they're late. The last thing I need is some vapid nineteen-year-old calling the shots on my set. It appears this one is no different. I've never worked with her before and was ready to give her the benefit of the doubt until she walked in and offered apologies with that sweet voice. She probably gets away with murder with a voice like that.

"Mrs. Hart, let's do this. My crew is ready," I demand. The manicured director gives me a playful glare before she steps back to glance at the model. *All right*, I'll ease up. It's just that timing is everything with these shoots. Those women can curl hair all day if no one stops them. It's my job to keep the shoot running on time. On the other hand, I don't want to piss Mrs. Hart off. She likes me for whatever reason, and I'd like to keep it that way.

The studio we're using was designed so that the prep teams operate behind a large partition. It offers the models privacy as the crew fits and tailors their clothing, and it keeps the set a bit more controlled. Models lose focus with so many people rushing around them and I always make sure my shoots are closed to anyone who isn't absolutely necessary. Today, the crew will remain behind the partition while Mrs. Hart and I direct the model. *The model*. I guess I should learn her name. I can't very well call her *Model* when I'm ordering her around. I'm not a complete brute.

"Flawless," I hear Mrs. Hart chime behind me as she assesses the first outfit, and I turn toward her voice.

"Good, let's go," I bark, waiting for her to look over so I can give her a sly wink. She's easily twenty years my senior, but I'm sure if she were closer to my age and single, I'd be her type—and you better believe I use that fact to my advantage.

She rolls her eyes playfully at my bad attitude at the

same moment the model steps out from behind the partition behind her.

In a whoosh, the air evacuates from my lungs, leaving me gasping for a deep breath to no avail.

Fuck.

She's not the *model*.

She's the blonde from the club last night. Just like that, every ounce of resolve I built last night on my run melts into a puddle at my feet. There's a shifting feeling, almost a pang near my heart as I take her in.

My body flexes in recognition and I have to grip my camera tighter in my palm for fear it'll clatter to the ground and I'll look like a complete dunce.

What the hell are the odds? Of course she's a fucking model. She's too gorgeous to be real and any other job wouldn't suit her. All of a sudden the voice seems absolutely fitting. It's as sweet as honey and matches her perfectly.

I watch her step onto the set and walk toward me, but I don't register the movements. Instead, I take in every single detail about her. I didn't get to see her up close last night, and I now realize that if I had, I never would have left without meeting her. She has bright blue eyes that compliment her glowing skin. Her pale blonde hair is twisted up off her neck, but a few shorter pieces frame her face. So much beauty is framed between those tendrils of hair, and I have to clench my fist for fear that I'll reach out and touch her. Her body is wrapped in a gown that hugs the alluring curvature of her body. She's on the short end of the spectrum for models, maybe 5'7, which I'm assuming is why she's doing print work rather than walking the runway.

Holy hell. I want her.

I gaze down at her red lips and I instantly imagine what

her mouth would look like wrapped around my cock. Would her red lipstick smear across my skin?

"...ley" Oh shit. I glance up and notice she's been speaking this entire time. That's when I realize her petite hand is outstretched in front of her, aimed directly at me like a white flag. Too bad I'm not thinking of surrender.

I cough, standing a little taller. "I didn't catch that."

She shifts her weight and speaks softly. "I was just introducing myself. I'm Charley."

I reach out to shake her hand and like fireworks, her skin crackles against mine. She smiles coyly, glancing down at her high-heeled feet. I want to force that chin up so badly my body physically aches.

"Once again, I'm sorry I was late, but I promise I'll stay focused for you," she murmurs shyly.

For me.

Repeat after me: you do *not* date models.

"Nice to meet you, Charley. I'm Jude," I croak like a fucking fourteen-year-old boy. I clear my throat gruffly and try speaking again. "It's no problem, but we need to get started."

My hand runs through my hair to wipe away the residual tingling from my palm as she steps onto the set. My gaze lingers on her longingly as she walks away from me, and the sappy gesture snaps me back to reality. This day will be impossible to get through unless I put these bizarre feelings aside. I've never had a problem dealing with models before, but then again, I've never been affected by one the way Charley affects me.

"Let's get some music going. This place is too quiet," I bark toward my assistants. A few seconds later, Bastille's "Pompeii" floods the studio with an upbeat rhythm.

"There we go," I breathe, letting the music move

through me, reminding me of the job I need to do. My camera feels like an extension of my hand as I move closer to the white draping. Charley's already moving with soft, fluid steps, getting a feel for her gown and the scene. It's a simple set. The focus is meant to be on the dress she's wearing, so when I angle the camera's viewfinder in front of my eye, I only see Charley, outlined by a white backdrop and nothing more.

Her soft blue eyes glance up at me from beneath her black lashes. Her mouth parts slightly, waiting for my cue. I've no doubt I'll fantasize about this very moment later tonight. The moment when she finally stood before me, ready for me to command her movements and coax out her every emotion. I know she'll be receptive; she looks submissive and beautiful, ready for every bit of pleasure I'd allow her to feel.

"These first few shots need to be simple. No smile. Captivating eyes, focused straight on me," I demand, already enjoying the feeling of ordering this angel around.

"Okay," she murmurs, stepping into character.

Chapter three

Charley

HE SHOULD BE on the other side of the lens. He's too handsome to be a photographer—but on the other hand, he might even be too handsome to be a model. I know that seems strange, but it's true. This photographer, Jude, is one hundred percent *man* and thinking about him posing awkwardly in styled clothing forces me to shove down a giggle.

"Sharper face, Charley. No smiling yet," he instructs as I watch him crouch low on his heels.

Focus.

God, he's gorgeous *and* bossy. He's got that dark, second-day stubble that gives him just the right amount of ruggedness. He looks like a perfect combination of a New York intellectual and a sexy Bear Grylls, like he would read the Times while starting a fire with two dry sticks and a piece of flint. Does such a thing even exist?

I've never found my job quite so easy. He wants me to focus on him and that's what I'll do.

With pleasure.

Naomi will want to know every detail about the first man I've found attractive in quite some time, so I start at his feet, taking in the worn leather of his MacAlister boots. I know it's petty, but I can't help but judge a guy based on his choice of footwear. Luckily, Jude completely passes the test. His boots rest beneath dark wash jeans that sit perfectly low on his hips. He's wearing a vintage Yankees t-shirt that stretches across his broad shoulders and slim waist. His arms shift and flex as he moves the camera—strong, toned arms, the kind of arms you get from lifting weights and then running to counteract the overt bulkiness.

Damn. Where do they keep guys like this and why couldn't he have been at the club last night?

Yeah right. I would've still turned him down. It's the way it has to be right now. I have to focus on healing myself first.

But in the meantime, I can ogle my photographer, right? I have to be here anyway, so I might as well enjoy the view.

I lift a hand and wrap it elegantly around my neck.

"Hold there, Charley. That's perfect," he comments, and I hear Mrs. Hart agree from the sidelines. I'd forgotten she was there for a moment.

Posing is second nature to me at this point. I let the music guide me as I hit various positions, trying to show off the silky cream gown from the best angles. Florence + the Machine's "Shake it Out" blasts from the speakers and I move seductively for the camera…or maybe it's for Jude. He stays silent and keeps clicking away, so I know I'm giving him good poses.

After quite a few shots, I relax my arms by my side. Jude pulls the camera away from his face and scrolls through the last few images. With a sigh, he glances up and narrows his eyes, as if considering what we're missing. His studious pose gives me a chance to see his gaze without the bulky camera lens in the way. He's got the bluest eyes— bright aqua, maybe even lighter than mine. I've never dated a guy with blue eyes before, but that's probably because I don't date *at all.*

He shoves his hand through his unruly dark brown hair again and I have to hide a smile. Each time he does that it makes his hair even sexier, and the gesture sends a shot of lust straight to my core.

"We have great shots of the dress, but I think we should mix it up a bit." Jude's deep voice filters through the room as he turns toward Mrs. Hart.

"I agree. The Dior gown is sexy and so far these images have been beautiful but…restrained." Mrs. Hart interlaces her hands and steeples her index fingers beneath her chin in thought.

A moment later, her eyes light up and she snaps her fingers. Before I know it, she's stepping toward me with fierce determination.

"Charley, turn around and I'll unzip the dress. The draping on the back is beautiful and I think we could get a sexy shot of you showing a bit more skin."

What?

My heartbeat races as though it's losing a fight with the blood circulating through my system. My eyes dart over to Jude, but he's glancing down at his camera wearing a mask of indifference. It's not as if I haven't shown skin at a shoot before—if anything, most of these high-end fashion magazines prefer you to be completely naked while holding their products. I'm usually posing with an equally nude male model, but for some reason, Jude's eyes seem more penetrating than any I've felt before. Unable to stop myself, I second-guess Mrs. Hart's opinion.

"Are you sure? The front of the dress is so lovely." The look she shoots me says it all: it's not a model's job to direct the photo shoot. I'm meant to comply quickly and gracefully, like a life-size Barbie doll.

My hands tremble as I turn away from Jude. I can feel his eyes on me now as if he's finally catching up to the events taking place. My skin blazes under his gaze. Mrs. Hart comes to stand directly behind me, and when her chilled fingers touch my neck, I jump slightly. Pretend this is a different shoot with a different photographer, I tell myself, trying to lose focus on the white backdrop that now lies before me.

"Wait." His dark voice cascades over my skin and I clutch my eyes closed. Does he want her to stop too?

Both Mrs. Hart and I twist back to look at him. He's got his camera held deftly against his hip and he's gesturing out with his right hand.

"Only unzip the top, where Charley can't reach. I want her to do the rest. The pictures will be more seductive if she's undressing herself," he commands. Jeez. His unyielding tone demands compliance. I know Mrs. Hart will agree with his idea, but I have a feeling she would go along with his instructions even if she didn't. He has a sort of animal magnetism about him. He's the type of guy that commands immediate respect and I doubt any female is very good at telling him no.

"Absolutely," Mrs. Hart says breathily, reaching up to pull my zipper down an inch or so, only until I can reach around and touch the zipper's metal teeth with my fingers.

Mrs. Hart backs away, off the set, and I'm left alone to glance back toward Jude over my shoulder. Nerves bloom in stomach as I realize I don't have a bra on beneath the dress. It's not that I don't need one—my C-cups definitely do—but it would have been visible through the sides of the gown and Mrs. Hart opted to leave me without one. It's not usual on sets, but today it presents quite the interesting predicament.

Does he even realize? Probably not.

He drags his fingers along his bottom lip and I study his gesture intently, losing myself in the beguiling sight. My lips part and I hear myself exhale softly as a wave of light-headedness hits me. His lips look just supple enough that I wish I could feel them on every inch of my body.

"Listen carefully, Charley," Jude begins, but then he waits until I offer a delicate nod before continuing. He wants all my attention and I'm more than happy to give it to him. My body still faces away from him, but I'm twisting my neck to look over my shoulder with an arched back. The pose makes me feel alluring and I let the sensation wash over me as he stares me down.

"I want you to keep your gaze on me. Never look away as I instruct you on exactly what to do. Understand?" His voice is hard and stern, as if he's dealing with a child.

I mash my lips together, feeling my heartbeat pound against my chest.

"Charley, do you understand?" he asks again, more demanding this time. I chance a glance toward his blue eyes. They look like a summer sky—infinite and full of possibilities.

"Y-yes," I stutter, surprised by the desire laced through my voice. Can he tell?

My entire body stands motionless as he turns back to

the studio's partition. "Switch the music, Jon. Put on that Charlie Mars CD I brought. 'Nothing but the Rain' should be one of the first tracks."

A moment later, a soft melody fills the studio. It's captivating and I find myself having to press a hand to my belly as a heady mixture of nerves and excitement floods my veins.

"Don't move your head, Charley," he commands as our eyes lock together once again. The pure intensity radiating off him makes me glance down. It's as if I'll go blind if I gaze into his blue irises long enough. "Reach up with your left hand and tuck your pointer finger under your right strap, like you're about to push it off."

I do as he says, fingering the silky material until it begins to inch off my delicate shoulder.

"Good, keep looking at me," he goads gently, and I hear his camera begin to click. His expression is hidden behind his lens once again, but I want to know what he sees. I want to know if this is affecting him the way it's affecting me.

"Arch your back gently and push the strap all the way off your shoulder." His voice is steady, as if he's asking me to clap my hands rather than strip off my clothing.

The silky material causes goose bumps to rise across my skin as it slips down lower on my arm. I can't help but glance down at the naked flesh. It's completely erotic moving for him like this, knowing he's telling me to pull the strap of my dress down.

"Good. Hold it." The camera clicks in a quick succession. Each snap seems to be synchronized with the hurried rate of my heart. *Click, click, click.*

"We're going to move to the other strap now, but stop in the middle with your back to me." I start to follow his instructions and he continues giving orders. "Close your eyes and tilt your head as if you're in the throes of passion, Charley." The way my name cascades off his tongue makes it so I barely have to pretend. As I twist my body, the gown's strap falls down farther and I slide into the new pose with unbridled passion.

My back arches even more and I lace my fingers through my hair, elongating my neck for the camera.

"How beautiful, Charley," Mrs. Hart comments, and I feel a blush tinge my cheeks. I'm glad I'm not facing them right now. This show isn't for her, and if I think about her watching it'll be harder to let go and hit the poses naturally.

Jude doesn't respond to Mrs. Hart. Instead, he clicks away through the shots with a professional cadence.

"You need to remove the other strap now, Charley. Do it just the way you did it before, but I want you to bite down on your lip and make eye contact with the camera while you do it."

His words make my legs feel like Jell-O, but I take a deep breath and force myself to turn toward him again. He's standing up now, leaning on his right leg and angling the camera so it hits me from slightly above.

He must be six or seven feet away from me, but it feels like a hemisphere. My eyes lock onto his face and I watch his brow furrow intently as I push down the other strap. I take my sweet time, reveling in this fierce vixen I'm pretending to be.

She would bite her bright red lips seductively just as I'm pretending to do. She would narrow her eyes invitingly on the man she's about to go to bed with. I imagine we've just come home from some fancy fundraiser. He's wanted me for months and tonight we'll finally have each other. The thin strap slides down my arm and soon my entire back is exposed as the top half of the dress folds down over my hips in the front.

The cold studio air sends a shiver through my body and my nipples tighten into little buds. I swear I hear Jude whisper, "Fucking beautiful," but his expression remains detached so I decide I'm probably imagining it.

The top of the creamy fabric drapes around my legs, juxtaposed against my naked torso. My breasts are completely exposed to the world, but my body is still angled toward the back of the studio, so neither Jude nor Mrs. Hart can see them. Still, I reach my arms around, trying to conceal them with alluring grace. I bite my lip hard, never breaking eye contact with Jude—or rather, his camera lens.

A pool of lust settles within me, awakening every part of my body. I try to use the intimate emotions to my advantage as I focus on this dangerously sexy man pulling me out of my comfort zone with hardly any effort.

"Pull your arms down around the front of your body," he instructs hoarsely. My first instinct is to protest, but there's no denying the whims of this man. My hands tremble as I wrap my arms around my body so they hold my quivering stomach, but he doesn't start clicking away like normal. He shakes his head, places the camera down on the media table, and then turns back toward me with sharp focus.

A sinking realization hits my gut. Oh god, he's going to come adjust my pose.

My stomach twists into a ball of anxiety as his footsteps echo against the studio floor. My eyes grow wide and I wonder if he plans on adjusting me from the front. Oh god, oh god. *Relax*.

This is my job. Plenty of photographers and stylists have seen my naked body before. The photos never end up exposing anything, and I've never posed for anything too risqué, but I don't know what will happen if Jude comes closer. I want him to touch me so badly, but I don't think I'll be able to hold up my facade if he does. I can practically feel myself wilting toward him and he hasn't even touched me yet.

I lick my lips instinctively and watch him step closer until he's right behind me. His scent immediately invades my senses. It's a hint of deodorant mixed with his natural aroma. The combination is fresh and intoxicating. I immediately crave more—more of his scent overwhelming my psyche as his body presses against mine.

His breath touches the back of my neck and I jump slightly, realizing that even in my heels he's got a few inches on me. If he craned his neck a hair to the left he could see past my shoulders to my bare chest, but I think he's letting me keep my privacy on purpose. Why?

My eyes fall to the floor as I try to gather resolve, waiting for his touch. I focus on my slow exhale, trying to ignore his warm breath against my naked back.

His touch never comes. I flick open my eyelids and look up to see him standing inches behind me with his hands clenched at his sides.

His blue eyes bore into mine. "Unwrap your arms from around your waist, Charley."

My grip loosens immediately, as if his vocal cords are connected to my body's synapses, and I let my arms fall. I hadn't even realized I was clutching the dress so tightly.

"Interlace your fingers gently in front of your hips instead," he instructs.

I don't break his eye contact even though his blue eyes seem to jar every nerve ending in my body. It feels like a challenge having him this close to me. Just as I move to lace my fingers together, my thumb trails across the sensitive flesh between my legs. Even though my skin is cloaked beneath my underwear and the gown, a rush of pleasure forces my eyes closed as my body shutters. What the hell is he doing to me? *I'm on set.*

His almost inaudible sigh tells me he's aware of how turned on I am from this little game. *He's doing it on purpose.* He wants a good photo and he knows what he has to do to get it.

Just as I think he's going to turn back for his camera, he leans in gently and whispers in my ear, sending chills across my flesh.

"Bend your elbows a bit; the arc of your torso is alluring and I don't want you to hide it." He bites out the instructions as if angry with me for concealing it in the first place.

I didn't think he was going to touch me. I thought he'd walk away, which is why I can't prevent the soft moan that escapes my lips when his hands wrap around the side of my torso. His warm palms ignite the skin just under my shoulder blades. The tips of his long fingers hit the sides of my breasts. His touch sets my skin on fire, and I close my eyes, wanting to block out every other sense. I'm not at a photo shoot. I'm not in a Dior gown posing for my photographer. I'm hardly sentient. His touch turns me into a pile of tingling sensations, throbbing need laced with adrenaline and lust. His touch is the only thing that matters. I love the difference in texture, my skin soft and smooth against his strong, calloused hands—hands that practically wrap around my entire body.

"Do you feel that, Charley?"

I feel nothing, not the floor beneath my feet or the studio lighting against my skin—only his touch.

When I don't respond, his hands slide slowly down the length of my torso, sending delicious shivers down my spine.

"Yes," I whisper so gently I'm sure he doesn't hear.

I clear my throat, trying to temper the lust building within me. His hand gently squeezes my waist, demanding a reply.

"Yes," I murmur, a little louder this time.

"Show the camera what you feel, Charley," he commands in my ear before dropping his hands and walking away. The moment he cuts off his touch, my surroundings rush back in like a crashing wave. My body cries out in protest as my eyes flash open and a deep inhale floods my lungs. Was I holding my breath that whole time?

Chapter Four

Charley

"MY APARTMENT IS eerily quiet this morning. Normally the sounds from the corner bakery next door drift up to my room, but I'm awake earlier than usual. I doubt the bakery has even unlocked its friendly yellow doors yet.

I've lived in Greenwich Village for the past two years. It feels more like home than anywhere I've lived before, including the sprawling townhouse on the Upper West Side that I shared with my parents for eighteen years. That place can't be considered a home. Not anymore.

My apartment, or rather my tiny room, combines a bedroom, bathroom, and kitchen into one open area. There's no space for a real painting area, but I make do. The apartment is inside an old townhouse my landlord, Mrs. Jenkins, remodeled after her husband passed away. There are four separate apartments on the bottom floor.

Mrs. Jenkins kept the second story for herself. She's a sweet woman and there would be many nights I'd go hungry if she wasn't there tapping on my door with extra pasta or a casserole in tow.

It's not that I purposely forget to eat. I lost my appetite four years ago and most of the time I have to remind myself to nourish my body. I should take better care of myself, but usually I'm lost in a painting and can't be bothered, especially when I never *feel* hungry.

The strange thing is, no matter how little I eat, my body still has the energy to run. It craves it. Every morning I get up and traverse my neighborhood streets. I have a strict route and I adhere to it like my life depends on it.

Except on Saturday mornings.

Every Saturday I drag Naomi to Central Park and we bask in the beautiful landscape as we do our weekly run together. I'll admit, I usually have to persuade her to go, but she doesn't fight much once we start.

In an hour or two I'll meet her outside her apartment and we'll take the subway up to 60th Street. We'll hop out at the bottom edge of the sprawling green space, stretch out, and start our run.

The only problem is, I'm not sure what to do to occupy my time until then.

I have two hours to glance numbly around my empty apartment.

I don't like these gaps of time in my life. I keep my schedule filled to the brim with activities, carefully planning each hour of my day. These unforeseen quiet moments are when my thoughts drift toward the blackness I've fought so hard to leave behind. The phrase *An idle mind is the devil's playground* repeats in my head as I glance down at my phone to see it's only a quarter after five in the morning.

I know I woke up early today because of *him*—because of Jude. I could barely get to sleep last night. Every memory of the day replayed behind my closed eyes, keeping my senses tingling and my mind racing.

After the gown 'incident', he practically ignored me. Mrs. Hart directed most of the remaining shoot, which ended up wrapping earlier than I was expecting. She loved the first shots so much the next few outfits only took a few minutes to shoot. By the time I'd returned from scrubbing off my makeup and changing back into my clothes, the set had been all but deserted. Jude's assistants were meandering around, breaking down lights and packing up diffusers; Jude was nowhere to be found.

I guess his work was done.

With a sigh, I roll onto my side to examine the early morning light casting shadows across my room. I would try to forget about him completely, but our photo shoot recommences on Monday after Mrs. Hart and her team finalize the fall fashion pieces they want to feature. Will he be there Monday?

I was actually sad when I realized he was gone.

But what was I expecting? He works with models all day, every day. It's clear any attraction felt was strictly one sided. I tug a hand through my hair to jar me from the embarrassing realization. Enough.

Before my brain can protest, I jump up and throw on my black capri leggings and blue Lululemon pullover then lace up my sneakers. I've got to get out of here. I'll check my mail and then see if Mrs. Jenkins is awake. She's always eager to chitchat, especially when I agree to eat some coffee cake with her.

• • •

The red line is empty when we board at the Greenwich Village stop. Naomi and I plop down next to each other on a pair of orange plastic chairs. She always lets me have the window seat so I can stare out and watch the dark tunnel whip by.

"I hate you, did I mention that already?"

Breaking my trance, I smile over at her and pretend to look up toward the subway's worn metal roof in recollection.

"Umm, once when I dragged your ass out of bed, then again when I literally had to tie your sneakers for you, and a third time when a tiny tear rolled down your cheek as you realized that today we have to run an extra mile to make up for last week."

Naomi has quite the flair for the dramatic. I secretly think she has to act so normal at her accounting job that she bottles up all her craziness and unloads it all at once as soon as we're together.

My sassy list makes her crack a smile, and she wraps an arm around my shoulders, bringing me toward her for a side hug.

"I think that should suffice then," she quips happily, apparently done with her pity party for now.

"I should just let you get fat," I tease, leaving my head against her shoulder.

"Impossible. My mother's English and my father's Swiss and Nigerian. Due to my lack of fat-ass American genes, I will have this killer bod until the day I die."

I shake my head because sadly, I know she's right.

Naomi is sickeningly gorgeous. Her lightly tanned skin and warm brown eyes are the kind every girl covets.

"Leave it up to the Swiss to produce a baby as cute as you," I tease, as I pinch her cheek.

She shoots me a playful glare and I sigh, happy to be in this element with her. Naomi makes me feel light, like nothing bad has ever happened or will ever happen. I soak up her happiness like a sponge, hoping it'll fuel me long after we've separated for the day.

We sit in silence for a few minutes as she checks her phone and twists a finger through her glossy ponytail. As we get closer to Central Park, the subway steadily fills and once again, I find myself daydreaming out the square window. The memory of Mrs. Jenkins' cinnamon swirl cake from earlier almost puts a smile on my face, but then I remember what was waiting for me in my mail this morning. On the very top of the stack of bills and junk lay a thick, eggshell white envelope engraved with my mother's initials in swirly calligraphy.

I guess I'd lost track of time. Usually I expect her "quarterly check-ins" a few days in advance, but her letter caught me off guard this morning. Her notes wouldn't come at all, except for the fact that I caved two years ago and told her my address. She wouldn't stop hounding me and even threatened to call the police and place a missing persons report, so I thought it'd be easier to just give in. However, each time one of her monogrammed letters arrives, I regret that decision all over again.

The cops would have been a nice change of pace to be honest.

With unsteady hands I tore the envelope open and peeked in to see her standard stationery tucked in front of a check made out to me. I didn't even glance at the amount. I walked back into my apartment, pulled the battered memory box from my closet, and placed the letter and check behind all the others.

Nice talking to you mother, do visit again soon.

"So, do you want to tell me more about Photographer Boy?" Naomi asks, breaking me out of my mother-filled reverie.

My heart instantly leaps at the memory of Jude. I don't look at her right away for fear that she'll see the emotions written across my face. The memory of his touch makes my body instantly feel warm and I know Naomi will see the flush on my cheeks. My eyes stay glued to the tunnel walls as they whip by my window.

"Not really, no," I mutter, barely loud enough for her to hear me over the rumbling of the subways tracks.

She knows better than to push me, but she's probably still upset that I've closed the subject off so suddenly. I'd texted her yesterday during a break in the shoot to give her quick details about Jude, but when he left abruptly I changed my mind about discussing him with her.

"All right, but for the record, he sounded seriously hot."

I don't respond because there's nothing to say other than *you have no idea*.

The subway screeches to a stop and more New Yorkers file into the confined space. An elderly Latino woman sinks into the seat in front of us, clutching her oversized purse on top of her feeble lap. I focus on her, studying the colorful pattern on her bag and the beautiful mix of charcoal and ashen tones in her hair. She's a nice distraction from Naomi's prudent stare, which I feel burning a hole into the side of my face.

When I'm silent for another minute, Naomi finally nudges my shoulder. "I forgot to tell you my friend from work is playing a soccer game in Central Park today. I told him we'd run by and say hello if we got the chance."

I don't really feel like meeting her friends, but it doesn't matter. I already closed up the option of discussing Jude and saying no to chatting with her friend would hurt her feelings.

So, I plaster on a simple smile and turn toward her.

"Sounds good. Have I met him before?"

"Nope. He works in a different department and we only met last week during one of our company-wide meetings. His name's Bennett."

I mull over the name, trying to recall if I knew any Bennetts growing up, but no one comes to mind. "Sounds cute," I confer. "Is he a friend-friend? Or a friend-soontobedating-friend?"

Her lips curl into a private smile and her honey-brown eyes stay pinned to her leggings. Even without a reply, it's obvious she's excited about potentially running into him.

"Good, at least one of us is going to get some," I wink as the subway pulls up to our stop.

• • •

"He said they're on the Great Lawn near 85th Street," Naomi declares between shallow breaths as we stop for water.

I brush away the drop of sweat trickling down my forehead with the back of my hand. "Sounds good. Let's take the outer loop and we'll cut across to the lawn."

She nods in agreement and pulls the plastic water bottle from her mouth, but then she hesitates. Her shoulders slump and her dark brows furrow in thought.

"Am I an idiot for agreeing to meet up with him after I've gone running?" she asks. It's rare to see the vulnerable side of Naomi and I never quite know how to approach it.

"Why? You look athletic and glowing!" I assure her, and she does actually. The whore.

"I don't believe you," she huffs as we start to jog again. We pull out onto the trail behind a group of moms pushing strollers and running full speed as if they're competing in a marathon. *Only in New York.*

"You look double skinny, like dehydrated-chic," I try to tell her with a straight face, but then we both crumble into hysterical laughter.

All joking aside, I can count on one hand the number of insecure moments Naomi has had in the four years we've been best friends.

"Naomi, do you honestly think I would let you meet this guy if you looked anything but gorgeous right now? Hasn't it been proven that men like the smell of women after they've worked out? Something about the pheromones." She's smiling by this point, so I know I've got her hooked.

"I'm pretty sure men like women if they have the correct hip to waist ratio for making babies." She drawls out her speech, saying the word *babies* like an old burly man would. We both burst out laughing once again as we run and I have to grip my side as a sharp cramp forms. Why do I think trying to run with her is a good idea?

I sigh. "God…why does that sound so gross to me?"

"Because it's weird. If I remember correctly from freshman psych, we like men when they smell like they've worked out because we know they can take care of us…evolutionarily speaking. It's like survival of the fuckable-est," she adds with a wink.

Just then, an overly tanned, muscly man straight off the

Jersey Shore runs by in a bright neon green tracksuit. I glance over toward Naomi the second he's out of earshot.

"Oh, yeah. I bet he could take care of me. He looks like an alpha hunter-gatherer for sure…" I raise my eyebrows suggestively and we both erupt in another fit of giggles.

"Don't even go there."

Not even in my dry spell would I go for a man like that. Wait—can you call it a dry spell when you haven't had sex in three years? More like the freaking Dust Bowl.

The Great Lawn is gorgeous. It's what most people imagine when they think of Central Park. A multitude of trails wind throughout most of the park, but the Great Lawn is a huge undivided space with fresh, soft grass, rimmed with maple and pine trees.

Today it's even more magical than usual because the seasons are changing; the air has been doused with a crisp chill, leaving the sweltering heat of July and August in our distant memories.

Fall in New York is a sight to behold. The city's trees transform from dark green to bright hues of copper and gold. Then practically overnight their leaves drop to the ground in heavy piles. I love hearing the sharp crunch beneath my shoes as we tread over the fallen leaves that dot the trail like red tears.

Naomi and I wander around, cooling off from our run while trying to spy her friend. People are spread out everywhere and I assume it has to do with the temperature. I can't imagine anyone staying indoors on a day like this. Families are having picnics and groups are spread out, playing Frisbee and baseball. I take in a cluster of middle-aged men dressed in matching raglan shirts that sport their names printed boldly on the back.

"He said he's with a group of ten guys," Naomi offers

as she scans the crowd. We weave through a line of children jumping rope and then round a little row of pine trees. When we step to the other side, Naomi freezes in her tracks and I feel her nerves practically crackle through the air. Her brown eyes are wide and she's staring straight ahead as if she sees a ghost. I slowly follow her gaze and lock onto the most beautiful sight I have ever seen.

"If we get to choose, I definitely want this to be my heaven," I quip as I take in the group.

Ten guys are spread out in the clearing. Not a single one of them is wearing a shirt, and even from a distance I can see the sweat dripping down their bodies. This is not your run-of-the-mill soccer team. No, these guys look as if they've just stepped off the pages of Sports Illustrated. David Beckham, eat your heart out.

"Please, dear god, tell me that is Bennett's group," I implore dreamily, pulling my gaze from the men.

Naomi still looks like a deer caught in headlights and I'm glad we're far away. It's clearly the right group, but if we wandered over now, she would make a complete fool of herself. I whip myself in front of her and put my hands on her shoulders, gripping them gently.

I stare into her chocolate brown eyes and shake some sense into her. "Yes, that is a group of sexy, sexy men, but you are one sexy female and could have your pick of any of them," I declare confidently. As I speak, the glossiness behind her gaze lifts and a wicked grin forms on her lips. The little minx is back.

"Let's go." She winks and pulls me forward. We're still a couple yards off and I use the distance as an opportunity to ogle the men as much as I want. Of course, the common denominator is that they all have rippling soccer bodies, but that's where the similarities end. They're clearly all from different cultures and different walks of life. One of the guys has wild, curly hair, and I find myself smiling as he does a silly victory dance after blocking a shot in the goal he's tending.

"Bennett's the blond guy playing midfield," Naomi explains as we get closer. I pull my eyes away from the curly-haired goalkeeper to find the man she's referring to. He's gorgeous, of course, with short blond hair and sharp features, but that's not what makes me clutch my hand to my throat. No, that reaction stems from the man Bennett is standing next to—Jude.

They rest there, catching their breaths and talking without even realizing we're approaching. They look like an erotic fantasy, standing close together like that. There's no comparison though; Jude is hands down the sexiest man on the field. He's got a few inches on Bennett and his dark, unruly hair yanks at the strings of my desire before I've even scanned down his naked torso.

My lips curl into a private smirk as I recollect my theories from yesterday. I knew he worked out and his chiseled body now confirms it. The morning sun glistens off his tanned chest and I have to clench my eyes closed in defeat.

"What's wrong?" Naomi asks, and I nearly jump at her words.

"Jeez. Settle down." She puts her hand on my shoulder and I can feel myself trembling against her palm beneath my tight running shirt.

"Bennett is talking to Photographer Boy," I peep quietly as I pry my eyes open. The look on Naomi's face is absolutely priceless.

In slow motion, her mouth drops open and her head swivels to where the two guys stand.

"No. Way. No. Freaking. Way."

"That guy is too sexy to be real." Her head snaps back to me and I shake my head, glancing down to the ground. I stare toward the golden leaves crunching underneath my neon-colored sneakers. Yes. Freaking. Way.

"Do you want to leave? We can go right now, Charley," she offers, and her sweet tone finally makes me lift my gaze. Bennett and Jude are glancing over at us, along with the other eight guys. I gulp; it's too late to leave now.

"No. No, it's fine. We've come this far and Bennett already noticed you." His wide smile shows exactly how happy he is to see her and it's almost bright enough to block out Jude's confused scowl.

Without another word, we start walking again and I try to focus on anything other than Jude. It doesn't work though. He draws my attention as though he's the sun, and I'm helpless against his overpowering rays. The chiseled v-line of his obliques leads down to his navy soccer shorts. I think that's called an Adonis belt, and god—now I know why. His shorts sit low on his hips and then cut off above his knee, revealing his mouth-watering legs and chiseled abs. Both of his strong hands grip his waist in a closed stance, making it clear I'm far from welcome.

"Naomi!" Bennett calls as we approach. He jogs over to greet us and I have to look away. The scene is practically nauseating as they meet midway and he kisses her on the cheek. I give them maybe a week before it's official.

"This is my friend, Charley," Naomi offers, and I force myself to look up and be polite. I really am happy for her. Naomi has had a string of bad relationships and this guy seems genuinely excited she's here; I can't help but like him.

I run my hand through my long ponytail and step

forward. With a big smile, I offer my hand. "Nice to meet you, Bennett." His hazel eyes lock onto mine and in that brief moment I understand I'm not a complete stranger to him. Jude either filled him in yesterday or just a minute ago as we walked up. Either way, the mischievous glint in his eyes tells me I won't get to pretend Jude doesn't exist.

"Nice to meet you too, Charley." He smiles knowingly. "Thanks for forcing Naomi out of bed this morning." He shifts his eyes to Naomi, and I swear I can see a blush form beneath her tan skin. Naomi, you little sap.

Suddenly a voice booms behind us. "Are you two going to play or what?" I look up just in time to see the curly-haired goalkeeper run over with a lazy smile. As he steps close, I realize he's handsome beneath his crazy hair and something about his easygoing attitude makes me lower my guard.

"Only if you teach me that little victory dance of yours," I muse with a grin. My compliment lights up his face, and for a moment I ignore the sensation of Jude's eyes pinned on me.

"Looks like we got a keeper, Bennett!" he quips with a slight accent threaded through his words, pronouncing keeper as *keepa*.

"I'm Tom by the way," he offers.

"Are you from Australia?" I ask with a smile.

His hand claps against his chest as he feigns heartbreak. "New Zealand! I'm a Kiwi, love!"

The gesture is so over the top I can't help but laugh.

Tom dribbles the ball between his feet. "So you are guys going to join?"

"I think we'll just watch if that's okay?" Naomi interjects, glancing toward me for backup. She has nothing to worry about; I'm not running around pretending I know

48

a thing about soccer with Jude watching. Over my dead body.

"Sounds good." I smile, glancing toward the center of the field. Jude hasn't moved an inch. His bright blue eyes are focused directly on me and he shakes his head once, slowly. Excuse me, you don't own Central Park.

"What's his problem?" Naomi asks as we walk together toward the side of the field. We didn't bring a blanket or chairs, so we sprawl out on the dry grass to watch the remainder of their game.

"I have no idea…"

Jude

"So is she single?" Tom asks with a hopeful tone.

"How would I know?" I bite out gruffly.

The four other guys on my team stand around me in a tight circle. We're meant to be discussing strategy for the second half of the game, but all four of them practically started salivating the moment the girls walked up. Why the hell is she here? The universe seems to be playing a cruel joke by forcing our paths to cross three times within the three days—although technically, she doesn't know about that first time at the club, and that's the way I'll keep it.

Josh narrows his eyes on Charley. "There's no way a girl like that is single. Although her friend is pretty, too. I guess Bennett already claimed her?"

"Claimed her? Who talks like that?" I snap a little too angrily.

The guys shuffle around on their feet until Tom breaks the silence.

"Yeah well, sorry mates, but I already made Charley laugh, so I guess that settles it, right?"

"Oh, fuck off, Tom," Josh laughs, punching his arm.

I want to kill them all.

I left the photo shoot yesterday the moment Mrs. Hart was satisfied with the shots we got. I shouldn't have touched Charley. I didn't plan on doing it when I walked over to adjust her pose, but I lost control the moment I stepped close to her. Her skin was so beautiful and I just needed to know what she felt like, how her radiant skin felt beneath my touch. She responded to it, blossoming like a flower, and it killed me to have to walk away. I hate myself for getting that close. I was a fool to think I could contain myself around her and now she's here, testing my will again all too soon.

Fuck.

I chance a glance over my shoulder. I just want to look at her. I know I shouldn't, but when she's wearing an outfit like that, there's not a man alive that could resist.

Her tight running top sticks to her skin, hugging her breasts. Her long, toned legs are stretched out in front of her as she leans back onto her palms. Her friend says something and I watch with steadied focus as Charley tips her head back and laughs freely. The sun highlights her golden hair and even without a stitch of makeup, she's the most gorgeous woman I've ever seen. I want to make her laugh like that. I want her to smile for me the way she smiles for her friend.

"Hey team captain, wake up! Aren't you meant to be leading us?" Josh quips, and I roll my eyes at being caught staring. Fuck them. I don't care what they think. Besides, they know the kind of lifestyle I live. There's no way they'd be able to guess the kind of thoughts running through my mind right now.

After all, *Jude* and *monogamy* don't even belong in the same conversation.

I glance back at the guys and notice Tom studying me intently.

"So she was the model on your shoot yesterday?" He's goading me and I know it.

"No, it was your mother, Tom," I answer flatly, but the guys all laugh anyway.

"Yeah, yeah." He groans, brushing my lame comeback aside. "Is she fair game?" he asks, tilting his head to the side, clearly not willing to give up yet. Four pairs of eyes stare back at me, waiting for my reply, and every nerve ending screams for me to say no. No, she's not fair game. She's mine. She belongs to me and she's off limits.

But I can't say that.

"Go for it. I don't date models, remember?" God, I'm a terrible liar. I don't think I could be locking my jaw or clutching my fists any tighter, and I know Tom can tell.

I groan angrily. "Can we play soccer already? You guys can fight over her later. Let's go!"

I reel back and yell for Bennett, "Is your team ready?"

Charley's head pops up at the sound of my voice, but I don't glance over. I know my tone is harsh, but I can't seem to control any part of my body at the moment, which is only pissing me off more.

"You'll have to excuse my friend, ladies. It's not often he's around such beautiful women." Bennett winks over to the girls and I hear them laugh. Charley's giggle sends a shiver down my spine and I have to shake out my shoulders to get rid of the foreign sensation.

After a brief word, we break from our huddle and move around the field to take our positions. I end up in midfield, a few feet from Charley. By the time I'm in place, everyone is still getting to their spots, so I hunch over, resting my hands on my knees and steadying my breath before the game starts again. I glance around to see that the guys are all busy fixing their shoes or stretching out, so I know I have this moment to myself. I grip my hands on top of my knees even tighter, and before I think better of it, I twist my head toward Charley. She's sitting a few feet away from me so my movement catches her attention. Within a second, she's staring up at me with wide blue eyes, as if she can't possibly pull her gaze from mine. Her innocent expression makes it impossible to hold back my grin, and without a second thought, I shoot her a slow wink.

Her mouth literally drops and my grin spreads even wider across my face. I know I must be an enigma to her. I'm a complete jackass one minute and then I wink at her the next, but that's the way it has to be. I want her, but she should just stay away from me.

Then why are you winking at her, asshole?

I shake my head harshly and turn away without a second glance. Luckily, Tom tosses the soccer ball across the field and the game begins, saving me from making anymore mistakes. For the next thirty minutes I'm going to focus on soccer and not the angel on the sidelines who is stirring up feelings in my hardened heart.

Chapter Five

Charley

"SO WE'LL MEET at The Village Tavern around nine?" Bennett asks Naomi.

The soccer game ended a few minutes ago and everyone's sitting in a circle swapping out their cleats for sneakers and shrugging on t-shirts, much to my chagrin. Goodbye heavenly dream.

"Sounds good. That place is really close to where Charley and I live." She smiles over at me and I offer a small nod. It's intimidating being in a group with so many attractive men, not to mention the man sitting directly across from me. I can't meet his eyes and we haven't said a single word to each other this whole time. Is he purposely ignoring me? Did I make him mad yesterday? No. He can probably just tell how much he affects me and he doesn't want to lead me on. But what about that wink? Naomi saw him do it too, so I know we'll break it down the second we're alone.

A few of the guys start to stand and say their goodbyes. Before he leaves, Tom offers me a wide grin and tells me he'll see me later. I'm happy he'll be at the bar. He's easy to be around, unlike *some* people.

A beat later, Bennett hops up and walks over to stand in between Naomi and me so he can grab our hands and pull us up. Naomi giggles like a schoolgirl. She seems to really like him and I can't wait to tell her how much I approve. All my instincts tell me he's a good guy.

After Bennett drops my hand so he can wrap both around Naomi, I reach down to grab my water bottle. The moment I stand, Jude's intoxicating scent wraps around me and I inhale deeply before standing back up. He's finally going to acknowledge me. I shift my gaze up to see him standing a few inches away. Instinctively, I turn toward Naomi for help, but she's wrapped up in whatever Bennett's saying.

"How's your endurance, Charley?"

My mouth hangs open as I turn back to Jude.

What? What the hell kind of question is that?

"What?" I don't even try to hide the shock in my voice.

I watch as his innuendo settles in and he has the decency to glance down at his feet before meeting my eyes again. No. Stop. Stop being charming.

"I meant, do you run every day?" he clarifies with a sly smile. I watch the corners of his lips curl up with intense concentration. His mouth looks like it was made for whispering dark thoughts in dark corners.

"Every morning," I answer in a clipped tone, trying to conserve my composure. Then I feel bad for cutting the conversation off, so I add, "It looks like you work out a lot too."

His smile widens and adorable dimples dot his cheeks.

"I try to stay in shape…"

My eyes drift down his body. Obviously he does.

"Will you be at the photo shoot on Monday?" I ask, wanting to know if I should prepare myself for his presence.

"Of course. Why wouldn't I be there? It's a two day shoot."

"Oh, you just left so quickly yesterday." I chew on my lip. Should I have acted like I didn't notice?

"There was nothing left for me to do. My assistants handle the grunt work."

He doesn't mean for his words to slice me, but they do. They cut right through me and I can no longer meet his eyes.

"Ah," I murmur, twisting the lid on and off my water bottle.

He clears his throat and I glance up to watch him wring out his hands. "Will you be at the bar later?"

I slide my gaze toward Naomi and Bennett. I know she'll make me go even if I'd rather not. "Looks like it," I answer, tilting my head to the lovebirds. His eyes slide in their direction and he smirks gently before recovering his cool demeanor. I guess we'll both be there against our will. How romantic.

"Then I'll see you later," he clips sternly, as though we're planning a business meeting. My water bottle crinkles as I wring my hands around the hard plastic.

I chew on my lip and nod, but I don't reply. Instead, I turn on my heel to grab Naomi so we can begin the trek home.

"Oh, and Charley," Jude calls behind me. I turn around

to see the sun glinting off his icy blue eyes. "That running gear might be even *sexier* than that first gown you wore for the shoot."

His words—delivered so confidently in what I will later realize to be his trademark arrogant demeanor—practically burn my body into a pile of crumbled ash on the spot.

• • •

"Nothing about him makes sense. He's completely cold and distant one minute and the next he's winking at me or telling me I look good in my running gear. I feel like I get whiplash when I'm around him and I don't know how to handle it. Most guys are easier. I can read their personality and mold to the situation, but Jude keeps me on my toes. I never know if he's going to tell me to fuck him or fuck off."

"And which would you like to do?" Naomi mocks in a therapist tone before breaking out in giggles.

"Neither!" I huff, pulling the bathroom curtain closed.

"You know it doesn't really count as a dramatic exit when you don't even have a door separating your bathroom from your bedroom."

"Yeah, well pretend I slammed my door really loudly because you're supposed to be on my side!"

"I am!" she assures me, ripping back the curtain and looking at me with her puppy dog eyes. "Charley, don't let him get to you. Yes, he might be the hottest man we've ever seen, but he's too complicated! Relationships shouldn't be complicated. They should make you happy. Like Tom. He made you happy right? And he's cute underneath that mop of hair."

"*And* he has an accent," I add meekly.

"See! Just stick close to Tom and you'll be fine. Jude probably won't even come."

But he told me he'd be there.

"Fine," I huff. "Will you pour me another shot?" I ask, batting my eyelashes up at her. I've been ready for the past half hour, and I've used the remaining time building up my liquid courage.

"Charley," she reprimands me like my mother. "You're tiny and you never drink. Do you think another shot is a good idea?"

I give her a pointed stare. "Do you want me to go with you tonight, Naomi?"

"Absolutely."

"Then please, my sweet, exotic bonita, pour me another shot."

"That sentence doesn't even make sense." But it works because I watch her walk over to the cheap bottle of tequila and pour another few ounces into my 'I Love NY' shot glass.

"Oh, but doesn't it?" I cock an eyebrow seductively.

"Nope. Still doesn't," she laughs before stepping closer with a determined pace. "Can I make your eye makeup darker? Your lip gloss and mascara combo could be worn by a thirteen-year-old."

"Be my guests," I say before tipping back my fifth shot. I know I'll be toast before we even make it to the bar, but that's not my problem. Or is it? I can't seem to decide in my tipsy stupor.

"God, are you already drunk? You just pluralized 'guest'. You realize that, right?"

I place my hands on her shoulders and try to focus. "Naomi. Work your magic and give me a sultry look. I want Jude to realize what he's missing."

I expect her to laugh off my comment, but I think she can tell that deep down I'm dead serious. I want to be the sexy vixen I was pretending to be during the photo shoot. I want the part of Jude that thinks I look good in my workout clothes to fawn all over me tonight. His demeanor might be all over the place, but I know what I want and with the aid of alcohol, I'm confident enough—or just inebriated enough—to let myself realize it.

• • •

"C'mon, Charley." Naomi tugs my hand lightly as we step inside the dim bar. I know we're running late because Naomi repeated it three times in the cab on the way over and then she practically tumbled out of the cab before the driver even stopped near the curb.

She took forever with my eye makeup, but I'm secretly glad. It was just the right amount of time to allow the alcohol to hit me like a slow, seductive wave. I'm just the right amount of tipsy. You know, the point at which you wink at the bouncer when you hand him your ID, but you don't throw up on his patent leather loafers. I feel good. Naomi let me stick with the clothes I'd already picked out. My skinny jeans are tucked into light gray suede ankle boots and I've got on my favorite black off-the-shoulder sweater.

The Village Tavern is a low-key bar, but it's still packed on a Saturday night. Warm bodies move against one another, vying for the bartender's attention. Just as I step up to join the ranks, Naomi tugs my arm.

"Not yet. Let's find the guys." She raises her eyebrow

challengingly and I know I don't want to pick this battle. I'll just get a drink when we sit down. "Sexy 'bonitas' don't buy drinks for themselves, Charley," she adds with a silly eye roll.

I'm not usually like this. Alcohol always reminds me of my mother, but tonight I'm pushing those memories aside and indulging in the blissful euphoria swirling around me. All I know is before I started drinking, my stomach was in knots about seeing Jude again, but now I'm excited. I *hope* he's at the table with the guys. Bring on your sexy broodiness, Jude.

"Naomi, is broodiness a word?" I ask through tipsy giggles.

She glares back at me, but I still see the hint of a smile. She's nervous about seeing Bennett; I can feel the tension emanating from her and I wish I could reassure her of his interest, but nothing I say gets through to her.

"Charley!" I hear someone call behind us, and I twist around to see Tom walking back from the bar. He's balancing a few beers in his hand, so I assume he's getting the first round for everyone. Everything about him puts me at ease. He's wearing a plaid flannel button-down and his curly hair hangs over his forehead. His smile widens even more as he gets closer to us.

"You guys look great!" he shouts over the music. I laugh, thinking about how bars are such funny places. Too loud to hear what anyone is saying, too dark to see what anyone looks like, but at the end of the night everyone gets laid anyway.

Naomi nudges her sharp elbow into my back and pulls me out of my random musing.

Oh, right.

"Thanks, Tom. You look cute too," I offer because it's

true. He looks happy and carefree—just like what I plan to be tonight.

"Sorry I didn't get you guys a drink, but I'll walk you to the table and then head back to the bar," he offers with a side grin.

"Sounds good," Naomi says quickly, obviously wanting to make it to the table sooner rather than later. I've never seen her like this.

"Lead the way." I gesture and fall in line behind the two of them. I stick close to Naomi so I don't lose them in the crowd and as I crush myself between bodies, my bracelets cling together; I glance down to make sure they aren't falling off. I always wear bracelets and rings, having perfected the art of layering from watching the stylists do it so often. I swap jewelry out all the time, but my grandmother's antique ring always dots the middle finger of my left hand.

"You guys made it!" I hear Bennett call in front of us with unmasked elation. He's not playing the role of cool, calm, and collected. His emotions for Naomi read across his face like an open book, and I watch as she rounds the table to take the seat next to him. He leans in to kiss her on the cheek and Tom takes the open seat on the other side of her…which leaves me to pick between sitting by myself on the other end of the table or sitting sandwiched between Tom and Jude. Of course.

My eyes sweep over Jude quickly, taking in his dark jeans and the white t-shirt peeking out from under his heather gray v-neck sweater. He's got the sleeves tugged up just enough so I can see the toned muscles of his forearm. I'm practically salivating by the time I remember to breathe.

"Looks like you're stuck with me," I lean down and

whisper into Jude's ear as I take the seat next to him.

He glances up with an amused look, as if surprised by my boldness. I like that I've caught him off guard, as if I'm the one controlling things for a change.

I keep watching him as I string my bag along the back of my chair, expecting him to offer a retort, but I'm left hanging. Instead, he turns toward the beers Tom placed on the table. He leans forward to grab a bottle and brings it to his lips in one fluid move. His sharp gaze flits back over to me as the bottle reaches his mouth and I watch, completely enamored as the liquid slides down his throat.

A slow, sexy grin spreads across his mouth and somehow without uttering a single word, he's stolen all the power once again.

"That doesn't seem so bad," he murmurs, glancing at me out of the corner of his eye with amusement.

He's going be the death of me.

"You're kind of a smug bastard sometimes," I accuse with a skeptical glare.

Did I actually just say that?

"Sometimes?" he asks, licking a drop of beer off his lips and placing the bottle back down on the table.

Drunk off cheap shots and determination, I reach forward and take the beer, repeating the same exact move he just did for me—except I'm taking *his* beer, and the look on his face says I'm going to pay for the rebellious behavior.

My entire body shivers with anticipation. What would he do in front of all these people? Take my bait? Kiss me? No. That would only happen in my fantasies.

"It appears our little Charley is drunk." He smiles sardonically, looking toward Tom.

Fuck him.

I drop the beer haphazardly onto the table in front of Jude and he has to reach out to stabilize the bottle before it tips over. The whirling of the beer's rim on the wooden table is the only sound I hear as I try to calm my nerves.

"Tom," I ooze sweetly, glancing up at him from under my lashes. "Would you like to go get that drink with me now?"

I glance back toward Jude and notice his jaw clench. His blue eyes drift from my face down to the exposed skin afforded by my off-the-shoulder sweater. He's hardly a foot away, and I swear I can feel his warm breath caress the arc of my collarbone. What would his lips feel like against the delicate skin at the base of my neck?

"Oh, sure, yeah." Tom hops up and a sudden pang of guilt hits me. I only asked him to go with me to piss Jude off. What kind of person does that? Right then I resolve to be polite, but careful not to lead Tom on. I actually think we could be good friends if he was up for it.

After a calming breath, I stand and straighten my sweater. The world spins slightly from the quick change in position, but I reach out to grab the back of my chair before anyone notices.

"Ready?" I ask with a friendly smile.

"Here, I'll get this round." Jude pulls out his wallet even though Tom protests. Jude doesn't pay attention to him; he pulls out cash and looks directly at me. "I insist."

Something about him uttering that phrase while his eyes are locked on mine makes my insides tingle with need. I don't know how long I stand there like that, staring down at him with soft focus, but eventually Tom clears his throat and I laugh. I laugh because there's nothing else to do. This situation is completely out of my comfort zone and I need more alcohol. Stat.

"How sweet of you, Jude," I say slowly, reaching for the cash. I know it wasn't necessary to say his name, but I wanted to know what it felt like. As I turn on my heel to head for the bar, I know I made the right decision. The lust that washed over his blue eyes confessed exactly how erotic it was to hear his name on my lips.

• • •

Jude

I reach down and adjust myself beneath my pants. That freaking woman will be the death of me. Just when I had her figured out, she showed up tipsy and completely threw me off. I watch her walking away and I'm reminded of how drop-dead gorgeous she is. She has that sexy, fuck-me hair that tumbles down her back in loose, natural waves, and her top—that hint of skin is a complete tease, making it so I can't help but want to rip off the rest of the material.

She knew what she was doing when she said my name like that and just as she intended, my dick hardened as if her sweet little hand was wrapped around it.

"What's up, man?" I hear Josh say behind me as his hand pats my shoulder. My body immediately stiffens as though he can feel how worked up I am. He and two other guys from our soccer team slide around the table and fill in the remaining seats.

"Hey guys." I tip my beer bottle toward them in greeting before taking a swig. A hint of Charley's lip gloss stuck to the rim and I can't help but want to lick it off.

Vanilla. My new favorite flavor.

"Is Tom here already?" Josh asks, forcing my focus back to the present.

"Yeah, he and Charley went to grab a drink."

"Smart man," he chuckles before glancing over at Naomi and Bennett. They've had their heads tucked together since she and Charley arrived. I've never seen Bennett like this with any girl. Hell, a couple nights ago we were in the club picking up women, and now look at him. The boy's in love and it looks like I might be losing my wingman.

"Are you excited about that photo shoot in Hawaii you've got coming up?" Josh asks, leaning back in his chair and getting comfortable.

I nod. "It'll be work, but the days should wrap up pretty early and then I'll have time to explore the island."

"That sounds awesome, man. Too bad you don't date models or that'd be the best weekend ever."

Too bad.

I shrug off his statement and take another swig of beer. In the past, my rule was in place to keep my professional integrity intact. I don't want to walk onto a set and have to worry about the model being pissy about the fact that I never bothered to call her back. Don't fucking shit where you eat. It's always been simple…until now.

A familiar giggle fills my ears and I tilt my head slightly to watch Charley break through the crowd. Tom has his hand on the small of her back, leading her to the table, and I have to physically push past the urge to break his fingers. As I take a gulp of my domestic, I try to remind myself for the last time that I don't give a fuck.

I don't know what they've done in the past five minutes, but she somehow looks even more tipsy and neither one of them has a drink in their hand.

"Hi everyone!" she sings as her gaze falls over Josh and the guys. They all sit up a little straighter as she nears and mutter awkward hellos. For a moment, their schoolboy reactions make me think maybe I don't even feel anything for her; maybe this is the effect she has on every man. I let that thought settle in for a minute, and although the idea of going back to my old life sounds compelling, I know I'm wrong. She's gorgeous, yes, but there's something about her—her softness, her hidden complexities, her humble nature—that has woven its way around my mind, threatening to undo me. I want to know everything about her. I want to know what she's hiding behind those captivating blue eyes.

Fuck.

I watch her slide into the chair next to me less gracefully than she did a few minutes ago, and I can almost taste the tequila in the air.

"Did you guys take shots at the bar?" I ask, annoyed at the edge in my voice.

She looks up at me with her innocent doe eyes.

"She made me, Jude!" Tom laughs behind me. I want to kill him.

Charley giggles with him and gently sways in her chair. I can't imagine how a girl her size could force anyone to do anything—not to mention, he should have noticed how drunk she was already.

"I'm curious, how did she force you?" I'm asking Tom, but my gaze never leaves Charley.

She bites her lip and angles her eyes at me accusingly. "I can be *very* persuasive."

The rest of the guys laugh off her comment and start talking about some football game scheduled for the next day, but I can't turn away from her. She's bewitched me and there's no hope of breaking the spell.

Her eyes flit quickly around the table and by the time they flash back to me, I can see the concern written across them. She leans in closely and folds her hands over her stomach.

"I don't feel so good."

Of course you don't, I want to say, but I bite my tongue.

"Did you eat dinner?" I ask softly, surprised at how quickly my anger turns to concern.

She mashes her lips together and shakes her head.

"Charley, you can't drink like this and not eat dinner before," I chide, but the moment I get the words out I instantly regret them. All of a sudden she looks so young and innocent. I want to make her feel better. I don't care if she is naive, she doesn't deserve to be sick.

I wrap my arm around the back of her chair and lean in. "Do you want to go home?" I ask. I watch her eyes grow wide in shock, and I can't help but chuckle.

"Not with me. Do you want me to take you to your home and then I'll go back to mine?" I clarify, but I'm not sure if I'm trying to convince her or myself. I won't want to leave her if she's sick.

"Ummm…" she hums, glancing across the table toward Naomi. I follow her gaze to find her friend in the middle of a heated make-out session with Bennett. He has Naomi practically pinned to the chair as she drags her hands through his once perfectly gelled hair. Jeez, that escalated quickly.

"I could probably just go home by myself," Charley says, nodding once and then twice as if she's trying to convince herself that's what she should do.

"I can't let you do that, Charley."

I can't add her life to my guilty conscience. There's no more room.

"No, really, Jude. I don't want to inconvenience you," she adds, already standing and looking around at the group.

"I'm gonna head home," she announces to the table. "I have to, uh, wake up early in the morning. Naomi, I'll text you tomorrow," she offers with a weak smile. Tom begins to stand and I shoot him a death stare. He is not going to take her home. I should have stepped up this morning and told the guys she was off limits, but I'm not going to make the same mistake again.

Tom stands frozen for a moment, unsure of what to do.

"I've got her." My tone couldn't be clearer. I'm not going to fight Tom about this; he needs to back down. "I'll see you guys next week."

By the time I'm moving after her, Charley's already halfway through the bar and I have to jog to catch up. When I slide beside her, she glances up at me with a timid smile.

"How can you move so quickly?" I murmur, wrapping my hand around her waist. The touch is too intimate, but it makes me feel like I've got a real hold on her. I don't want her to trip and fall in those boots. Surprisingly, she doesn't move away. Instead, she pushes back into me, giving me her weight and pressing her soft curves against me.

My arm practically engulfs her petite frame and I exhale thinking of what could have happened if she'd left by herself. Does she usually walk around alone at night? Surely Naomi sticks with her most of the time.

I hear her hum into my chest and I glance down. "I'm glad you're coming with me," she offers, and then looks down at the floor as if embarrassed she's told me the truth.

I gently lift her chin, just like I wanted to do at the

photo shoot. "Are you sure you don't want Tom to take you home?" I ask because I'm genuinely curious about what her reaction will be. Jealousy is a new feeling for me and I'm beginning to realize just how possessive I feel of this angel.

She chews on her lip but doesn't meet my eyes. Instead, her gentle gaze is focused on my stubble as she nods slowly.

"Say it, Charley."

Her lips part gently and she breathes in a slow inhale.

"I want you to take me."

Chapter Six

Jude

CHARLEY'S LAST SEMBLANCE of sobriety dissipates during the cab ride home. The shots she took at the bar sink in, adding to the alcohol already coursing through her system. I am not this guy. I don't sleep with drunk women, therefore I don't take care of drunk women—yet here I sit, cradling Charley against me and praying she won't be sick before we get to her apartment.

"How many shots did you and Tom take?"

"Two." She puckers her lips and drags out the *oo* sound.

"And I took a few shots before leaving home," she clarifies, rolling her head toward the window. I've got a good hold on her, but I'm pretty sure if I let her go she'd slide right on down to the floor of the taxi.

"Do you normally drink that much?" I ask gently. I won't judge her for it, but it concerns me that she didn't think to eat more before she started.

"Never," she whispers, and it's impossible to ignore the sadness suddenly clouding her blue eyes. She looks hopelessly lost in that moment.

I squeeze her shoulder reassuringly, uncertain of where her mind is starting to wander. She's watching the New York landscape flash by through the window. It's a few minutes later when she finally murmurs, "My mom drank a lot."

Her confession catches me off guard. She looks too polished to come from a rotten past. The taxi pulls up to a stop sign and Charley watches a family taking their dog on a late night walk. What was her family like?

"I'd come home from school and usually she'd already have started on her second bottle of wine for the night. I know because she used to let me play with the corks," she laughs sadly.

Her words are hazy as though they're spilling from her mind like a daydream. Does she know she's speaking out loud? She doesn't look at me as she talks, and I don't interrupt her. I want to know why there's so much sadness in those eyes.

"She wasn't like an *alcoholic* alcoholic," she laughs, but it doesn't sound carefree. It sounds pained and hollow, so I pull her closer to me, trying to shield the sad memories.

"She functioned perfectly fine and had everybody in her social group fooled. She was poised and polished around them, but around me she turned into a nasty drunk. She'd say the meanest things to me. Drunk minds speak sober thoughts, right?" She pauses for a beat. "God, I hate her."

The city lights illuminate the sudden paleness of her features as a tear slides down her delicate cheek. I reach out to swipe it away, for once not caring about the consequences of my actions. Tomorrow I'll go back to being the old Jude, but right now I just want to be there for her.

"I'm sorry, Charley," I whisper in her ear, watching the goose bumps bloom down her neck.

My words break through her daydream and she suddenly tries to scoot away. "Why am I telling you this?" She shakes away her thoughts and then leans her head back against the seat. The moment is gone and I can already feel her reserve against the world building once again.

She isn't opening up to me; she is letting drunken memories slip out to blend with the hazy night air.

"Jude, I feel sick," she groans, squinting her eyes closed in pain.

"I know," I soothe. "We'll be home soon." I keep running my fingers through the silky strands of her hair as silence fills the confined space of the taxi.

When we're almost to the address she gave the cabdriver, I watch a sloppy smile unpeel across her lips. I can't keep up with her drunken moods. She's crying one minute and smiling the next. Will she remember any of this in the morning?

"Jude, will this be like it is in the movies, where you start to undress me because I'm too drunk to do it myself, but then we have sex because I suddenly sober up?"

Her words are sloppy, but I can't help the fact that hearing her say the word 'sex' still makes my dick stir. She's *that* enticing.

"Is that how it happens in movies?" I ask, trying to appease her.

"Mhmm," she mumbles, keeping her eyes closed and her head tilted back. "But just so you know, I'm definitely going to throw up when we get home, and you'll be disgusted, so we should probably not have the sex if that's okay."

I laugh, completely losing myself in the drunken allure of this woman.

"All right, Charley, guess I'll just have to settle for a rain check then," I retort, wishing my words weren't a joke.

Her smile spreads across her cheeks, highlighting her little dimples, and I lose myself in the innocence of them.

But the moment washes away when the cabdriver pulls up in front an old townhouse. I pay his fare quickly and then help a clumsy Charley out of the backseat.

It's hell trying to get her from the cab to her front door. Once we're there, she leans against me as she rifles through her purse for her keys. My neck cranes back to view the two-story house. Ivy winds up the brick facade and friendly plant holders dot the outside of each window. Does she live in this place by herself? It's huge.

A frustrated sigh breaks through her throat and I glance back down. "Charley, do you want me to get the keys for you?" I ask lightly, not wanting to push her amiable mood.

Her tongue peeks out of the edge of her mouth as she focuses on finding the keys. I have to fight the urge to just take the damn purse out of her hands.

"No. No, I can get them," she slurs. If this was any other girl… *No.* I don't even know what I'd be doing because we wouldn't be here right now. We'd be at my apartment finishing up so I could call a cab and send her on her way.

Suddenly a light flicks on in the foyer and the image of a short gray-haired woman appears through the frosted glass.

"Mrs. Jenkins!" Charley shouts, much too loudly for the middle of the night.

The door creaks open and the woman I assume to be Mrs. Jenkins eyes me with cold skepticism. If Charley doesn't drink often, then I'm sure she usually brings guys home in a much more sober state. I don't know why I care, but I don't want this woman thinking I'm trying to take advantage of her.

Old hinges squeak to life as the elderly woman opens the door wider and steps back so I can help Charley through.

"Thank you for your help. Charley isn't feeling well so I wanted to make sure she got home okay," I offer as Mrs. Jenkins eyes me up and down. She nods slowly and waves her arm for us to follow without a word. She's wearing a patterned muumuu and well-worn house slippers. Her back slumps over at a sharp angle as though her spine can no longer support the weight of her upper body.

"Mrs. Jenkins, you don't have to worry. Jude here doesn't even find me atttractiveee!"

I snap my gaze to Charley. Even in her drunken slur, her words annoy me. It doesn't help when Mrs. Jenkins sends me a glare over her shoulder. What? What am I supposed to do? Confess what I really feel for Charley while she stumbles drunkenly through the hallway? I don't even know where she's getting that idea from anyway.

When we arrive at a cherry-red door at the end of the hall, I begin to piece together that this is a boarding house of sorts. Mrs. Jenkins uses her set of keys to unlock the faded copper lock and then turns around, keeping her concerned gaze on Charley.

"Do you want me to come down and check on you in a little bit?" she asks, her warm expression making it clear that she adores Charley. Suddenly I don't mind her as much. I'm glad someone will be here to check on her later.

"No. No. I'll come over in the morning if you want."

"That'd be lovely. Goodnight, Charley. Feel better." She offers me a tight-lipped smile as she moves around us and heads up the old wooden staircase in the corner of the foyer.

"She seems nice," I note with sincerity as I hold the door open for Charley to enter.

But Charley doesn't answer. The moment we're inside, she runs to the toilet and collapses before it with a heavy groan. I bolt over and lift the lid and seat, brushing her hair away from her face. She isn't sick right away. She sits there for a moment trying to will the nausea to pass, but sadly nothing will help but getting the alcohol out of her system.

I don't know what to do. I've never sat with someone while they've thrown up before, but I try to remember what my mom did when I was little. I rub Charley's back the way my mother would, around and around in small circles, and I hope it soothes her a bit.

After a few minutes, her stomach is empty and the dry heaves subside. She leans back on her heels.

"I don't think there's anything left." Her hands rest on her legs and her bottom lip protrudes slightly; it's subtle, but enough to make my heart break at the sight. She won't look at me and I know she probably feels embarrassed.

"Do you have a washcloth somewhere?" I ask, pushing off the ground.

"There are a few in the basket under the sink." She gestures to the porcelain sink against the wall, which is barely two feet away from where we sit. That's when I realize just how tiny Charley's apartment is. Her kitchen and bathroom are crammed together against the wall before me. When I twist my head, I see that her entire life is crammed into this one room. It doesn't feel sad; no, it feels like a home, and I don't mind the small space one bit.

I wet the washcloth and bring it back to Charley, handing it over so she can dab her lips. She looks utterly drained as she lifts the towel, so I reach over and help her, dragging the warm cloth against her cheeks. I stand up and rinse it quickly, then turn it to the clean side to wipe away her makeup. She was wearing too much anyway. She looked breathtaking, but I like her blue eyes without makeup even more.

After she's cleaned up, I stand to make an exit, knowing she probably wants some privacy.

"You could've looked at my boobs, but you didn't. What kind of guy doesn't look?" she asks out of the blue as she shoves off the ground and moves toward a dresser next to her twin bed.

Whoa. What?

"What are you talking about, Charley?" I rack my brain through the events of the night, but not a single thing comes to mind.

"At the photo shoot. You were so close to me and I wanted you so badly, but you didn't even look!" I watch her pull out a t-shirt and a pair of flannel pajama pants.

Is that why she doesn't think I find her attractive?

I stand up and tug my hand through my hair. "I didn't want to, Charley. You weren't naked because you wanted to be. You were naked because you were modeling on set." I'm not a fucking pervert.

"But you touched me like you wanted me, Jude," she bites out, turning toward me when she says my name; it cuts to my heart.

The old Jude would have lied and told her it was part of the job, but she was honest with me in the cab. She opened up about her mom and the least I can do is be honest with her.

"I *did* want you." My words sound momentous, but my tone is cold and insensitive, as if my callous heart isn't ready for lyrical confessions just yet.

Her eyes grow wide. She looks down at the clothes in her hand as if hoping they'll supply her with the answers to her drunken musings. Her beautiful lips mash together in thought. Is she turned on? Pissed off? Does she want me to leave? It doesn't matter.

"I don't date models, Charley." My mouth feels dry and my heart hammers against my chest. Why? Why am I fighting against what I feel for this girl?

Long, torturous seconds pass as I wait for her to react, and it's just enough time for me to realize I don't want to hurt this girl. She's too much, too much of everything. She burns away the loneliness and scar tissue encased around my heart every time her gentle blue eyes fall on me—which is why I have to walk away. She has her own issues, and I've got mine. She needs lightness, happiness, not someone who has their own demons.

Yet I can't peel my attention away from her. Instead, I watch her head lift and her eyes drag up my body with slow determination. I've seen those blue eyes flushed with a range of emotions but carnal desire takes me absolutely by surprise.

Fuck.

"I'm not on set right now," she whispers, looking up at me from under her lashes. She's absolutely beautiful and I want nothing more than to close the space between us and feel her skin against mine again. My fingers tingle in memory of what she felt like: smooth, magnetic, addicting.

Neither one of us says a word as she starts to peel her black sweater over her head. My dick hardens so quickly I think it may be conditioned solely for her use. As her hands pull the sweater off, I stand paralyzed, watching her strip for me, revealing a lacy black strapless bra. The swell of her breasts spilling over the top is the sexiest thing I've ever seen. She's breathing slow and steady and her trim, toned stomach quivers beneath my gaze as she tries to seduce me.

Fuck.

I blink, trying to break the spell she has over me. "We can't do this, Charley. You're drunk."

My entire body hums with desire and I feel like a live wire. I need to leave. I need to run or go to the gym. I have to get this energy out of me or I'm going to take advantage of this girl.

I tug my hand through my hair agitatedly and turn on my heels. Her kitchen—or lack thereof—is right behind me, so I reach for a glass and fill it with water before heading back over to the basket beneath her sink. I grab a bottle of aspirin and then walk to her nightstand. My movements are hurried and methodical, but she's watching me with enamored focus. I don't look at her until I've set everything down next to her bed. She'll appreciate the gesture in the morning even if she's too drunk to realize it now.

I have to leave.

My eyes implore her to listen to reason. "Charley, it's for the best," I try, knowing it's not what she wants to hear.

"Get out, Jude."

"Charl—"

"Get out!" she yells, pointing angrily to the door. I have no idea what she's thinking, but this is the way it has to be. She'll be happier in the long run and I just wish she could see that.

Running my hand across the hairline on my neck, I shake my head and walk to the door.

"You know, on second thought," she says, and her voice sounds bone-chillingly calm. I glance over my shoulder. She has her hands on her hips paired with a look of steely determination. I know she's closing herself off. I can feel the walls being built with brick and mortar around her heart.

"I was wrong earlier." She narrows her eyes for emphasis. "I should have picked Tom to bring me home."

Chapter Seven

Charley

"**I DON'T KNOW** what depression feels like. I know what my life feels like. I was diagnosed with clinical depression four years ago, after the *incident*, so is my entire life a "depression"? It can't be. I'm happy when I'm staying busy, running, and working, or when I'm with Naomi, but then there are times when I feel like the atoms inside my body are firing in every direction, rioting against me and boiling over until all I can do is scream. In those moments, I feel completely at a loss, not in control of my own body and mind. Most of the time, if I just expel the anger, I can start over, building my resolve once again. That's the reason I run every morning. I have to exert every muscle of my body into submission, willing my brain to comply for the day.

It's very simple. I don't look homeless. I don't look

crazy. Maybe that's life's greatest hoax: on the outside I'm a model, completely flawless, and on the inside, I'm a wack job.

The whole process was *easy* compared to everything else I was living through during the end of my senior year of high school. I smiled and took the anti-depressants until Dr. Francis asked me if I was ready to wean myself off them. I should have said no. I should have told him I had no appetite and never slept. Instead, I smiled politely and crossed my hands on top of my designer skirt. *"I'm ready to take control of my life. I feel so much better, Dr. Francis. You have no idea how much these past few months have changed me."* I said it so convincingly, and who doesn't trust a girl in designer clothes with perfectly applied makeup?

That's the reason I picked up painting in the first place. Dr. Francis suggested it for therapeutic purposes once he decided I could quit taking the prescriptions. It was either keep a journal, join a weekly support group—hell no—or pick up a hobby. Dr. Francis said it would help me work through my emotions, and in a way, it does.

The summer after high school I started painting. I lost touch with every friend—or rather, *acquaintance* I had from my old life, and I let the images in my mind take over. It wasn't enough though. It didn't sate me, so on the very first day of my freshman year at Columbia, I swapped out of honors finance and into fine arts.

I've painted ever since. I don't have a strict medium; everything collides together and usually I let the work lead me. Each time I start a new painting, my heart beats wildly and my limbs feel light. My stomach quivers and a high spreads through my veins like a drug.

But then every time I finish, I step back, tilt my head,

and feel the spiraling downfall carry me back to the darkness of my life. Every single time I finish a piece, I think the same thing: "This is all there is?"

But then I begin anew, grabbing a fresh canvas and racing for the next high.

• • •

Mrs. Jenkins came by earlier, but I brushed off her leftover coffee cake and told her I still wasn't feeling well. I stayed in bed and skipped my morning run. I can't help but replay last night in my mind. I was tipsy when we got to the bar and those shots pushed me over the edge, yet, sadly, I still remember everything. I remember practically throwing myself at Jude. What guy watches a girl strip and then leaves? Every time I think about it a new wave of nausea hits me. He could see the sadness beneath the thin layer of makeup. That's why he left. Why would he want to be with someone as messed up as I am?

Naomi called me last night and a few times this morning. I know she'll be over soon if I don't respond to her texts. We've been friends long enough for her to see me when I'm low, but for some reason I just want to file away last night in the recesses of my mind. It's embarrassing and I'm sure I'll have to see Jude again if Naomi and Bennett are serious about each other. That thought makes me dip my brush into the paint I mixed earlier and spread it harshly across the canvas.

I have a splitting headache, but I don't take the aspirin Jude left out me last night. I relish the pain; I use it when I choose a brush. I use it when I mix the acrylic paint until I end up with a deep red hue. It's beautiful and sad, like a wilting rose. I've heard every single argument concerning whether or not abstract painting can be considered art, and to be honest, I don't give a shit what anyone thinks. I stood in front of my first Rothko painting when I was eighteen years old and it broke my heart. It tore at the sadness I felt every day the summer my father died. I sat on the floor of the museum with my knees tucked toward my chest and wept.

I didn't go to his funeral.

Staring at that painting was the first time I'd acknowledged his death anywhere outside of Dr. Francis' office.

Rothko's canvas stood floor to ceiling, painted a solid black. There was nothing else, no abstract elements, no faces or shapes. Just a dark, rich black. The spotlight in the museum highlighted the texture of the paint on the canvas, the way Rothko had streaked the lines. The brush strokes were visible, alive, organic, and they spoke to my soul.

I let myself feel more that day in the cold museum than I did in a year and a half of therapy.

• • •

"Open this door, Charley, or I will bust through it. I'm serious," Naomi calls as she hammers on the door to my apartment. It's almost seven at night and I've avoided talking to her all day. I shot her a text saying all was well, but of course she saw through it.

I hover on the other side with my cheek pushed against the cold wood. "Naomi, I'm fine."

"Charley, let me in," she begs, and her voice cuts through me. I don't mean to make her sad; I don't mean to make anyone sad. This is why I wish she'd just leave. I hate being the friend that brings everyone down. It's not fair that she's always the happy one trying to cheer me up.

A second later a slip of paper slides under my door, hitting my foot. I glance down to read her chicken scratch. ***Naomi + Charley = bad bitches for life (no exceptions, not even on the sad days)***

I let a smile break through the cloudiness and unlock the door. Dr. Francis said part of recovering was choosing to be happy, allowing people in and accepting their kindness.

"I'm doing this for your sake, Naomi," I say as I crack the door open and let her walk past. "Can't you see that you should be sexing Bennett right now, not hanging out with me?"

I shut the door and whip around to look at her, but she completely ignores my logic. A timid smile dots her face and she reaches out to show me the contents of her intervention. I cup a hand over my mouth, trying to quell my emotions. She has all the essentials because she's amazing, and I love her. It's that simple. I have to accept her kindness because she gives it willingly and without strings attached.

"Dinner," she says, holding up a white cardboard box. "Obviously pizza because what else would you want?"

I smile gently as she puts the box down and grabs her purse. She pulls out a DVD and holds it up. "Best of SNL with Tina Fey and Amy Poehler." She tosses it over and I have to think fast to catch it.

"And lastly, some sleeping pills." She knows me so well that sometimes I swear she's an extension of myself.

"I'm going to force you to eat, we're going to laugh our asses off, and then I'm staying with you until you pass out. You're *allowed* sad days, Charley. I wouldn't expect anything less, but you aren't allowed to have a sad life." Her warm brown eyes see straight through me, and I nod gently. "I'm cutting you off. Starting tomorrow, you're going to wake up refreshed and you're going to rock that photo shoot. I'm not going to ask about Photographer Boy because he doesn't get to add to your sad days. Tina and Amy are the only people we need tonight," she states, finally cracking a smile.

I brush away a tear, but it's different from the sad tears that filled my day before she arrived. She's like a guardian angel and I thank my lucky stars she walked into my life our freshman year at Columbia. Without a word, I walk over to her and hug her with every ounce of strength I have. I want her to know how important she is, how much her kindness affects these sad days.

Chapter Eight

Charley

I BRUSH A stray strand of hair away from my face as I weave through the crowded sidewalk. I feel better. I know I'll have more lows. After all, my newfound resolve is only skin deep, but on days like this it's hard to remember just how sad I felt yesterday. A good night's sleep is exactly what I needed.

As I head into MILK Studios fifteen minutes early, I smile and take a deep breath. Jude did the right thing. He saw that I arrived home safely and he left when he felt uncomfortable. It was an honorable thing to do and I see that now. Yes, I wanted to jump his bones, and yes, he walked away after I took my shirt off for him, but that doesn't mean I should have yelled at him.

"Morning, Charley!" Joanie chirps as I walk out of the elevator.

"Morning, Joanie," I wave, genuinely happy to see her again.

Most of the crew has already arrived. I wrap my hand around the strap of my purse, trying to spy Jude among all the frantic people. I shouldn't be surprised to find him in the same location he occupied on Friday: tucked behind the media table, scrolling through proofs.

As I approach the table, he looks up and wets his lips. I take in his dark stubble, his tousled brown hair, and his blue button-down shirt. He's got the first two buttons undone and a shadow of brown chest hair is just barely visible. His expression is reserved, maybe even hesitant, but when I offer what I hope to be a truce smile, his shoulders relax.

"Hi." I swallow and adjust my purse strap.

His smile grows even wider. "Hi."

I glance around to the assistants who've all paused their work and are looking at us with bemused expressions. I shake my head, smile, and look back to Jude.

"Could we talk for a quick second?" I ask with a hopeful tone.

He raises his eyebrows in surprise, but quickly recovers. "Oh, sure."

Once we're away from prying eyes and ears, I clear my throat and begin, "I'm really sorry about Saturday night. I was rude to you after you were nothing but a complete gentleman." My cheeks redden from the sincerity behind my words, and I look to the floor for a moment. I have no clue what he thinks of me after that night; I just hope my apology isn't falling on deaf ears. I push past the thought and continue.

"I don't know if you remember me saying I usually don't drink that much...or really at all," I offer, trying to skirt around the subject of whether or not he was listening to me talk about my mother.

"Charley, you don't need to apologize. We've all been there…and yes, I remember everything you told me that night." His voice is level, but when I glance up into his blue eyes, they're warm and sincere. He's being so much nicer than I was expecting. He should hate me after what I said to him.

"Um, also…I am still glad you were the one to take me home. That was a silly thing for me to say and I only think of Tom as a friend." I know I'm speaking too fast and rambling, but I want to clear the air before I lose my nerve. "You didn't have to leave the bar to take me home. You don't even know me and you took care of me." I run a hand through my hair and laugh pitifully. "And then I threw myself at you. I'm so, so sor—"

"Charley, do you want to get coffee with me?" He cuts off my sentence, not letting me finish my apology.

What did he just say?

I shuffle back a step as my stomach flutters. "Coffee?"

His head tilts to the side and he gives me a dimpled grin. "It's a type of beverage. Most people tend to drink it in the morning. I like it black, but…" He pauses and pretends to scrutinize me. "I think you would maybe want it with cream and sugar."

I shake my head and laugh, narrowing my eyes playfully.

"Good thing you're a photographer because you have pretty poor detective skills. I prefer vanilla lattes." I cross my arms in front of my chest, knowing I still haven't answered his question.

My default answer for the past four years has been no, a solid no, so why isn't a polite decline springing from my lips now? He hasn't asked me on a date; maybe it would be okay if we just got coffee. No big deal.

"Ah, like your lip gloss," he murmurs, glancing down to my mouth. Something tingles across my flesh. Anticipation? Hope? I suck my bottom lip between my teeth and meet his gaze.

"How'd you...?"

"You drank my beer." He shrugs confidently, but I swear I see a subtle blush grace his handsome features. I can't believe he would have been able to taste my lip gloss on the rim of that beer, but the thought sends a shot of lust through me. I like knowing he's tasted a tiny part of me. With a resigned sigh, he shoves his hands into his pockets and shakes the thoughts from his head. What was he thinking about? The way it tasted? I have that same vanilla lip gloss on now...

I drop my gaze, unable to look at him anymore.

"So, I guess I have to accept your offer since I owe you a drink now." I pull the strap of my purse harder, unable to stand still under his gaze. I don't know why, but for some reason a simple "yes" won't cut it with Jude. I can't just give in to his charm and dimples—a girl could get lost in those bad boys.

"It is the least you could do," he agrees with a seductive smile. "Should I grab your number?"

My eyes flit around the studio before I answer. "Have Bennett get it from Naomi."

His eyes search my face, almost begging to learn the mysteries I keep tucked away. "You aren't making this easy."

I smile and shrug, trying to hide my excitement behind my calm facade. Nothing about this is easy. I'm the match head and he has every power to ignite me, to strike me and watch me erupt into flames. I just hope I get to burn long enough to get him out of my system before he decides to move on. I stand mute and fidget from one leg to the next.

He starts to retreat so he can get back to work, but he keeps his blue eyes pinned on me, making my stomach feel hollow and tingly all at once. "Wednesday afternoon, Charley. Pencil it in as busy because you and I are having coffee and I know just the place to take you."

In that moment, Jude's charm steals a piece of my heart and carries it away with him. I can't help but wonder what he'll choose to do with it.

I shouldn't have agreed to coffee.

• • •

Jude

Thirty. Thirty-one. Thirty-two.

"Take it easy, man. We still have a few more rounds," Bennett warns as he spots me behind the bench. With one final heave, I shoot the bench press bar back into its metal holders and sit up.

"I feel like I'm going insane," I groan. The towel soaks up every drop of sweat as I forcefully drag it across my forehead. Our upscale gym is packed with the after-work crowd. Women in tight pants and tank tops swarm around us, but I don't look at a single one of them. They do nothing for me anymore. Dammit.

"Because of Charley?" Bennett asks as he rounds the

bench press so we can swap places.

"Who the hell else would it be?" I snap. I've been acting like a complete asshole to Bennett lately, but I can't help it. I have so many pent-up feelings—desire, anticipation, need, guilt—and it's pissing me off. No matter how much I run or hit the gym, I can't get her out of my head.

"Cool off, lover boy. You're having coffee with her tomorrow, right? That's a good start."

"I have no clue what I'm doing. If this was any other girl, I'd buy her a coffee and then we'd have sex in the coffee shop's bathroom." I toss the towel down onto my gym bag. "I'm not meant for relationships."

"That's true, you're one moody asshole. I almost feel bad for Charley." He shoots me a grin as he starts his reps.

"Yeah, yeah," I mock, rolling my eyes.

He breathes heavily as he lifts the bar in quick succession. "I don't know what's going on in your head, but don't fuck Charley over." He exhales as he lowers the bar to his chest. "I actually like Naomi, and I can't imagine she'll keep seeing me if you screw over her best friend."

I tug a hand angrily through my hair. "What do you think I'm doing, Bennett? She literally stripped when I took her home Saturday and I *left*. I left so I wouldn't screw it up and she hated me for it. I saw the hurt in her eyes and it killed me to leave her like that."

Bennett rests the bar back into the sockets and sits up, twisting around to face me. "I cannot believe I just heard you say that. Who *are* you?"

I puff my chest, trying to recover from my sappy admission. "You're one to talk, Bennett."

"Yeah, Jude. I'm the first to admit that our lifestyles were shallow, but I'm not running from what I feel for

Naomi. I really like her and I'm not wasting time with games."

I sigh angrily. "It's not the same for me." I move around to start another round of presses, wanting this sappy conversation to end already, but Bennett keeps going.

"I know. I know you have your own problems to work out. You chose that fast lifestyle to keep away the prying questions and unwanted sympathy. I just chose it because it was easy..." His cocky smile makes me relax and I try to focus on the weight of the bar above me. "Just figure out what you want before it's too late."

• • •

I don't think Bennett meant to scare the shit out of me last night, but ever since our conversation, my stomach hasn't stopped churning. It feels like someone's wringing out my organs and won't let go. It's not like Bennett said anything revolutionary, but hearing everything laid out so simply made it feel real, inevitable, final. I can't toy with Charley. She's not the type of girl you bang out of your system. She's the type of girl that becomes your muse, the inspiration for your entire life. She makes me want to live a life that's worthy of her, but I can't change the past no matter how hard I try, so maybe that's not even possible.

"Is this seat taken?" a woman asks, breaking me out of my thoughts. I look up to see her pointing to the vintage armchair next to mine. She's smiling invitingly and it's clear she wants to strike up a conversation.

"Oh, yes, sorry. I'm waiting on a friend." The liquid spark in her eye dwindles before she nods and turns to find another seat. I watch her walk away with soft focus, but then the cafe's front doors open. With a burst of bright light, Charley steps through the threshold. The sun still shines through the glass behind her, illuminating her silhouette, making her appear ethereal and intangible.

I watch her blue eyes span the bustling room, trying to find me, and my pulse spikes. I offered to meet at her apartment so we could take the subway together, but she wanted to meet here. Now that I'm watching her, I think she might have known something I didn't. Seeing her across a crowded room sends a thrill through me and I wish so badly that she was mine, that she would see me from afar and a slow, sexy smile would grace her delicate features. She would cross the room slowly, purposefully. I would stand to greet her and when she drew near, I'd pull her into my arms and envelope myself in her sweet scent. She'd kiss me on the neck with a feather-like touch and murmur a hello into my ear.

The whirring of the coffee machine pulls me out of my reverie, but I'm left with one residual thought: I'll make her mine. I have to.

Her eyes finally land on me and in that moment, it feels like she exists solely for me. She offers me a shy smile before glancing down to her feet and heading over. She darts between tables. I stand slowly, studying her graceful movements. She looks effortlessly sexy in her ripped up jeans, white tank, scarf, and fitted leather jacket—so much so that I haven't even collected my thoughts by the time she's standing in front of me. We end up lingering there silently for a moment, soaking in each other's presence and smiling like fools.

"Hi, Charley," I murmur as my body itches to step closer. She leans forward on her tiptoes and kisses my cheek. The sweet gesture is fleeting, over faster than I could've imagined. The skin she kissed still feels alive, like her lips and my cheek are magnetic poles trying to draw toward one another again.

"Hi, Jude," she hums softly, and my insides liquefy.

"I got you a vanilla latte." I twist around to point to the table sandwiched between our two armchairs. "But if you want something else I can go grab it." I shove my hands into my pockets nervously and turn back toward her.

"That's perfect, thank you." She sighs, seemingly surprised I remembered her drink of choice. The sweet glow behind her eyes makes me want to purchase a dozen more lattes for her just to prolong the effect.

In a flourish of graceful movements, she folds herself into the chair as I sit down in silence. She unwraps her navy scarf from around her neck and I try to slyly study her over the brim of my coffee cup. The moment the silky material slips away, the radiant skin between her neck and the top of her shirt is finally revealed. It's tantalizing, a little sliver of milky perfection.

She sighs, breaking my trance, and picks up her latte. With a glance to the right and left, she nods. "This place is really cool."

We're in one of my favorite coffee shops in New York. It's tucked away behind an old bookstore and most people walk by the worn brick building without a second thought. I stumbled in a few years ago on a rainy day and was completely hooked. The chairs are comfortable and inviting, the lights are bright enough to read but low enough to feel intimate, and mellow music is always playing softly in the background.

"I usually hide away in here on the weekends."

She glances up at me with a bemused smile, as if she can't picture me actually doing that. Does she expect me to prowl for women every moment of my life?

"Are you a reader?"

I nod slowly. "I devour books like candy." She licks her lips when I say the word devour and I let myself dream that she wants me as badly as I do her.

"Same here. Who's your favorite author?"

"I don't have one; it's too hard to pick."

After taking a sip of her latte, she sets the cup down. "Interesting."

"Is it?" I beckon with a half smile.

She props her elbow on the side of the overstuffed armchair and rests her chin on her palm. "What are you reading right now?"

"The Count of Monte Cristo."

She cocks one of her eyebrows. "Are you a classics man?"

I run my fingers against my short stubble. "I haven't decided yet. Sometimes I find myself liking contemporary fiction more. I never get tired of a good mystery." I take a long drag of my black coffee.

She's intentionally keeping the conversation aimed on me, but I want to know about her. "What about you, Charley? What book are you reading right now?"

"'I Was Told There'd Be Cake' by Sloane Crosley. It's a collection of her essays." A shadow of a smile graces her lips. "I'm only a quarter of the way through, but it's really funny so far."

I nod. "Have you read Sedaris?"

She grins. "Love him."

"Yeah, I can tear through his books in a few hours."

"Maybe you can let me borrow one of your mystery books sometime."

I nod. "Definitely—although I'll warn you, I usually

end up having the weirdest dreams if I read a thriller right before going to bed."

"That happens to me too! I'm always being chased or having to flee the country or something." She laughs before narrowing her eyes on me and reaching over to take another sip of her coffee. I don't know what she's thinking, but it seems like I wasn't what she was expecting. Did she think we'd have nothing in common?

After we take our sips, I glance over at her and ask a question I hadn't thought of before now.

"Is Charley a nickname?"

The moment the question hangs in the air between us, I see her entire demeanor change. Her shoulders slump and her eyes flash down to her drink.

The pad of her finger drags along the brim of her cup and her eyes study its thin trail intently. "No."

What? Does she not like her name?

Her peculiar response leaves me briefly flustered and I can't think of anything to say, so we sit in silence for a moment. I didn't mean to bring up a negative subject; I want her to be happy with me. I scroll through my mental Rolodex of small-talk topics and land on music, but just when I'm about to ask about her favorite band, her eyes slide up my body.

"Is Jude a nickname?"

Her sly smile tells me she's pushed away those sad feelings and is trying to turn her mood around. Another time I hope she'll open up to me about them instead.

I chuckle. "No. My dad is a big Beatles fan." I smile, thinking of my parents.

She lets out a soft, carefree laugh and my heart constricts as if she has a direct grip on it. "That's awesome! He picked a great song."

I nod. "Yeah. I like the lyrics."

Her question brings me back to a memory of my dad, and for some reason I find myself starting to share it with her. "My dad plays the guitar"—I seesaw my hand—"sort of. Anyway, on Saturday mornings, when my brother and I were really little, he'd wake up early and make us eggs and bacon and then grab his guitar. Man, we hated him so much at the time. He'd kick open our doors and strum that acoustic guitar, breaking out into a choppy version of 'Here Comes The Sun'." I glance up to find her blue eyes focused intently on me. She smiles and nods for me to continue.

"It didn't matter how many times he played that song, he never seemed to get it completely right. Some cord or another would always be off. He'd sing the lyrics obnoxiously loud, never stopping to fix his mistakes."

"My brother and I would protest more and more as we got older, saying we needed our sleep, and I can't remember when, but he eventually stopped playing it for us." I nod at my coffee and take a sip. "It's one of my favorite memories from my childhood."

"Do you think he knows that?" Her voice sounds like a soft melody.

I glance up and slide my hand across my dark stubble. "Y'know, I'm not sure."

She glances into the air, thinking for a moment before her eyes light up. "You should buy him the sheet music sometime... Maybe he'd connect the dots without you having to jeopardize your masculinity."

I offer her genuine smile. "That's a good idea. My dad is not the mushy type."

"Is he in New York?"

"Nah. Both of my parents and my brother still live in Boston. My parents bought a house in the suburbs almost thirty years ago and they still live there."

"Thirty years!" She twists her long hair through her fingers and pushes it over her shoulder, exposing her elegant neck. "That's crazy!"

I shrug, realizing thirty years with Charley doesn't seem like it'd be enough. "They're old school. My father was a police officer until he retired and my brother's still with the force."

"Is your mom retired as well?"

"She taught second grade until she had my brother and me. Then I think my dad referred to her full-time job as 'nagging him'."

She throws her head back and laughs and I find myself chuckling along with her because the sound is infectious and addicting.

"He loves her though. My father completely adores the ground my mother walks on."

She nods her head, looking off in the distance. "That's so sweet. They sound great."

I remember her talking about her mom's drinking problem, so I stick to neutral territory. "What about you? Did you grow up on the island?"

"Born and bred," she says with a wide smile. "I love this city."

"Did you grow up in Greenwich Village?"

Her eyes cloud over for a moment. "Nope. I lived on the Upper West Side until I went to Columbia and moved in with Naomi."

"That's where you guys met?"

"My first day on campus." She smiles in recollection. "They paired us as roommates because we were both in the finance program, but when she found out I was actually doing fine arts, she flipped and threatened to swap." She laughs. "She thought I was going to be some crazy hippie, doing drugs in the dorm and stuff." She grins and glances up at me from under her lashes conspiratorially. "Let's just say I wasn't the one who partied the hardest that year."

I laugh, not surprised by her revelation. "I like Naomi. I think Bennett has completely fallen for her."

She leans back in the armchair, kicks off her boots, and tucks her socked feet up under her legs. The gesture seems so endearing, but I can't figure out why—maybe because she would only do it if she were beginning to feel comfortable around me?

"Yeah. She seems pretty smitten with him too."

"Poor saps." I wink, and she rewards me with a bright, dimpled smile.

I cock my head to the side. "Y'know, I went to Columbia as well. That's why I moved away from Boston."

"Oh really? What did you study?"

"Photojournalism, but I'm twenty-seven so I don't think we were on campus at the same time."

"Guess not. I'm only twenty-three."

I wonder what the boys on that campus thought of her. It's probably best we weren't there together. I wouldn't have let her go a single date with anyone but me.

She clears her throat. "Did you always want to be fashion photographer?"

Her question catches me off guard. I shake my head as memories buffet me from all sides—hungry children, bloody wounds, burnt villages. My fists instinctively clench around the armchair as I shove the thoughts aside.

"No. I stumbled into it two years ago and decided it could be a good fit. It's easy work compared to what I used to do." That's all I'll say; this conversation has been too good for me to bring up my demons now.

My subconscious shouts at me to change the subject.

"I saw those paintings in your apartment. They were amazing. Is that what you studied at Columbia?" I slide into asking about her art flawlessly, but she doesn't answer right away. She eyes me skeptically, clearly aware of the forced transition. I know she sees the desperation written across my features, but no one wants to talk about heavy stuff on the first date. First date…is this a date?

"Yes. I started painting after high school and lov—"

"Clarissa!" someone shouts a few feet away from us, and Charley's head snaps up to follow the sound.

"Clarissa!"

I stare at Charley, confused. The frat guy moving toward us definitely recognizes her and Charley's wide-eyed expression seems to say the same.

"Hudson?" she asks with a confused scowl.

He doesn't seem to mind her lack of enthusiasm.

"I can't believe this. I haven't seen you in five years and I run into you in this crappy coffee shop of all places?" I bristle at his assessment and Charley shoots me an apologetic glance.

"How have you been?" she asks with an awkward smile.

"I've been so good. I've missed you though. The whole gang misses you." The guy, Hudson, finally glances over at me but he seems to barely register my existence. My blood boils and I have to fight the instinct to stand up and force him to look at me.

Charley clears her throat. "Ah well…Hudson, this is Jude…a photographer I work with." She gestures over to me and Hudson throws me a wave. The son of a bitch doesn't even shake my hand—and what the hell? *A photographer I work with?* How about *friend* at the very least?

His cheesy country-club smile splits even wider when he realizes I'm not her boyfriend. "Oh yeah! I've seen you in tons of magazines. You're even more beautiful than you were in high school, Clarissa."

She blushes at his compliment and I crack my neck. It's not something I ever do, but I want to deck this guy and I need something to do with my body so I don't make a scene in front of Charley and the rest of the coffee shop.

When Charley doesn't respond, Hudson continues, "You know, I'm glad I ran into you. I have a club opening up on Friday and I don't have a date yet..." Oh, fucking hell. Who does this guy think he is?

Charley rubs the back of her neck and bites her lip. Everything about her body language screams how uncomfortable she feels, but Hudson doesn't even seem to notice.

"That's so great, Hudson," she coos with fake enthusiasm. How can he not tell?

"Why don't you come?" His eyes flicker over to me with disdain. "And you can bring your *friends* too. I'll put you guys in the VIP section and drinks will be on me, of course."

He pointedly drags out *friends* as though his blanket term couldn't possibly be referring to me. No, he means fellow Upper West Side WASPs. This guy can't be real.

Charley glances over at me with uncertainty in her eyes. What does she want? My approval? Does she want me to speak up and claim her? I'm your *photographer*, Charley, remember? I tip my brow and shrug before sipping my now cold coffee. It tastes like shit, but I need something to occupy my mind so I don't have to watch her agree to go on a date with this douchebag.

"Um, okay. That sounds good, Hudson."

Her words grate my heart and I squeeze the coffee cup so tightly I think the ceramic might shatter beneath my fingers.

"Here, let me get your number and I'll give you all the details before Friday." He grabs his phone out of his tailored chinos, and at that, I stand and leave to go to the bathroom. I can't sit there and watch her accept a guy's date while we're having coffee.

"Jude?" Charley asks, her soft voice nearly breaking my heart. I almost didn't turn around, but for the fucking life of me, I can't say no to the girl.

"I'm just running to the bathroom really quick." I should leave. This is too much, but I swear the way she looks at me in that moment could melt the ice caps. During her entire conversation with Hudson she didn't show anywhere near the amount of feeling she's giving me with that one look. *There's still hope.*

Chapter Nine

Charley

"WHAT THE HELL Charley!?" Naomi shouts through the phone.

"I didn't want to be rude! What was I supposed to do?" I argue, flipping through the pages of my sketchbook, trying to simultaneously sketch and appease Naomi all at once.

I swear the groan she emits just then could be heard across the Atlantic. "Tell him you're on a date with another guy and it's rude to ask you out like that!"

I huff, falling back on my bed with a thud and scattering my sketchbook to the floor. I cringe thinking of the bent corners I've just caused.

"Jude never said it was a date! And I tried to get him to look at me, to give me some sign that I should say no, but he shrugged it off. He didn't care, and I felt like a complete idiot, so I said yes."

"What happened after Hudson left?" she asks, as if she's a detective interrogating me under a harsh bulb.

I swallow and try to say the next sentence as calmly as possible. "I invited Jude to go with us to the club. He said he'd invite a date and we could all go *as a group.*" No, saying it slowly didn't make the phrase sound any better out loud. "Which proves everything, Naomi. If he wants to invite a date, he isn't upset Hudson invited me."

The sinking feeling in my stomach threatens to consume me as silence fills the phone call. I focus on the world through my window, contemplating mind over matter. If I tell my stomach and my heart and my legs and my eyes and my ears to stop pining for Jude, shouldn't I be able to do it?

"You're a fool. He said that to protect himself. He wants you, or he wouldn't have invited you to get coffee— which means you're going to look freaking sexy tomorrow, and you're going to prove to Jude that you want him and not dumb Hudson."

"I don't know, Naomi… Last time I attempted that it didn't turn out so well." My cheeks still burn looking at the spot near my nightstand where I drunkenly stood and stripped for Jude. I should wrap caution tape around the spot like it's a crime scene; Lord knows I've avoided it as though physical remnants of my pride lay concealed under the varnished wood.

I drag a hand feebly down my face, wishing Naomi would let me go back to sketching already.

"This is different, really. I'm going to leave work at noon tomorrow and use a few personal hours so we can go shopping. You just have that catalog shoot in the morning, right?"

"Yes," I murmur, knowing her mind is already made up, and maybe she's right. I haven't purchased any new clothes in a while because I've been saving all my modeling money. A new dress *would* be nice.

"Perfect," she chimes happily. "Let's meet at Barney's around one, okay?"

"Sounds good."

"And Charley, do not give up yet. We'll figure this out. He wants you. I know it."

Her confident rallying speech makes me feel like we're in the middle of Rocky. I half expect her to show up outside my door in a moment with boxing gloves and an iPod playing "Eye of the Tiger".

• • •

Naomi and I are scrubbed, buffed, waxed, and plucked. There is not a strand of unwanted hair on either of our bodies, and the hair that's *left* is lying in big, silky waves down our backs. After we found the perfect dresses in Barneys, we treated ourselves to a spa day and got our hair and makeup done. It's been ages since I've pampered myself and I feel sexy—too sexy, but Naomi assures me the dress isn't too much. Obviously, I don't believe her, but I'm rolling with it because even *I* think I look edible.

My gorgeous cream lace dress has three-quarter-length sleeves and a plunging v-neck. It has a tank dress lining and a sheer, open back. The tight dress hits my legs literally a few inches under my ass, but it's practically vacuum-sealed to my body so I don't have to worry about the cool fall air exposing my underwear (or lack thereof). The dress is too tight for anything other than a tiny thong, but at least my lady parts are covered. I just won't be doing any bending over at the club. Naomi, bless her gorgeous self, has the same size feet as me and let me borrow her four-inch nude Louboutin pumps to finish off the look.

"This is going to be such a good night," Naomi declares from the other side of the cab's back seat. I turn toward her and smile.

"I love that lipstick color on you, especially when everything else is so *nude.*" She wiggles her eyebrows playfully and I laugh.

"It's called 'Heat Wave'. They used it on me at my photo shoot the other day so I picked some up on my way home."

"Mmm, you look like a sex vixen," Naomi mocks in a horrible Russian accent, making me laugh even more. The cab driver eyes us skeptically through the rearview mirror, and I can't stop the giggles from taking over. I'm completely giddy with the anticipation of seeing Jude soon. I don't care that he'll have a date. I just want to look at him. Know he's real. That a guy is *actually* that sexy. I loved our conversation on Wednesday. It felt so natural to sit with him like that, tucked away in the corner of a coffee shop.

Naomi's phone vibrates in her hand and her chocolate brown waves conceal her face as she bends to check it. "The guys just got there," she says as she reads her text message.

"Cool," I say, feigning calmness as I glance through the cab window. "Guess I should let Hudson know I'm on my way," I mumble, even though that's the last thing I want to do.

Naomi checks her lip gloss in her small silver compact before stuffing it back into her clutch. "I'm glad it's cold enough for coats. That way, when we get inside the club, we can take them off and make a *real* entrance."

I smile, shifting my gaze back toward her. "Why am I

not surprised that Miss Drama Queen would love a grand entrance?"

She winks at me and slings her coat open to reveal her long-sleeved black bodycon dress. "Please. With dresses like these"—she points her finger between us—"you can't *NOT* have a dramatic entrance."

I shake my head slowly. "Remind me to sign you up for a reality show when we get home. You'd be a celebrity in no time."

"You wouldn't dare," she huffs dramatically, although I know it's secretly her dream job. Getting paid to be crazy? She would never leave. "Not unless the Kardashians need a new sister. I'd have to change my name to Kaomi, but it'd be worth it."

I'm still laughing at her fake name when the cab pulls up in front of Hudson's new club, but the moment I spy Jude through the window, every ounce of humor is completely wiped from my body. *Holy...*

He and Bennett are standing outside on the curb talking to Hudson. There's a winding line of people waiting to get into the swanky club that wraps around the entire building. Girls shiver in their short skirts, checking their makeup and complaining constantly, no doubt. Guys shuffle back and forth impatiently, checking out those same short skirts and trying to move closer to their prey for the night.

I knew Hudson's club opening would be packed, but this is insane. Naomi reaches over to pay the cabdriver since I bought our lunches at the spa earlier, and I follow her out into the chilly night air. Music pounds from the club doors, reverberating through my body and joining the already pulsing rhythm of my heartbeat.

Then my eyes fall on *him* again and everything else melts away.

Dark tousled hair, dark stubble, and icy blue eyes. Black fatigue jacket, a white t-shirt pulling taut against his muscled abs leading down to dark jeans, and his sexy leather boots. I lick my lips, tasting the sweetness of my bright red lipstick. He hasn't seen me yet. He's turned toward Hudson and Bennett with his hands tucked into the front pockets of his jeans. I would have stood there all night, frozen in desire, but Naomi pulls me forward and I follow blindly. As we walk up, catcalls sound from the crowd of people waiting in line and the guys turn toward the commotion. There are dozens of people on the sidewalk, but I don't notice them because *our* eyes meet and the air ignites between us. His searing gaze glides from my eyes, to my lips, to my jacket, and then slowly down my long, exposed legs. I want to squirm beneath his appraisal, but I can't move. He's got every motor unit in my body on lockdown. When he finally meets my eyes again, a fiery need burns behind his blue gaze and I can't help but smirk. He hasn't even seen the dress yet.

Just then, Hudson glides in front of me, cutting off the magnificent view and dousing the once sizzling air. He reaches out to grip my shoulder in greeting, but his hand feels cold and my first instinct is to shirk away from his touch. I keep my eyes focused on the lapel of his black suit jacket as I try to will myself to plaster on a genuine smile.

"You look great, Clarissa," he offers as his eyes peruse the same path Jude's did only seconds earlier. Can he see that my skin's already been set ablaze by someone else? I barely glance over his preppy suit and tie, but I offer him a friendly smile. His dirty blonde hair is gelled back, displaying all his handsome features, but strangely I don't see the appeal like I once did.

"Hi Hudson, thanks so much for inviting us. This place

is packed." I tuck my hands into my coat pocket, realizing how chilly the night air is without Jude's eyes warming my body. "And actually I go by Charley now," I clarify, hoping he'll accept the transition without question.

A brief scowl covers his features before he offers a curt nod and turns toward the group.

"C'mon guys, let's go inside." Naomi squeals in excitement as Hudson's hand hits the small of my back over my coat and dress. It's not a crude gesture, but my eyes immediately dart to Jude as a wave of guilt hits me. Do I expect him to be upset? If so, I should be relieved to see him lift his eyebrows and smile before turning on his heel and leading the way inside.

Heavyset bouncers man the entry, allowing clusters of people to enter every now and then. When our group walks up, they quickly part the crowd and let us enter with a quick flourish of velvet rope.

Everyone in line boos in protest behind us. I doubt they realize Hudson is one of the owners. They probably just think we're VIPs or something, which I guess tonight we are. That thought should excite me more and it really was nice of him to invite us, but I'm not sure what he's expecting from me. Surely he'll be too busy to actually spend time with us.

The moment we enter the club, the flashing lights and music consume my senses. Sexy dancers in spandex shorts and crop tops dance on platforms as hoards of club-goers circle around the bar and dance floor. There must be hundreds of people inside, but it's hard to tell in the sexy darkness of the club. Neon lights strobe above the room, illuminating certain areas and casting others into darkness. Our group doesn't stop until we reach a set of glossy black stairs that can only lead to trouble.

"We'll check your coat in VIP. It'll take less time to get them later on," Hudson shouts in my ear, and I nod. I'd forgotten I was even wearing it. The club isn't hot, but I imagine once we hit the dance floor we'll warm up nicely.

The glossy stairs don't take us to another floor. The seven steps simply raise the VIP area above the rest of the club so we're on an exclusive level. A thin glass railing rims the parameter of the VIP section, further dividing the club between the haves and the have-nots.

Just as my nude Louboutins step onto the second stair, a fast beat takes over the sound system and the entire club erupts in shouts. I twist toward the noise, forcing Hudson's hand from my back on accident, and spot a house DJ spinning on a stage a few feet away. He's got a flat-billed hat turned backward and a bright neon shirt over sagging jeans. I recognize his upbeat mix from the radio and the crowd is going wild so I know he must be famous.

Okay, this is *pretty* cool. Naomi turns around and the absolute joy written across her face says it all.

After we all check out the DJ, Hudson leads the group to a table in the center of the VIP area and a pretty waitress appears to grab our coats. Naomi and I unbutton them and just as I let the wool material drift down my arms, I feel Jude's gaze practically devouring me, heating the air and caressing my skin with unspoken desire. I can't look at him; I let my sexy curls hide my face as I try to remember to breathe.

"Wow." Hudson's tongue practically falls to the floor as his eyes hover a beat too long on the v-neck of my dress; I know it's revealing quite a handful of cleavage. *Damn you, Naomi.*

I glance up toward my traitorous friend and watch her mouth, "Own it." Easier said than done, but she's right. I *should* own it. I flip my hair behind my shoulder and glance up. Everyone's seated at the table now except for Hudson and me, so I tuck my hands behind the back of my dress and slide into the seat directly opposite Jude. He's eyeing me with a wicked grin and smoldering eyes; I wish I knew what was going through his thoughts right now. Everything seemed platonic at the coffee shop, even though my emotions were going haywire. Tonight feels different, like we're both letting our guards slip and forgetting about the repercussions.

I don't have time to wonder about it further though because Hudson turns to me, leaning in and pulling me into a private conversation. That's when it hits me. Jude didn't bring a date. What the hell? He didn't bring a date. I glance up briefly. He's chatting with Naomi and Bennett, but maybe his date will meet us here?

"Charley," Hudson says slowly, trying out my new name and pulling my attention back to him. "How have you been since high school? I mean obviously you've done well for yourself. You're looking sexy as hell." His breath carries remnants of tobacco and a vision of my mother prancing around the house with a glass of wine while nursing her second pack of cigarettes for the day pops into my mind.

"I've been good." I fidget awkwardly before folding my hands over my lap. I shouldn't mind his compliment, but for some reason it seems overly slick.

"You seem like you're doing well too. Do you own many clubs?" I ask as my eyes glance around to take in my surroundings. They keep VIP so secluded I can hardly see what the rest of the club looks like.

"This is the first. My dad wanted to diversify the business."

"Well you guys did a great job. This place is really cool."

Hudson's gaze flits around everywhere as we talk. At first I assume he's multi-tasking, trying to make sure his club's opening is running smoothly while attempting to keep me entertained, but after a few minutes, I find myself following his gaze out of curiosity. My eyes land on a gorgeous brunette at the bar. She's smiling over at him, practically eye-fucking him even as I look on. I can't help but laugh. I don't mind; I don't particularly want his attention on *me*, but we literally just got here.

"Oh, thanks. My dad and I worked really hard the last few months," he answers, only half interested.

I nod, trying to salvage the remnants of our conversation and stay focused on him rather than Jude, but it's becoming harder by the second.

"I hope your father is doing well." My words are completely lost on him as the brunette from the bar walks over and starts to whisper in his ear. He smiles and wraps his hand around her waist, squeezing her ample curves and making her squeal in delight. I feel like a voyeur watching them like this, but as I'm about to get up and offer her my seat, the brunette walks off and Hudson eyes me once again. Damn.

"So do you like modeling?" he asks, running his smooth hand across my shoulder. My skin bristles under his touch and I have to fight the urge to pull away once again. He *just* had that hand wrapped around some girl's ass.

Does he not realize how slimy that is? I can feel Jude's gaze on me, but I don't want to look over. I don't want him to witness Hudson treating me like a toy, so easily disposable.

"Um, yes. It's a means to an end," I say flatly.

"That's great!" he responds overenthusiastically, and I realize he's not listening to a word I say. He's glancing over my shoulder making sexy eyes with a redhead at the next table. Does this guy have ADD or what? Luckily, the same waitress that took our coats comes back at that moment with a round of drinks, saving me from this strange purgatory.

"Awesome," Bennett shouts, reaching for a drink.

"Don't forget to make eye contact when you toast or you'll have seven years of bad sex!" Naomi shouts, and we all laugh as we take our glasses.

She turns to Bennett and they playfully stare into each other's eyes and tilt forward until they end up face to face. Bennett leans in, closing the gap, and gives her a sweet kiss. I smile and clink glasses with Hudson quickly, before he gets the same idea, then with Bennett and Naomi, purposely leaving Jude for last. He leans over the small table and looks directly into my eyes as our glasses clink. His gaze is completely unreadable. Is that anger clouding his blue eyes?

"We wouldn't want that," he murmurs huskily as our glasses unite. His tone and sexy words completely catch me off guard and as I start to pull my glass away, the mixed drink spills over onto my trembling hand. Before I can reach to get a napkin, Jude is there, grabbing my hand and bringing it to his warm lips. Every person at the table watches him gently suck the alcohol off my skin and with a whoosh, all the oxygen leaves the room. My entire body reacts: my lungs hang in suspension, my mouth drops open, and the throbbing between my legs feels untamable. I cannot believe he just did that, and I cannot believe how good his lips felt on my skin.

The line has officially been crossed.

"Damn, Jude!" Naomi laughs, breaking the moment and lightening the mood. He laughs as if it was just a game and then drops my hand. The movement causes my nipples to pull against the lacy fabric of my dress and I feel the wetness now dampening my thong. His lips were on my skin for less than a second and he turned my entire body into a ball of hot desire. *Smug bastard.*

As I adjust my dress and awkwardly take my seat, Hudson's arm hits the back of my chair with a thud. I can't meet his eyes or Jude's. Guilt hits my stomach and I'm not sure who it's for, Jude or Hudson? I can feel the tension emanating around the table. Hudson's hostility practically blankets my skin, but he doesn't really have the right. We clearly aren't here on a date.

"What's up, Hudson!" A voice booms behind us and I inwardly sigh, relieved to have a distraction from my swirling thoughts, but the reprieve is short-lived when I realize how many people are trailing after that voice. In a flash of movement and screeching chairs, our tiny table is overtaken and suddenly we're in the middle of a rowdy group of Hudson's friends. Bodies envelope us from all sides, patting Hudson on the back and offering greetings. I nod my head and offer introductions, but I can't remember a single name after it's all said and done—except for one: Olivia. That's only because she went to the same high school as Hudson and me. I shouldn't be surprised she stayed in touch with Hudson; they ran in the same crowd.

Olivia was one of my good friends growing up, but we went our separate ways after junior high. She turned into a heavy partier and I focused on dance and studying to get into Columbia. She's still as gorgeous as ever with her rich brown hair and classical features.

"No way! I can't believe *you're* actually at a club! I

thought you fell off the face of the planet after high school, after everything went *down...*" she drawls as we awkwardly greet each other. Her words are masked with a sing-songy high-pitched voice that makes my ears ring.

I plaster on a fake smile and quickly fill in the lull at the end of her sentence before she can say another word. "I haven't seen you in forever. How have you been, Olivia?" I ask, knowing the surest way to avoid things I'd rather not discuss is to turn the conversation toward her. At least girls like her are predictable in that sense.

"I'm good. Just working in PR, but I'm sure you knew that." She gives my body a onceover, but we aren't in high school anymore and she can't intimidate me the way she used to. Her eyebrows rise in approval as she appraises the nude Louboutins. Thank you, thank you, Naomi.

"Oh, I didn't know, but that's so great," I ooze before glancing down at my light blue cocktail. Would I have turned out like her in another life?

"Yeah. I'm with one of the best firms in New York," she says with a bored tone before scanning the group because, clearly, I'm not worthy of her time. When her head stops swiveling and her almond brown eyes narrow, I already know who she's locked onto: Jude. He's nodding and his head is dipped low, listening intently to one of Hudson's friends. The gesture shadows half of his face in the club lighting, making him appear even sexier and more mysterious.

"Excuse me a minute," she clips out, waving her hand in front of my face and moving away before I can even reply.

Well then.

I watch her move toward him in her slinky black dress and I think for one long second about tipping my drink onto her so she has to go clean it off in the bathroom…but this isn't Mean Girls and I'm not a capricious teenager—sadly.

"Hey, Charley! Come meet my friends." Hudson beckons me over with a manicured hand. His gaudy, diamond-encrusted watch shines in the strobe lights like a disco ball, momentarily blinding me. Who is he trying to emulate? Jay-Z?

For the next five minutes, I stand stoically as Hudson and his friends toss back liquor and discuss the hottest ass they've "pounded" lately. I try my damnedest to keep my gaze from falling on Jude. Olivia cornered him right after she left our conversation and I'm pretty sure if she stepped any closer she'd be inhaling his sexy, fucking flawless stubble. Dammit.

Look away.

Naomi and Bennett are off canoodling, otherwise I would have used her as a scapegoat the second Hudson's friends started comparing dick sizes. Oh, I'm sorry, maybe it was yacht sizes. I don't want to force myself onto her and Bennett as the third wheel. She's been so supportive lately; she deserves some alone time with her new guy.

"So where have you been keeping this one, Hudson?" One of his friends asks with a slurred smile. I decide on the spot that his plucked eyebrows and fake tan have to be part of an early Halloween costume.

"Yeah. She's too hot for you." Another friend chimes in with a signature grunt. Hudson folds his arms over one another and the edges of his mouth curl up at his friends' approval of me.

Have they completely forgotten I'm standing right here? Have we suddenly traveled back to the 1950s?

"Wasn't she on Maxim's hot list this year? Damn."

"Shut up," Hudson huffs shallowly, clearly not *actually*

wanting them to stop. *Oh stop—no, I didn't mean stop. Keep going.*

"She wouldn't go for either of you," he declares proudly with his chin raised as though he has the winning hand.

How do any of these guys pick up women? Do girls really look past their complete ineptitude because they have greasy suits and flashy watches? No thanks. My vibrator has more charm than the three of them put together.

I roll my eyes and look around for an escape.

I could go to the bathroom and just not come back to VIP after. If I have to listen to these guys or watch Jude and Olivia for another second, I'll throw up on the spot. I must be glutton for punishment because I can't help but look over at *him* just one last time—and I see he's not focused on Olivia. She's rambling on, her hands gesturing wildly in the air, and all the while, Jude's eyes are fixed on me. The moment I find him staring, his smirk widens and one seductive dimple appears. He tilts his head and looks over at the VIP stairs.

I scowl in confusion. Does he want to leave?

My eyebrows knit together. "What?" I mouth with a ghost of a smile across my lips. We clearly need Morse code.

He tips his head again, deeper this time, and I can't help but laugh. How is Olivia not picking up on this? Oh, right. She's completely absorbed in her own ramblings. I think he wants to go talk in private, and the thought sends fresh butterflies through my belly.

"I'll see you later, Hudson. I'm going to go find the bathroom," I offer politely, even though a part of me just wants to walk off without another word.

"There's a VIP restroom over there," he says, pointing his finger behind the bar.

"Oh, it's no problem. I think I see a friend on the dance floor and I want to say hi."

He nods, believing my lie and already losing himself in the sight of another girl. "If it's a hot chick, bring her up."

I shake my head and mumble under my breath, "I wouldn't want to ruin the nice circle jerk you guys have going on." Was Hudson like that when we dated in high school? For some reason I can't remember.

I don't know if Jude will follow me, but I want to leave VIP regardless. I didn't get to explore the club earlier, and I want to find the ladies' room and reapply my lipstick.

As I weave through the club, I try to put the last few minutes behind me. This night can still be salvaged if I completely avoid VIP at all costs. Hell, even if I just sit in a corner and fantasize about Jude's lips on my hand, it'd be a great way to spend the rest of the night.

The restroom is packed by the time I reach it, so I stand behind a long line of girls trying to fix their hair and makeup using fogged mirrors and confined space. After a hellish wait, I finally push through the exit and am greeted by one of the most beautiful sights I've ever seen: Jude leaning against the wall in the dim hallway with his arms and ankles crossed. He looks so damn relaxed and confident I want to attack him on the spot, push myself against him and feel the hard planes of his body against the lace of my dress. He's ditched his jacket and his coiled arm muscles press against the sleeves of his rolled up shirt.

"I have to hand it to you, Charley. You put up with much more from that guy than I would have expected," he praises. I'm surprised there's no hint of jealously or anger, but I suppose he realizes Hudson isn't competition.

I shrug. "I didn't want to brush him off. He's an old friend and he *did* get us into VIP after all."

117

His jaw tightens faintly. "He's an asshole. He took you for granted. If you had been talking to me back there, I wouldn't have been able concentrate on anything else."

I flinch in embarrassment. "Was he that obvious?"

Jude pushes off the wall and takes a step closer to me— a dangerous, suggestive step. "Only because I couldn't take my eyes off you."

"Olivia was pretty good at grabbing your attention." I test the water with a sly grin.

He gives me a wicked smile and takes another step toward me. His scent wraps around me and his dominant demeanor sends a shiver down my back. "Was that her name?"

"Jude…" I chide.

"I don't want *her*…" He lets the last word drag, as if willing me to fill in the second half of his thought. He wants me.

I blush and glance down at my pumps.

How did we get here?

He lifts my chin, forcing me to look up into his blue eyes. "That dress should be illegal. I almost had a heart attack when you took your coat off earlier."

My mouth goes dry as his words sink in. Every modicum of coyness apparently evaporated the moment we stepped into the club. The thumping of my heart in my ears overshadows the music pulsing around us. I clinch my fists tightly, feeling a delicious heat spread through my limbs.

"How much have you had to drink?" I need to know if it's sober Jude or drunk Jude that wants me, not because I'll let that stop me—hell no—I just desperately hope he isn't drunk. I don't want him to forget this moment in the morning.

"That one mixed drink. You?" he demands, licking his

lips.

"I only took a sip," I peep, feeling heat flush my cheeks. Where do we go from here?

"Then it looks like there's no reason you shouldn't dance with me."

He doesn't wait for my answer, he just reaches for my hand and tugs me toward the dark dance floor. I have to walk fast to keep up with his long gait, but when we arrive, we bypass the perimeter and delve deeper into the swell of sweaty bodies.

Of course Jude would lead me into the very center of the packed dance floor. He set my life on fire the moment I saw him at that photo shoot. He pushes my limits, and every time I'm around him, I feel like I'm on the knife edge of desire.

We push through one final ring of dancers and I glance up toward the house lights. There are dozens of them, all whirling in circles with the beat of the music. I lose myself in their neon dance as Jude twists himself behind me. His hand drags along my stomach, leaving a trail of lust in its wake as he pulls my body close to him. His arms are so strong and controlling, pinning my body to him. I feel the firmness of his chest against my back. As the song's beat hits the crescendo, we grind our bodies together, trying to unite every single cell.

"I can feel every inch of you beneath that dress," he murmurs as his warm breath cascades down my neck and lands on the bare skin between my breasts. I follow its path and watch my breasts heave and strain against the tight fabric.

"I wore it for you," I murmur, pushing my hair behind my shoulder and offering him my neck in a moment of boldness. I'm rewarded when he bends down and trails his lips along my delicate skin. This isn't us; this is what would happen if everything were easy and right in the world. This can't be real. His hand tightens around my waist as he grinds his hips against me—hard. I don't know when it happened, when we began to acknowledge the inferno building between us, but a moan escapes me as I meet his body push for push in a dangerous, seductive dance.

"You moaned just like that at the photo shoot. I was running my hands down your body and I just barely touched your breasts. You moaned so softly I doubt anyone else heard. It was so hard not to look at you, Charley. I need you..." He trails feather-light kisses up to my ear.

His words send my body into overdrive. Raw passion is laced through each of his syllables, making my panties drip with wetness. I need him. Here. On the dance floor. Now I know he needs me too.

Before logic sets in, I reach my hands up and link my fingers behind his neck, pulling him down to me. My breasts push together. The lace from my tight dress grazes my nipples, eliciting another soft moan.

"God, you're so sexy," he whispers into my ear as his free hand trails down, past my dress, and grips my bare thigh. I love that he takes what he wants. His warm touch shocks my core and I jerk back against him. His touch is hot, demanding, and begging me to open up for him. I don't care that we're in public; no one's paying attention to us. The lighting on the dance floor makes it impossible to even see a few inches beyond yourself. We're alone in a crowd.

Once his hand grips me, he leaves it there and I know he wants encouragement. He needs me to say it's okay.

I lean my head back against his chest and push my ass against the thick erection straining through his jeans.

"Touch me, Jude," I whisper, hoping he'll push his hand

up my thigh. I want him to feel how wet I am, how much he turns me on.

Instead, his hand drags up over my dress, touching the thin valley between my breasts. A sliver of naked skin is exposed by the deep neckline. His finger skims the scalloped edge of my dress before he slides past the lacy material, dangerously close to my nipple.

I'm playing with fire and I want to be burned.

A ragged moan breaks through him. "No bra, Charley?"

I bite my lip and look up into his eyes with feigned innocence. "It wouldn't have worked with the dress."

His finger trails over my nipple and I bite down harder, needing a release.

"When you were getting dressed earlier, did you think about me touching you like this?" I close my eyes as his hand slides under the lace material and cups my bare breast. *Holy fuck*. My back arches instinctively, filling his hand with my aching chest. He growls into my ear as he kneads my overly sensitive flesh slowly and seductively. Desire ricochets through me as the world begins to fade. There's only touch, Jude's touch, arousing my every cell.

Suddenly, his fingers find my nipple and he tweaks it hard. My eyes flick open and I cry out with a mixture of pleasure and pain.

"Answer me, Charley," he demands huskily.

His sensuality is intoxicating, leaving me a heap of tingling nerves, but I manage to muster a small yes.

Chapter Ten

Jude

THE LIGHTS ILLUMINATED her skin as if she's some erotic fantasy brought to life before me. She arches into me like a flower straining toward the sun and I can't help myself. She wants me—her entire body screams it. Her nipples harden into tight buds beneath my touch. Her mouth gapes open as her head tilts back onto my chest. The way her hips press against my dick makes me want to take her right here, but I can't. This can't go that far, and I have to be the one to make sure of it.

I know this, but when she pushes her ass against my erection, the move threatens to undo me. I twist her around, push her against me, and capture her cherry-red lips roughly. I've wanted to kiss her since the photo shoot, and now that her mouth is connected with mine, I know I'll never get my fill. Her tongue sweeps across my bottom lip, capturing my soul and gripping it in her delicate hands. A hard, carnal growl moves through my throat and she pushes her body flush against mine. My hands slip through her soft curls, holding her neck and tugging her closer as I deepen the kiss.

Our hearts beat wildly, pressed together and pounding against one another. I'm trying to control my reaction to her but it's hopeless. I'm leading the kiss, controlling her and possessing her mouth, but when she shudders against me, every thought slips from my mind. Our bodies move of their own accord. She threads her hands through my hair and pulls hard, showing me what she wants. She needs a release as badly as I do, but she's scared to tell me, scared to do something so scandalous in a club full of people, even if those people are drunk and consumed by their own dancing.

A dangerous thought spurs me forward. She might be threatening every facet of my old life, but pleasuring a woman is something the last few years have taught me well and I intend on showing her exactly how adept I am.

Charley

His tongue drags along my lips, begging for entrance, and the moment I let him, my world flips upside down. Heat floods my body and I can't keep the moans from escaping my mouth as our tongues collide. Holy hell. His kiss seizes my mind, and when his hand drifts down the front of my dress, I almost cry out in anticipation. We're molded so close together that no one could even see his hand tugging the bottom of my dress up. I've never done anything like this. I've never even wanted to, but I'd rather die than have him stop now. I don't care if light suddenly floods the club and everyone's attention turns toward us; I'd still let him consume me because that's what Jude does to me. He makes me *feel*. He pushes thoughts and reason away and gives me things I can only experience with my five senses. Smelling his erotic aroma of lust and cologne. Hearing his moans rock through his body, telling me just how turned on I'm making him. Seeing the fierce desire clouding his handsome features. Tasting his minty breath as our mouths collide. Most of all, touching and feeling. Feeling his hand slip down the front of my dress and slide up the inside of my thigh.

He spins small circles on the sensitive flesh just below my thong and my mind goes black. I can't process anything except the tingles of pleasure radiating from his touch. He hasn't felt my wet thong, yet I'm about to come undone.

Goose bumps bloom across my skin as he leans close to my ear. "Open your legs for me, Charley."

I tuck my head under his chin as my feet spread, ever so slightly, just enough for his hand to slide upward, so luxuriously slowly I think I might go insane. I'm breathing raggedly, trying to concentrate on slowing my heart, but then his fingers find my thong and I gasp as my body spasms instinctively.

"Oh, Charley. You're so wet. So ready for me." His ragged words collide into me as his fingers run possessively up and down my center.

"Please," I moan huskily into his mouth, overwhelmed with need.

He slides two fingers across my inner thigh, teasing my

thong aside, and I cry out, but Jude's there capturing my mouth and feeding off my cries as his fingers slide across my wetness.

"Oh, please." I sound pained, tortured, needy.

He's barely touched me, but I'm so close to the edge. It's been so long since someone's touched me like this. His hands move so seductively, as if he knows exactly where to linger, where to drag the pad of his thumb to send delicious waves of pleasure coursing through me. His finger teases my entrance, but he won't take it that far. We don't have the luxury of time and Jude knows it.

Instead, he spins small, mindboggling circles around and around, teasing out my desire.

"Come for me, Angel," his words demand, and I know my body will comply because he's in control of me, of my world.

He rubs right where I need it the most. I bite down on his neck to muffle my cries, yet even then I can hear the faint echoes of my, "Oh, yes. Oh, god. Yes, Jude," as I fall over the edge. My entire body greedily rocks against his skilled fingers. My world shatters into a never-ending bliss and Jude is right there with me, murmuring in my ear and coaxing every last drop of my orgasm out of me.

As the waves of my desire-induced delusion wane, the world around me begins to slowly filter back in. The blaring sounds of the music, the dancing people, the entire room that exists around me. Holy. Hell. I can't believe I just did that. Jude's arm is still locked around me, but I feel like I've just awoken from a dream as it fades away, out of reach, leaving me in this scary reality. Where do we go from here?

I stay tucked under his chin, willing the world to stop turning, to go back to the moment before. What's he thinking? Surely he needs his release as well, but that won't be quite as easy in the middle of the dance floor.

Finally, I will myself to glance up and find Jude looking down at me with such sweet desire written across his features that a shot of lust spirals through me. My body is so in tune with his commands, but we hardly know each other. When did it learn that he was in control? Before or after he coaxed out the most delicious orgasm I've ever had?

"We should get back to the group. Naomi's probably worried about you," he admits with a look of disdain as he straightens the bottom of my dress. His touch is so sweet and innocent, as if he wasn't the one pulling it up indecently only moments before.

"What about you?" I ask, dropping my hand to the outside of his jeans. He's so large and his excitement is impossible to ignore when I'm pressed so close to him. With a growl, he captures my hand and shakes his head.

"Later," he promises, placing a gentle kiss to my wrist.

I pout with a silly frown. "Not fair."

"Hmm," he hums, bending down to capture my pouty lip and tease another seductive kiss out of me. That's what it feels like when he kisses me: him leading our mouths, coaxing out my desire before I even realize I have any to give.

"I want you, Charley." His mouth trails over my cheek and down to the sensitive skin just under my earlobe. "Come home with me."

His revelation and his request are everything I wanted to hear and I find myself nodding before thinking it over. Yes. Yes. Yes.

Without another word, he twines his fingers through mine and pulls us back to the VIP section. Something had shifted between us; I can feel it swirling in the musky club air. I expect him to drop my hand once we get back to everyone, but he tugs me closer, wrapping his arm around my waist and keeping me pinned to his side.

"Oh, hold on. You've got some of my lipstick on your mouth and cheek." I dip my thumb into my mouth and swipe it across his skin, cleaning him off.

"It was worth it to get to taste that delicious mouth of yours." His blue eyes are already heating up again and I have to laugh and lighten the mood or we'll be kicked out of the club for indecent exposure.

After the lipstick is gone, he leans down to offer a chaste kiss on my cheek. When I look up, Bennett, Hudson, Naomi, and half the VIP group are all staring at us with befuddled expressions. Can they see the orgasm written across my features? Is my hair wild and untamed, or am I imagining things?

I wish I could ignore their gazes, but it's too late. Jude and I should have just left. The fun is over. It dissipated all too quickly, leaving a tight pressure in my chest that threatens to suffocate me on the spot. Before I fully realize my actions, I'm tugging myself free from Jude's sturdy arms and building the fortress around my heart.

I want to rewind, back to when decisions didn't need to be made, when I didn't need to separate myself from this man. God, why do I have to think so much? Why do I have to leave this situation before he leaves me? I have no clue what he's thinking, but I can't go back to when my life was a never-ending black fog. Those days were almost impossible to get through, and I can't let Jude drag me back there. I know he wouldn't mean to hurt me, but I know I'd be the one to care too much, feel too much, love too much. Nothing can protect me from a broken heart—not even his promises.

I already lost myself in his touch and something tells me it wouldn't compare to what would happen if I go home with him.

"Charley?" Jude whispers in my ear, begging me to look at him, but I don't. I can't.

I shrug him off. "I need to talk to Naomi really quick. I'll be right back." His warm breath slips away until all I can feel is the recycled club air. Naomi's eyebrows perk up as I move toward her and I hope she can see the silent plea written across my features. In an instant, she nods in understanding and extracts herself from Bennett so we can head over to grab our jackets from the coat check.

"Jeez. Were you with Jude that whole time?" she asks in a hushed tone.

I bite my lip and nod, not meeting her eyes.

"Well, you have to come home with me. If I leave with Bennett, we'll have sex, and I'm not ready yet. It's too soon." I almost laugh; it's the last thing I'd expected her to say. My shoulders relax and already my breathing comes a little easier. She's saving me without even realizing it.

"No problem. We'll share a cab back." My voice is oddly calm, but I know it's because I'm already burying the emotions Jude just resurrected from deep within me, tucking them away behind layers of lace and curls and red lipstick.

"Thank you so much!" She grabs her jacket and hands me mine with an inquisitive stare. "Did Jude finally make a move?"

I feel my complexion burn. "Something like that."

"Hey," she says, tugging my arm lightly. "Everything okay?"

"Yeah, Naomi. It's fine." Cold, dead waves—does my

voice always sound like that?

She nods and we pull on our coats as we head back to the guys. Everyone's either leaving to head home or to the after-party at Hudson's apartment. As I say goodbye to Hudson and thank him for the invitation, Jude's piercing gaze never leaves me. Naomi and Bennett head toward the exit and Jude falls in step beside me. My body yearns to move toward him, but I shove my hands into my shallow coat pocket.

"I can't go home with you," I state plainly. "Naomi needs me to share a cab with her so she doesn't go home with Bennett." I keep my eyes pinned on the concrete floor in front of my heels, but he isn't convinced. He steps closer to me, tugging my elbow so that I have to stop and look at him.

My face reveals nothing, not a single emotion. I've perfected this hollow glance; it's what I fed Dr. Francis for months.

"Don't do this, Charley." He rubs his stubbled chin with an exasperated sigh.

I feign confusion with a shrug and a narrowed gaze. "I'm not doing anything."

"I can feel it. Do you think those walls, that facade you're hiding behind is subtle?" He leans in dangerously close and a shot of fear and lust saturates my nerves. "I see straight through you, Charley. I'm scared too, but I'm not the one running. You are."

Before I even fully register his words, Jude is brushing past me. He nods to Bennett and Naomi before disappearing through the club, leaving me behind.

• • •

Jude

Does she think any part of this is easy? She doesn't realize how far I'm straying from the boundaries of my old life. There were no games; I told her exactly what I wanted on that dance floor.

It was the hardest hour of my life letting Hudson talk to her while I looked on from across the table. He didn't even pay attention to her. He treated her like I've treated every girl before her, like she was a dime a dozen. I needed her to know how wrong he was. That's why I licked her hand when she spilled her drink. I wanted her to feel beautiful and cherished, and it worked. Hudson's gaze could've sliced my body in half. Smug prick.

I would have stolen her away earlier, but I had to be sure she felt the same. If she had wanted to be there with Hudson I would have let her enjoy her night, but it didn't take long for me to realize he completely repulsed her—as he fucking should have. Then the brunette girl locked onto me as her prey for the night. I eventually just walked away from her; she was in the middle of a sentence, but I didn't give a shit. Charley looked up and I nodded to her, asking if she wanted to leave the VIP area. When she climbed down those black stairs, I followed right after her, not caring about a single other soul in that club.

Everything was falling into place; we were acknowledging the connection between us, we were thriving off of it. Then she withdrew. The second we returned to VIP, she recoiled and we moved back to square one. I feel like I'm at a complete loss. I want to force her to face her fears, but I know that won't work. She's like a wild horse; I have to slowly coax her away from the isolated life she's made for herself. I know she's had it hard—I can see it behind her eyes—but she can't hide forever, and I want to be the person that saves her. I want her to be mine.

The vibrations from my phone stir me out of my thoughts and I glance down to see it's a work call. Really, on a Sunday morning? Then I realize I'm in my office, checking work emails.

Whatever, they don't know that. I tap my thumb against the sleek, modern desk as I swipe a finger across the screen and answer the call.

Why is the director of my upcoming shoot calling me so early on the weekend? If they're changing the location from Hawaii, I'll drop. That's the only reason I agreed to do the job in the first place.

"What can I do for you, Ryan?" I ask in a clipped tone.

"Candace is out of the shoot."

"What? Are you joking? She was picked for the cover!" The shoot in Hawaii is for Sports Illustrated. Every year they do a swimsuit issue boasting some of the sexiest women in the entertainment world. Candace Hill was picked for the cover months ago after a painfully drawn-out elimination process.

"Yeah, well, when you're nursing injuries from a motorcycle accident, you can't really model bikinis," he barks. Oh man does he sound pissed. The photo shoot is next week and we're out a cover model.

"She rides a motorcycle?"

"Her rocker boyfriend was driving and she wasn't wearing leathers, so she has road rash, but nothing too serious."

I drag my hand through my hair, staring off at the canvas photo hanging across from my desk. A small boy with sad eyes stares back at me.

"So we'll bump one of the girls from a centerfold to the cover?" Normally photographers aren't involved with the casting process, but I've made a name for myself the past few years. I've got a good eye and it commands top dollar.

"Looks like we'll have to, but there's no one that feels right for it."

I close my eyes, envisioning crystal blue eyes, bright blonde hair, and golden ivory skin.

"Wait—Ryan, look up Charley Whitlock."

Oh shit. Did I really just offer her name to him? It was impulsive, spurred on by my desire for her, but now it's too late to ignore my suggestion. I lose focus on the photo across my desk once again, waiting for his reply.

"I've heard that name before," he admits. The sound of clicking echoes through the phone as he types her name into Google.

A moment later there's a loud thud, and I'm sure he's slammed his hand on the desk. "What the hell. Why wasn't she brought up when we were doing first rounds?"

"She isn't famous or *dating* a famous person."

"Yeah? Well she will be after this. She's got it. I want her for the cover."

"Good. You'd be an idiot to choose anyone else."

"I've gotta go call her agent. For all I know, she's already booked."

"See you on the plane."

"Yeah, thanks Anderson."

When the line goes dead, I toss the phone onto the table and recline back into my black leather chair. Was that a good idea, or did I just complicate things even more with Charley? If she accepts—she'd be insane not to—we'll be in Hawaii together for three days. So much for taking it slow.

Chapter Eleven

Charley

WITH A CONTENTED sigh I push my apartment door open and slip my heavy keys onto the chipped ceramic holder hanging on the wall. I woke up early and ran until my limbs ached. I hadn't realized how far I'd actually gone until I looked at my exercise watch a moment ago: 13 miles, almost half a marathon. I was hoping the run would take longer, but the endorphins definitely helped. I'll just have to ride on their momentum as long as possible.

Maybe after I shower I'll go down to a bookstore and browse around for something to take my mind off last night. I can't let myself think about it. Every few seconds, when something threatens to remind me of Jude, I shut it down and carve out a new thought from my brain. It's torturous but necessary if I don't want to spend the entire day wallowing in self-pity, which I don't.

The blinking screen on my phone catches my attention and my heart leaps in anticipation of seeing his name. As I approach, I sigh in defeat. It's just my agent, Janet.

"Morning, Janet." I try smiling into the phone so she won't be able to tell I was hoping it was someone else.

"Where the hell have you been?" she shouts into the phone excitedly.

What? What could have happened since I chatted with her on Friday?

"I was out on a run. What's up? You don't normally leave me a dozen voicemails before noon on a Sunday," I quip.

"Pack your bags, Charley!" she squeals through the phone.

"What? Why?" My hand clasps around my neck protectively.

"You booked a COVER! Of the freaking S.I. swimsuit issue!"

Silence fills the airwaves as I let her sentence sink in. No. There's no way.

"Are you insane? They pick celebrities for that." My heart races. There's no way they'd choose me. I'm a nobody. I didn't even have Janet send them my portfolio for review. I didn't think there was a point, and to be honest, that's the way I wanted it. I don't want to be a celebrity.

"Newsflash: you're sexier than any celebrity out there! You fly out on Friday—"

"This Friday!?" I squeeze my temple with the pads of fingers as I pace my tiny room.

"Yes! I had to move around a few other jobs to make it work. You cannot pass this up."

"Who's on the shoot?"

"The magazine will provide their own makeup and hair crew. Ryan Kelly is the shoot director. You've never worked with him before, but he's amazing. Everyone raves about his vision."

"Oh yeah, I've heard of him before."

"And Jude Anderson will be lead photographer."

I nearly drop the phone.

"You've got to be kidding me."

"I'm dead serious, babe. You get the sexiest photographer in all of New York for a three-day shoot in Hawaii. Thank the karma gods, Charley, because you must have been really good in your past life."

Fucking Jude.

"What if I don't want to take this shoot, Janet? What if I'm not ready for my life to change?"

"Charley, let's just say this one shoot will give you *plenty* of time to lie low and paint. You'd be crazy to turn down the amount they'll be paying you." And her. She doesn't say it, but I'd be the worst client ever if I turned down a commission that big for her. She's a great agent and deserves to have a payoff. I'll deal with any new fame the way I handle everything else: by hiding away from it.

After we hang up, there's one last piece of the puzzle nagging my mind, and it has Jude written all over it.

I look at my phone, scroll down to the Js, and tap.

Two slow rings later, his deep voice wraps around my senses.

"Hello." God, he says that word so alluringly I almost forget my anger. Almost.

"Did you have something to do with me landing this freaking job?" I snap.

He chuckles lightly. "Good morning, Charley. You sound radiant."

God I want him. No! Damn it.

"Jude! What the hell? Did I book this job because of you or because they actually wanted me?"

He pauses and I rub my hand anxiously along my hairline.

"They had originally booked Candace Hill, but she is injured and they needed a replacement. I mentioned your name to Ryan, yes. However, he chose you on his own. You should have been on the list, I just expedited the process."

"Dammit, Jude!"

"You sound even sexier when you're angry. Maybe I should piss you off more…"

"I hate you. This isn't a game!"

A sexy chuckle spills through the phone.

"Don't forget to pack a few bikinis, Charley. The weather is warm in Hawaii and we'll be staying in a hotel on the water."

With that, the line goes dead and I hurl my phone against the pillows on my bed. That bastard. This is a perfect example of why we shouldn't be in a relationship. The last thing I need to be worrying about is whether or not people in the industry assume I'm sleeping around to get jobs.

• • •

As the week drags slowly on, it begins to sink in just how much my life will change after this shoot. This magazine hits every newsstand across the nation and there's not a heterosexual male who doesn't own a copy the day it goes on sale. Am I ready for this? What if the world finds out who I truly am? Will my alias hold up? It's too late to change my mind. I'll just have to hope for the best and be ready for the consequences. I've gone into hiding once, and I can do it again.

Janet told me all the models and crew are meeting in New York and a private jet will be taking us to Hawaii; it's easier to coordinate if Ryan knows everyone is safe and sound. The last thing he needs is a delayed flight and a missing model. I haven't been on a private jet in years, since before my father's charges were announced, but I'm excited to experience it again—as long as I can avoid Jude and whichever model he decides to replace me with. He said he didn't date models, but we *quasi* dated so that can't be true. God, it kills me to think of him with another girl, but I keep reminding myself that that's insane. We've known each other for one week; that's not enough time to hand someone your heart. No, I've only handed him a few pieces, pieces I wish I could take back and protect under lock and key again.

Throughout the week, most of my free hours are spent preparing for the trip. I nab a few sundresses and light scarves, a new pair of flat, strappy sandals for walking on the beach, and some travel-sized bathroom essentials.

By Thursday night I feel confident with my packing progress, so I decide to meet Naomi and Bennett for an early dinner. I have to be at the airport at six in the morning because the flight is scheduled for an ungodly eleven hours, but fortunately we don't start shooting until Saturday. Hopefully I'll be able to catch up on some sleep during the flight.

Pushing open the heavy oak door, the scent from the oven-baked pizza stirs memories of forgotten hunger. Pizza was my favorite food growing up and sometimes the aroma carries me back to simpler times; I'm hoping that will be the case today. I've been running even more this week, and if anything, I should *gain* a pound or two before the shoot. My jeans feel less snug than they usually do.

I'm sure people assume I'm thin from the pressures of the modeling world, but my problem stems from my lack of appetite and general overthinking—like today, for instance, I was too busy running errands and packing. The only thing I've had to eat was a protein bar this morning. It's hard to remember to eat when you're never hungry.

Oh well. Naomi chose my favorite food for a reason. She knows I'm nervous about the shoot and am in desperate need of a proper meal. When I scan the restaurant, relief washes over me as I spot her and Bennett sitting in a booth along the side wall. I didn't think they'd lie to me, but a part of me figured Jude might have tagged along without me knowing. I'll see him bright and early tomorrow morning, but I need another few hours to build my strength before I have to look into those gorgeous blue eyes again.

"Hey guys." I smile and slide into the bench across from them. The two little lovebirds are squeezed together on one side of the booth. Their hands rest between them on the table, locked in a sweet display of affection. I wonder if I should I be looking for a bridesmaid's dress soon...

"There she is!" Naomi sings, pulling my attention away from their entwined hands.

Bennett casts me a wide smile. "Will we even get to hang out with you when you're rich and famous?"

I blush and tug a hand through my hair. "Oh, be quiet. You know I'm going to hide out as much as possible."

He laughs. "It's strange that a girl like you would get into such a public profession."

I nod because he's right, but there's more to it than that. "Yeah, well, if you saw the paycheck, you might not think that. I'm essentially selling my soul and my right to privacy for a burlap sack with a money sign on it."

"Ah." He waggles his eyebrows, making us laugh.

A beat later, my eyes fall on Bennett's tailored suit and Naomi's gorgeous ivory wrap dress. Suddenly I feel way underdressed in my slouchy jeans and knitted sweater, even if they are designer.

"Did you guys come straight from work?"

"Yeah," they say in unison and smile lovingly toward one another as if they're straight out of a 1950s afternoon special.

"Do you have to hide the relationship while you're there, or does it not matter since you two are in different departments?" I ask, curious about how their relationship pans out during the work day. What would it be like to work in an office with Jude? I can't imagine my days would be very productive. I'd be on edge the whole day, wondering when he would turn the corner and find me daydreaming about him, drooling like a sap at my desk.

Bennett sighs. "We haven't disclosed it with HR yet, but we should soon."

"Oh, yeah, we should," Naomi agrees, dropping her gaze. It's a strange reaction, but I'll let it slide for now. Maybe they've been avoiding discussing the topic. I'd imagine it's a big step to make their relationship public at work. It puts more pressure on the situation, and they probably don't want to be the topic of workplace gossip.

I clear my throat. "Do you guys already know what you want?"

"We were thinking of just splitting a large pizza. We need to fatten you up!" Naomi laughs, and I'm glad to see her light mood again.

"Ha ha. Sadly that's true. I've been too nervous to eat this week. I've never done a cover shoot before."

"You'll be great; don't worry about it, Charley," Naomi states confidently.

I nod and drag my eyes down the menu, reading over all the topping options.

"I'm good with whatever you guys want, as long as it has pepperoni," I decide, dropping the menu back onto the table and reaching for my water. I squeeze the lemon into the glass and swirl it around until the bitter citrus has dispersed completely.

When the waitress comes around, Bennett orders our large pizza with olives, mushrooms, spinach, and pepperoni. Just hearing him describe the ingredients makes my mouth salivate like one of Pavlov's dogs.

The second the waitress leaves, Naomi steeples her fingers and studies me with an air of concentration. The mood around the table instantly shifts from friendly dinner to shit's-about-to-get-real. When I glance between them, it's clear I'm about to be subjected to an intervention of sorts.

"Are you nervous about Jude being in Hawaii as well?" Naomi asks candidly, keeping her razor sharp gaze on me.

"Naomi…" I warn, not really wanting to discuss everything in front of Bennett. He's hardly an unbiased third party.

"Hey, don't worry about me," he offers, probably realizing his awkward position. "It's not like I haven't had to listen to Jude rambling on about you for the past two weeks."

"What?" I ask before I think better of it. "No, wait. It doesn't matter."

"Charley, he's obviously crazy about you," Naomi offers gently.

"Yeah, well, I'm not happy about his involvement in the casting of the shoot. It feels slimy and I hate having to second-guess my reasons for being hired. Those models are going to be the most gorgeous women in the world and they're going to judge the fact that I was given the cover."

"Don't let them bother you," Naomi advises. "Remember you're absolutely gorgeous, and yes, Jude might have introduced you to Ryan, but Ryan wouldn't have agreed with Jude if you weren't perfect. Why would he have? It's his name at stake if people don't like his cover."

"Maybe he owed Jude a favor…" My insecurities rear their ugly head, and then I bite back my words. "Whatever. I'm going to avoid him at all costs. He can party with the other models. I'll focus on the shoot and soaking up as much sun as I can. It'll be fine."

Bennett bites his lip and I know he's fighting an internal battle about whether he should speak up or not. When his mouth opens a moment later, I take a deep breath, preparing for his testimony.

"Charley, I don't think you should write Jude off just yet. He was being honest when he said he never dates models; you're the first he's ever cared to get to know. His dating habits weren't completely wholesome in the past"—my stomach twists in knots thinking about Jude with women before me—"but he's different around you." He pauses and then decides to continue on. "And there are things in his past that pushed him toward that way of life. They aren't my stories to tell, but there's more to Jude than what you see on the surface."

Dammit Bennett. Dammit. Dammit.

I don't want to hear any of this. I want Bennett's eyes to hold less sincerity, less honesty. I know he's telling me the truth, and as hard as I try to reinforce the walls around my heart, already I feel another small piece breaking apart for Jude, for this man that might have as many demons as I do.

Wiping my hand down my cheek in defeat, I sigh and meet his eyes. "Can we not talk about him for the rest of dinner if I promise I'll take your words to heart?"

My stomach is coiled into a tight knot and I just want to relax and eat some pizza.

Naomi reaches across the table and grabs my hand.

Looking into my eyes, she offers me a hopeful look. "I'm really excited for you. This is a good step. You deserve it; don't let your past ruin it for you."

Chapter twelve

Jude

THE PRIVATE AIRPLANE hangar is buzzing with activity even though it's hardly half past five in the morning. The world was silent on the cab ride over, but here, everyone's grabbing coffee and securing their luggage and carry-ons. I sigh, reclining back in the soft leather chair as my assistants confirm all our equipment is accounted for. It's cold in the lobby so I tug on my leather jacket, reminding myself that soon I'll be in Hawaii and away from the cold for three days. Perfect.

A stout, middle-aged flight attendant, dressed head to toe in navy blue, announces that we can begin to board the plane while we wait for the rest of the passengers. Leaning down to grab my luggage, I recheck my phone, trying to stall a moment longer because Charley hasn't arrived yet. I almost called her yesterday to insist that she let me pick her up or at least hire a car service for her, but I ended up deciding against it. When we talked on the phone about the shoot she told me she "hated me", and although I know those words couldn't be further from the truth, I wanted to give her some space.

I don't regret offering her name to Ryan. She should have booked the cover over Candace to begin with, and I'm glad everything worked out in the end. She can be angry with me all she wants—hell, it's a turn-on anyway. I smile wickedly thinking of her sexy voice during our phone conversation.

The stout flight attendant props open a pair of sleek glass doors that lead out onto the runway. Everyone begins filing past me, heading into the dark, foggy air to begin loading their luggage. I hang back for another moment, hoping Charley will appear. A few minutes pass. Nearly everyone has filtered out of the lobby and there's still no sign of her, so I decide to board and save two seats.

The cabin of the private jet is luxurious, with light brown leather seats lining a long aisle in pairs. Thankfully the rows aren't crammed together. There's enough room to recline fully so that the chairs form makeshift beds. I claim a row in the back of the plane, tossing my carry-on bag into the window seat to save it for her. If I had to guess, I'd assume Charley would want the opportunity to glance out the window. The thought makes me narrow my eyes toward the front of the plane in search of her.

All I see is a flurry of glimmering hair in varying colors as the other models flounce around the plane. I recognize most of them from the casting process or from previous photo shoots. I don't think I've actually held a real conversation with any of them, though it's not from their lack of perseverance. The moment I take my seat, a few of them hop up and make their way to toward my row like piranhas.

"Morning, Jude," a pretty redhead sings as she angles her body toward me. I have to fight the urge to pull out my phone and ignore her greeting all together. Don't feel bad for her—I've seen her jump from bed to bed on every shoot we've worked on together. She's not interested in my morning; she's interested in having a quickie in the plane's restroom. The girls keep talking but their words filter through the air unheard, as if my ears don't recognize the frequency in which they speak. I nod and offer simple greetings, but it's impossible to ignore their lingering gazes. A few of them even glance at my carry-on bag on the vacant seat, but I smile civilly and cut the conversations short. The last thing I need is for Charley to board right as one of them is trying to sink their claws into me. I don't need any more cards stacked against me when it comes to her.

They eventually wander off, and as the plane continues to fill, I smirk, pleased with myself for not ordering that car service after all. If I had, Charley would have been here ten minutes ago and she could have picked a seat anywhere on board. Now there are fewer spots available and the odds that she'll *have* to sit by me are looking better and better.

That is until I see Ryan board the plane a moment later with Charley in tow. Motherfucker. She's tilting her head back and smiling up at him—a perfectly beautiful smile, except it's aimed at the wrong person. Ryan's assistant, who boarded right after them, taps him on the shoulder and mutters something in his ear. He nods and takes out his cell phone, leaving Charley to wave goodbye and look up the aisle of the plane.

Her blue eyes find me and I watch her swallow slowly.

She hovers in the middle of the aisle, frozen until she realizes she's blocking everyone's path. She blushes and murmurs an apology before hiking her bag higher on her shoulder and walking toward the back of the plane, directly to me.

I stand as she approaches, taking in her sexy jeans and tight, white, long-sleeved shirt.

"Morning." I try to keep the smile off my lips, I really do, but I still feel the ends of my mouth curling up.

She narrows her eyes sharply in response and I know I'm not in the clear yet. I gesture over to the window. "I saved you a seat."

Twisting her head around, she takes in her other options. Most of the crew has paired off and a few of the models are chatting casually. Ryan's sitting with his assistant, which leaves Charley to choose between sitting by me or the chubby lighting director.

"But if you'd rather…" I goad, leaning in so that my breath tingles across her skin.

She rolls her eyes and brushes past me to get to the seat. I thought she was sexy on the phone, but seeing her pissed in real life feels like a wicked challenge I can't wait to take on. Her butt brushes against my thigh, barely grazing the front of my pants. I inhale and clench my fist. Surely she didn't do that on purpose, or she's playing much dirtier than I was expecting.

I grab my bag and shove it under my seat as she sits down and gets comfortable. I can smell vanilla lingering in the air she just occupied, and I wonder if that's the scent she chooses for body wash as well as lip gloss. I'm still fixated on that thought when she leans in, whispering so quietly no one else can hear. "I don't hate you."

The words aren't what stir my heart; it's the tone she

uses, as if she were murmuring sweet nothings into my ear instead of a white flag. I lick my lips, needing to adjust myself so I can sit more comfortably, but I don't want to give her the satisfaction. The past few weeks have been hell. I can't remember the last time I've gone this long without sex. I feel like I've reverted back to being a fourteen-year-old. The slightest touch from Charley and I'm a fucking goner.

Eyeing her out of the corner of my gaze, I see a slight smile gracing her lips. I don't know how long she'll be like this—open and receptive—but I'll take it slow. Bennett told me about their conversation last night; I know I'm walking a thin line with her and I'll be damned if I step over the edge until she's good and ready.

We sit in silence until the jet taxis down the runway and takes off. She's leaning on the palm of her hand and focusing on the expanse of pre-dawn darkness outside her window when I lean over.

"It's always darkest just before the dawn," I offer quietly, knowing a girl like her would appreciate the imagery in the proverb.

After a long pause, she asks, "How long until I see the light?"

"Sooner than everyone back on the ground. The plane is taking us to a higher perspective, so we'll rise to meet the sun."

"So we're literally *rising and shining*?" she asks with a sly smile, sliding her gaze toward me to see if I appreciate the nuances of her humor.

I can't help the overwhelming smile that grips my features.

"Was I right to think you prefer the window seat?"

She nods.

"I'm a daydreamer," she murmurs.

I mull over her revelation. "That doesn't surprise me one bit. Were you always like that?"

She chews on her lip in thought, angling toward me slightly. "More so in the past few years. I think that's why I like to run and paint. I run to get a break from my overactive imagination, and I paint so I can *use* that same imagination. I don't think I'd be able to function without a combination of the two."

I can see the beautiful heaviness of her soul when she explains things like that. "I know what you mean. I'm a runner as well.

She smiles. "I kind of guessed from the soccer game." Her eyes linger over my chest and abs. "And other *things*."

My hands grip the seat beneath her blatant appraisal of my body. Does she realize how obvious she is? How much she's turning me on?

"Have you ever done a marathon?" I ask, trying to ignore our volatile chemistry.

"No, but I've been thinking about it lately. Maybe I'll work my way up to one."

I slip my leather coat off. The cabin is much warmer than the hangar was. "You should. It's an amazing feeling when you cross that finish line."

"Have you done the New York Marathon?"

"And Boston. I'm not sure which I prefer."

She raises her eyebrows. "Impressive."

I nod, wanting to turn the conversation away from me.

"Bennett told me you guys got dinner last night."

"Yeah." She drags her hand through her hair and twists it into a little ballerina bun, highlighting her elegant cheekbones and neck. "I've been nervous about the shoot, so I was happy for the escape."

Why is she nervous?

"Since it's your first cover?" I ask.

She bites her lip. "Yeah. I'm just not sure what to expect." Her voice lowers to a whisper, but everyone's immersed in their own conversations, so she shouldn't be overheard. "I honestly feel a little out of my league," she says, turning back to the window. My stomach sinks. She's the most beautiful thing in the world and I hate that she can't see that at times. She knows she's pretty, but she shouldn't be intimidated by the models on this plane; they don't hold a candle to her beauty.

I turn my body toward her so my knees hit the side of her chair.

"On my first shoot for a fashion magazine, I didn't have a clue what I was doing. They hired me because of work I'd done for National Geographic and Time Magazine, but when I got to the set, I almost turned around on the spot. I wasn't ready to enter this world. Models are an *interesting* subject to photograph, and I've worked with my fair share of crazy ones"—I lean in closer—"some of which are on this plane with us."

She laughs and then curves her body toward me, bringing her knees to her chest and leaning her head back against the leather seat; I have her full attention.

I continue, "But I just focused on doing my job and it worked out."

"That sounds easy enough." She nods, but her eyes still shine a dark, murky blue, and I know she's wrestling with another thought.

A moment later, she explains, "I'm also nervous about the fame. I almost wish I could just be in the background of the shots."

Wanting a private life isn't peculiar, but for some

reason I don't think Charley's hiding from the spotlight for reasons quite so transparent.

"You don't have to do the cover if you don't want to," I offer. "Hell, you don't have to do the photo shoot if you don't want to. You can be my assistant." I wink at her and am rewarded with one of her heart-stopping grins.

"It's okay. My agent, Janet, put it in perspective for me. The money I'll be making will allow me to paint uninterrupted for a while, and that's what I've wanted all along."

Smart girl. "Would you ever want to exhibit your work?"

She mulls over the thought. "I'm not sure. When I first started, it was a deeply personal process. I never dreamed of sharing my work with anyone. But what's funny is that to an outsider, they're just abstract paintings. They have no clue what I was experiencing while I was working on them." She draws soft circles on the arm of the chair. "It's not as if I painted a self-portrait or anything."

A few moments pass as I chew on her words. "I think it could be a good step. Sometimes sharing things with the world can feel…freeing."

She soaks in my words as she studies the tan leather seat. The cabin's quieter now as conversations dwindle. It's still only half past six in the morning and everyone starts turning off their overhead lights and reclining their chairs in hopes of catching a few more hours of sleep.

"I'm too wired to sleep just yet," Charley whispers, scooting closer to me so her voice doesn't carry across the quiet cabin.

"I brought a mystery book with me if you want to read it?"

Her eyes light up. "Yes!" She leans forward under her

chair, reaching to pull a book out of her bag.

"Here, we can swap for the flight. I've read this before." I glance down to see Jonathan Safran Foer printed on the spine.

"Are you Jewish?" I ask, glancing up to her.

Her eyes brows furrow. "What? No?"

I smile, pointing down to the sticker placed on the top corner of the book: National Jewish Book Award.

She half smiles. "Oh, I hadn't noticed that. A lot of the story focuses on a Holocaust survivor..." She pauses. "But I'm not really...anything. Are you religious?"

I mull over her question, contemplating the cruelties of life that I've seen firsthand. "No, but I grew up Catholic. My parents and brother still practice." I draw a line around my neck. "My dad has worn a heavy gold crucifix since before I can remember."

She smiles at the idea. "How very Boston of him."

I laugh, a little too loud, and people turn to glare at us.

"It's only funny because it's true," I admit. "What about your dad, is he religious?" I purposely glaze over her mom; I don't want to upset her.

Her face falls so suddenly and harshly that she takes my heart with it. "He's dead, but he used to take me to church when I was younger."

I'm beginning to understand that being around Charley is like walking on a minefield, but it's worth the risk. It's worth treading lightly to unveil the girl behind those blue eyes.

"My mom never came because he insisted on taking us to one of the nondenominational community churches. Let's just say she did not approve. On any given Sunday, we'd sit crammed between a single mom of five and a homeless person. It was a humbling experience, and I'm grateful he took me. Even if the religion itself didn't stick, the lessons did."

"He sounds like a great dad," I murmur.

Turning back to look out through the window, she mumbles, "I thought so too."

"When did he pass away?"

She pauses a beat too long before answering, and I realize I'm once again treading on thin ice with her.

"Four years ago," she finally says before turning toward me. "Could I read that book now?"

• • •

We end up reclining our chairs and reading in silence for a while. Every now and then she gasps quietly, completely lost in her own world, and I can't help but watch her. Does she always get carried away in the books she reads, or only in thrillers? Either way, it's adorable. When her eyes grow wide and she mumbles "no way" under her breath, I can't resist the urge to make her show me what part she's on. Every time she angles the book toward me and points her finger to the sentence. I read the passage and give her a knowing glance before letting her get back to it.

Eventually, we sleep on and off for a few hours. Every time I wake up, Charley is sleeping soundlessly. She's wrapped in the blanket and pillow the airline supplied for each of us, and her blonde hair shimmers on top of the drab, gray wool. When we first went to sleep she was leaning away, toward the window, but I guess she moved closer while I napped because her sweet face angles toward me now.

Bright sunlight streams through the window covers,

highlighting a piece of wavy blonde hair that lies across her eyelid. I reach over to push it away, watching her peaceful inhales and exhales. When my hand touches her, I expect her to stir, but she hums and pushes her cheek against my palm affectionately. The act is so innocent, and I momentarily lose myself in her. Instead of pulling away, I leave my hand there, cupping her cheek and running my thumb gently along the soft skin of her cheekbone. The movements lull me back to sleep.

When I wake an hour later, my hand has fallen down to cup her neck. A small smile forms on my lips even before I blink to find her blue eyes staring back at me in amusement.

"Hi," she whispers.

I smile lazily, blinking my eyelids open.

"I thought your hand was part of my dream." Her words hold so much promise.

"Were you dreaming about me, Charley?" I ask with a dark tone.

She sucks in her bottom lip coyly and nods but never looks away. Maybe she's slowly beginning to trust me?

I lean forward until my lips brush her earlobe. "You were cuddled against the seat facing me; I thought you wanted me to touch you."

She blushes and laces her fingers with mine over her neck. We sit frozen, drowning in one another, enjoying the moment until her breathing changes and I feel her pulse quicken beneath my hand.

"I was mad at you." She pauses. "I'm still mad at you, for interfering with my career."

"I'll never do it again. I honestly didn't think about it from your perspective. I thought you'd be happy about it."

She nods and her chin brushes against my hand. "I am.

I'm confused, yes, but overall, I'm happy about being here."

"With me?"

Her breath hits the side of my face as I listen to her uneven inhales.

"Yes."

R.S. Grey

Chapter thirteen

Charley

THE HOTEL IS beyond my wildest expectations—although you can hardly even refer to it as a hotel. Hotel insinuates a multistory building with hundreds of rooms; the Kaunaou is an intimate resort boasting fewer than fifty guests at a time and a staff member dedicated to every suite. Our crew makes up more than half of the rooms, an the other patrons look like well-to-do families from all around the world. I wonder if they knew a swimsuit photo shoot would infiltrate their vacation.

I wasn't sure what to expect for the room situations, but it turns out that while some of the crew is sharing rooms, the models and important staff members get to enjoy the luxury of having their own suite. I'm smiling at the thought of how good it'll feel to sleep in a luxurious bed later when Jude strolls over to me with two room keys in hand. They aren't the standard electronic cards; they're intricate gold keys attached to a sand dollar key chain. I immediately wonder how long it'll be before I lose mine.

"Suites 11 and 12," he gloats, holding out one of the keys to our adjacent rooms.

"Coincidence?" I ask with a wink.

His delectable lips twist up into a smirk. "I think you know the answer to that."

I laugh. "Ah, is it one of the perks of being friends with the director?"

"Something like that. Let me get your bags." He reaches down and grabs my suitcase, but I keep my carry-on wrapped around my body.

"I got this." I smile, and he doesn't fight me on it as we start to wander toward our rooms. The journey takes us much longer than it should because we keep stopping to marvel at the absolute beauty that is Hawaii. We saw an aerial view of the islands from the airplane, but standing in paradise feels completely different. The resort is open and airy. There's no clear delineation between the outdoors and the interior of the building, just sloped roof structures and pillars every now and then. The crystal clear water practically laps up into the hotel and a rush of excitement passes through me at the idea of getting to swim in it tomorrow.

I wish we had the time today—after all, it's only three in the afternoon—but I have a few fittings and makeup tests before the shoot tomorrow morning. Those are the last things I want to do after hours of traveling, but it shouldn't take all night.

I pull my gaze from the beach and glance down the corridor. We pass room 15 then room 14, and I realize we're getting closer.

"Do you have a preference on rooms?"

I slide my eyes over to him and, with a smile, ask, "Am I allowed to pick after we see the views?"

"What!" His eyes dance with humor and he narrows them as a grin spreads across his lips. Suddenly the air between us sparks and the game is on.

In a flash, he drops my bags and takes off down the hallway with me at his heels. Sliding the key into the lock on room 12, he pushes the door open and I duck under his arm to inspect the room. It's completely breathtaking and without a doubt it has the same exact view as room 11, but it doesn't matter. We have to look at them both. I reach up and tug room 11's key out of his hand and dart out into the hall to unlock the next door. He's yelling behind me, but I heave the door open and smile when I see that there's no palm tree obstructing the view of the ocean from this room.

"Mine!" I yell, right as Jude screams, "This one's mine!"

We erupt in laughter, but I can't let him win. I run over and jump up onto the bed like a ten-year-old. "Sorry, Jude, but the room has been claimed!"

He waggles his eyebrows seductively and throws his leather jacket onto one of the nearby desk chairs. "Oh, really? Cause it looks like I've already put my jacket down." He shrugs his arms and cocks his brow, as if to say 'tough luck, kid'.

My arms cross over my chest and I stand a little taller. "Don't worry, I'll call room service and explain the situation. I'm sure they can hang up your jacket in room 12 because that's *your* room."

"Is that so, Whitlock?" His sharp blue eyes dare me to keep playing the game, and it's an offer I can't refuse.

My hip juts out to the side. "Looks like it, Anderson," I

spit with all the sass I wish I actually possessed.

He takes a predatory step forward and my body starts to tremble. All at once the memories from the dance floor flood my brain and I know I'm in over my head. This is Jude's game and his rules. He takes another step and then another, and already my heart is beating a wild rhythm.

"Sir. Sir?" A voice calls from the hallway. A moment later, a young bellboy arrives at the door holding our bags and eyeing us suspiciously. Our race down the hallway surely caused a commotion.

Jude turns around with a frustrated sigh, not happy about being interrupted, but when he sees the bellboy holding our bags, his demeanor relaxes. He strides over confidently to retrieve our luggage and tip the boy.

As he slips his wallet out of his back pocket, he shakes his head regretfully, but I can tell he's still being playful.

"Sorry about that." He angles his head back to me. "My friend and I were racing to see who could get to our rooms first. She's a bad influence on me." A loud chuckle escapes me and I clap my hands over my mouth. As Jude hands over some cash, the bellboy fleetingly glances up at me standing on the bed and his face reddens. Jude follows his glance with a wicked grin.

He tisks, shaking his head admonishingly. "Oh, don't worry. I'll punish her for hopping up on the bed like that." I think the bellboy's eyes almost bulge out of his head at Jude's joke, but then he turns on his heels and hurries down the hall before Jude can assure him he's kidding. Poor kid.

A soft chuckle sounds from Jude as he closes the door and turns back to me with a hungry gaze.

"You can *punish* me all you want, but the room's mine." I smirk.

Quicker than I could have imagined, Jude's across the

room and pulling my feet out from under me. I fall back onto the bed with a loud thud and gasp in surprise as the pillows catch my head. Before I can even think to react, he drags me down by my boots so my legs hang off the bed.

My heart is practically in my throat as he bends down to hover over me, placing each of his hands on either side of my head. I have no clue what we're doing, but I don't want him to stop. I feel like I'll spontaneously combust if he walks away now.

He holds his gaze steady with mine as I watch him bend down to tug the bottom of my sweater up. He gently nips my stomach with his teeth.

"Jude," I moan, scared of the power he has over me.

His teeth keep gently nipping higher and higher until he reaches my neck and then he grazes my earlobe. The sensation of his lips against that skin is so erotic that my eyes roll back into my head and my back arches.

His husky words break through my cloud of pleasure. "I think I should get some kind of *compensation* if you're getting the room with the better view."

My chest quivers as my lungs try desperately to expand fully. I have two options: I can give in and offer something, or I can keep playing his game. I choose option two.

"Should I arrange for a model to come by your room? They've been eyeing you this whole trip. Who do you want? That pretty brunette? I'll have her come *compensate* you after our fitting." I thrust my hips up so they meet his groin in a seductive wave as I drawl out the word *compensate*. I know I'm playing with fire.

He growls and cups my chin so I can't tilt my head away. The move should scare me, but instead, it turns me 'on, morphing me into a puddle of desire. I like this side of him, the side that won't let me get away with my snarky games. I want him to force me to open up to him—physically and emotionally.

With his hand on my chin, he grinds himself against me *there*, once, twice, over and over again until I feel like I'm going to lose my mind. "Are you listening to me, Charley?"

I gulp. "Yes." His pants and my jeans are the only barriers between us, but they feel transparent when he grinds hard like that.

"I. Don't. Want. Them," he bites out.

We stare into each other's eyes with a fierce intensity.

"Then take what you want, Jude," I whisper demandingly. His eyes glow with unspoken desire when those words slip out of my mouth. Did I really just say that?

His brow cocks and he sweeps his lips down over mine, so gently I'm not sure if they're actually on me or not. "I plan on it, Charley, but it's almost four and you have fittings." With that, he grabs my arms and hauls me up off the bed.

He's gone from the room before I even fully catch my breath. How does he do that? How does he turn my world completely upside down?

• • •

You can hardly even call them fittings—we're only modeling string bikinis and simple cover-ups—but they want to be sure they have everything in the correct size, so we're set up in a conference room inside the resort. Models fling clothes everywhere as they change into their swimsuits, and stylists flit around taking measurements and adjusting straps and ties.

They have a few styles picked out for me, but for tomorrow, I'll be in a white bikini that has a twisted bandeau top and a strappy Brazilian bottom. It's more revealing than any of the suits I packed for the trip, but it fits like a glove and it looks amazing paired with the delicate gold chain the stylists tie from my neck down to my waist. It looks like something a celebrity would wear as they're tromping around on their honeymoon. I tug gently on the thin chain as the stylists swarm around me.

"How the hell are your boobs that big when you're this size?" the small raven-haired girl asks as she adjusts my swimsuit bottom. I blush, peaking down at the top of the bathing suit. My breasts are spilling out of the tight top, and I have to fight the urge to adjust the material to cover them more.

"They aren't *that* big…" I try to assure myself—and anyone else in earshot—but the stylist huffs and steps back to inspect her work.

"Ugh, you lucky bitch." She laughs and whips around to go grab another suit. I use the opportunity to go stand in front of one of the numerous full-length mirrors positioned throughout the room. I gasp when I see my reflection. My tanned skin looks like it's glowing beneath the gold body-necklace even in the harsh resort lighting; I'm sure it'll be even better when we're out on the beach. I twist on the balls of my feet to check out the back and almost faint when I see how much of my ass is exposed. It's not a thong, thank God, but it cuts sharply, revealing quite a handful. Jude is going to freak and I can't help but smile at the thought.

"What a great suit," a sweet voice sounds behind me. I turn to see the brunette model that only an hour ago I was mentioning to Jude for *compensation*.

"Oh thanks." I smile. "I'm Charley by the way."

"Bella," she coos, taking my hand. She's absolutely beautiful with deeply tanned skin and long silky brown hair—not to mention I've seen her in dozens of magazines over the past year. Why didn't they choose her for the cover?

"So I saw you sitting with Jude on the plane." Her head tilts to the side gently and she rests her hand against her elbow. Wow, she really cuts to the chase. Her sentence wasn't posed as a question, but her tone insinuates that I should answer as though it was.

"Yeah, he's a friend," I answer curtly, unsure of where she's leading the conversation.

I guess my tone was overtly defensive because she holds her left hand up so that her beautiful ring glistens in the light. "Oh, you don't have to worry about me, but you should know that I've worked with him on a few other shoots. He's never dated any models that I know of, but let's just say some of these girls wouldn't mind being his first."

My eyes scan through the crowd as she speaks. It's not like I couldn't already see that, but I wonder why she wants to point it out to me.

"Why are you telling me this?" I ask with a slight smile so she doesn't think I'm angry with her.

"I saw you guys cuddling when I used the plane's bathroom. It was incredibly sweet and I don't presume to know what's going on, but if you *are* more than just friends, I wouldn't let these girls get to you."

I'm about to explain to her that we aren't more than friends, but I bite my lip. She's trying to help me out and I appreciate it. I'd be lying if I said I wasn't slightly intimidated by the thought of all these beautiful women pining for Jude. Damn him; if he weren't full of such dark sexiness, this wouldn't be a problem.

"I appreciate it, Bella." I smile before swapping the subject. "Where are you from?"

• • •

By the time the fittings are done and I'm back in my room, exhaustion has set in and nothing sounds better than a relaxing bubble bath before I crawl into my king-sized bed. The bath is practically overflowing, music streams from my phone, and I've dimmed the lights so shadows cast across the gleaming marble floor. The bathroom angles toward the ocean, and if I leave the door open I can see the rolling waves fading into the black night as I recline into the Jacuzzi-style tub. It's perfect and I let my mind wander as I soak myself into a pruned raisin.

The water turned lukewarm a while ago, but I haven't been able to force myself to get out. The only reason I stir at all is because the last song on my playlist cut off, silencing the room and awaking reality. The peace and quiet was just what I needed after the hectic day, even if a certain pair of dark eyes still wove their way into my thoughts the entire time.

Suddenly, a loud clap sounds at my door and I jump, sloshing water over the side of the tub. Who would be coming by? I didn't order room service, even though I should probably eat soon. I haven't thought to have dinner yet. I step out and grab my towel to dry off before quickly wrapping my body in one of the resort's plush robes. It's fluffy, white, and reaches the tips of my feet. I'm completely cocooned in its warmth as I trek to the door. I lean forward to look through the peephole, and my heart races when I see Jude's confident smile on the other side.

With my hand clutching the top of my robe closed, I unlock the door and slide it open.

"What are you doing here?" I ask, even though I can see the bags of food in his hand. Maybe he's just stopping by on the way to his room.

"You have to eat something," he answers, as if the situation between us is completely black and white.

I clutch the robe tighter. "How do you know I haven't eaten already?"

His eyes scan down my robe before landing back on my face with an easy smirk. "Charley, have you eaten yet?"

I suck in my bottom lip, trying to stall for time, but it doesn't work. "No," I answer simply.

He holds up the bags. "Don't worry, I won't keep you up late, I swear." He crosses his hand over his heart and my resolve melts ever so slightly.

I want him to come in. I do. I want him to so badly, but what happened earlier is still fresh in mind. If he comes in now, I'm scared of where it might lead. Or do I want it to lead there? I certainly did earlier…

"Okay, but only because I'm starving," I huff, as if I'm even slightly annoyed by his presence.

He winks as I hold the door open a little wider and let him pass by. "Oh, of course." His presumptuous tone makes me want to kick him out—just barely. Unfortunately, it also makes me want to jump his bones.

It's quite the predicament.

"You can set out the food while I change." I point over to the small dining room table in the corner of the room facing the large floor-to-ceiling windows.

He sets the bag down and glances at me over his

shoulder with smoldering eyes. "I think I like what you have on just fine."

"I'm sure you do," I retort with a scolding headshake. He chuckles as he starts to open the bags, and I quickly grab my yoga pants and a loose nightshirt.

"You should see what I'm wearing tomorrow. It's a really modest one piece," I joke as I walk back out from the bathroom, having changed and brushed out my long hair so it falls straight down my back. It'll only last for a few minutes though; the moment it starts to air dry, it'll turn into loose waves.

"Somehow I doubt that." He quirks his brow skeptically as he starts to scoop salad and chicken onto one of the plates. I smile, accepting the plate as I take one of the seats at the table. I wrap my legs up under me and as soon as my eyes take in the feast before me, my stomach grumbles loudly. It's a strange sensation after having lost my hunger so long ago.

"I guess I didn't realize how hungry I was." I blush, unwrapping one of the plastic forks.

"You seem to be forgetful when it comes to food," Jude remarks, but I just shrug, doubting he'd be able to understand.

Once he's sitting across from me and we've eaten a few bites, he pauses and glances up. "So tell me more about this suit."

"Well, it's covered by a really long skirt, so you can't see anything."

"Mhm," he mumbles.

"Don't believe me?" I cock my brow challengingly.

"Not in the slightest," he says, licking his lips between bites. My eyes follow its trail as I try to recall what he tastes like. Minty spice instantly comes to mind.

"Well, I guess you'll just see tomorrow." I shrug, knowing he'll freak even more now.

He nods, looking me straight in the eye as he murmurs, "I can't wait."

My cheeks flush as I quickly look down at my plate. "What did you do while I was in the fitting?"

"I had a meeting with the crew, but then I had a little bit of time to go explore the beach outside the hotel."

"Oh, I'm so jealous!"

He furrows his brows in concern. "We'll have time to go after the shoot tomorrow."

"Really?"

"Yeah. I'm not sure how tired we'll be, but maybe after a nap we can go swim or walk down the beach."

I chew the rest of my bite slowly before nodding. "That would be really fun."

After a few bites in silence he asks, "Did you get to meet any of the other models?"

"I met a girl named Bella. She was really nice and admitted to seeing us sleeping on the plane, so I'm sure she wasn't the only one."

"We weren't doing anything wrong," he answers with a sternness behind his blue gaze.

"Oh, no. I know," I clarify. "Well actually, I wasn't certain, but it didn't *feel* wrong to me."

"Good." He nods his head, and I can tell he likes my answer. "Was she nice to you?"

The way he asks makes it clear that if she wasn't, he'd be all too willing to rectify the situation. Suddenly, I'm glad she was sweet. I can't blame him for wanting to be protective of me; I'm just not sure why he feels the need to be. Maybe because he orchestrated this whole job so doesn't want me to have a horrible time?

"Oh, yeah. We chatted for a while actually." I pause, wondering if I want to tell him the next part. Will it boost his ego even more and remind him of all the other options he has available to him? "I'll be honest, she warned me about the other girls having crushes on you."

"Charley, we talked about that earlier."

"I know. I trust you, and jeez, it's not like I have some kind of deed on you. I just wanted you to know what she said."

He looks up at me thoughtfully. "Thanks for telling me."

"Do you like knowing they all find you attractive?" A small smile skims across my lips.

He shakes his head and stands to put his empty plate and silverware back into the brown paper to-go bag. "It sort of makes me more uncomfortable than anything else, but their opinions don't matter to me."

"Oh?"

"Yes. There's only one person whose opinion I would care to know."

"Well you don't have to worry. I'm sure your mom thinks you're handsome, Jude." I smile wide at my cheeky comment, knowing he'll bite back.

He leans back in his chair, folding his hands over what I know to be a very toned stomach. "You're funny, Charley, but I think you're avoiding answering my question."

"You expect me to lay all my cards out on the table?" I stand and fold up the rest of the trash before carting the paper bag over toward the door. When I'm done, I bypass the table and sit on the edge of the bed.

He shrugs. "I think it's fair. I've been honest with you thus far."

"Yes," I answer simply, folding my legs to sit with them

criss-crossed on top of the comforter.

"Yes?" he asks, standing from his chair and walking toward me.

My pulse spikes as he approaches and I wet my lips instinctively. "Jude, you can't honestly be that obtuse. Yes, I find you really freaking attractive." I fold my hands between my legs, watching a possessive smile take over his features, transforming him into the sexiest man I've ever seen.

"Uggh," I sigh, splaying back onto the bed.

Chapter Fourteen

Jude

"WELL THAT WASN'T so hard now was it? It's the least you could do after I brought you dinner."

She leans up, bending her arm, and rests her head on the palm of her hand. I mirror her actions so we're lying down, facing each other. "I really do appreciate you feeding me," she offers with a timid smile.

"I was happy for the company."

We lay in silence, soaking in the moment, testing the waters of what could happen next.

"What time are you going to sleep?"

She twists her neck to look at the ornate clock decorating her nightstand. "I can probably stay up for another thirty minutes, but then I need to be out like a light or you'll be whining about a model with bags under her eyes tomorrow morning."

"Never," I protest, taking in those gorgeous eyes now. I'd never complain about something that brings me so much joy.

"What are you thinking?" she asks dreamily.

"I was wondering how long I got to keep you," I answer honestly. The way I say "keep you" sounds more possessive than I meant it to, but when I see her plump lips part for a gentle inhale and her eyes dilate with arousal, I know she likes the idea as much as I do.

Oh, sweet girl. If I could take you now, I would, but thirty minutes is not enough time.

She's quiet for a few moments after that, trying to tamper the desire that's so easily read across her features. I watch her twirl the soft duvet cover around her finger. "Wouldn't it be nice if we were here for vacation and not for work?"

I smile. "I don't think you would have let me sweep you away to Hawaii on any other pretense."

"There *is* a photo shoot, right?" she teases.

I laugh before shrugging playfully and narrowing my eyes. "That information is classified, Ms. Whitlock."

After she's laughed herself out, I scoot an inch closer so we're only a foot or so away from each other. "Have you ever been to Hawaii?"

She shakes her head and her gaze falls on the wall behind me as memories cloud her expression.

"No. My mom always preferred Aspen or Europe. She wasn't a beach kind of lady." She wrinkles her nose. "Too much sand."

I reach out and twirl my finger on the back of her hand that rests on the bed between us. She doesn't pull away, but her eyes linger on my touch with a soft focus. "That's a shame. Europe is beautiful, but you seem like you belong on the beach."

She smiles wide. "I do. I love the water and the sun. I could sit out in the sun for hours."

I let my finger glide up over her delicate wrist and then slowly up her arm. "You're already radiant, but once you catch some sun tomorrow, you'll be glowing," I say admiringly, letting my hand pause at the top of her sleeve. She scoots a few inches closer to me, and I take the invitation to run my hands under the cotton shirt. Her skin is so soft, so inviting, and my hand feels as if it travels of its own accord, trying to get its fill of her.

I glide across her shoulder and down her shoulder blade, barely grazing her skin, but I still feel those familiar goose bumps blossom under my path.

She purrs softly and scoots another inch. "That feels amazing."

Her words undo any remaining resolve, but I don't want to ravage the poor girl. I take a deep breath and glide my hand back down to her arm to get a better angle. "Lie on your back, Charley," I instruct, gently pushing her down.

She complies willingly, her beautiful wet curls splaying out around her while her arms lay limp by her side. Her big blue eyes look up, searching my face for answers, but I'm not willing to give anything but these simple touches. Maybe tomorrow I'll take it further, but right now, this is perfect.

When my hand reaches the hem of her loose cotton shirt, I tug it up slowly, revealing an inch of her slim, tantalizing abs. I drag a finger across her skin, from hip to hip, watching as her stomach quivers in response. I love doing this. I love knowing my touch can cause so much lust to build within her. Tugging her shirt up another inch or two, I lean down and place a chaste kiss an inch away from her belly button. She arches ever so gently, enough to goad me forward until I've tugged the hem of her shirt up so that it rests a millimeter below her breasts. Everything about Charley is so delicate and pretty: the sweet curve of her torso, the dip of her belly button, the gentle line that slopes down her trim abs to the top of her black pants. We're both in a dreamy haze, letting the moment carry us, but I have no clue when one of us will snap out it.

With quick movements, I crawl over her, pinning her to the bed beneath my thighs and leaning forward to carry some of my weight on my hands. If I had my way, this is where she would stay all the time—pinned under me, ready and willing for me to take her.

I glance up toward her face. I would have expected her to protest by now, but she looks beyond words. Her entire body hums underneath me, lust practically seeping from her pores. I want to sate that lust, rev it to the breaking point and then push her over the edge over and over again.

"Please," she whispers under her breath.

Before I've even registered my movements, I've pinned her hands above her head and am leaning down to sweep my lips across her hers. She opens up for me so willingly it makes my dick ache. I need more as our tongues collide, trying to convey each ounce of yearning we're trying to hold back. My hips and mouth set a dangerous rhythm but she meets me grind for grind.

Clasping her wrists with one hand, I scrape down her shirt and tug it slowly over her beautiful breasts, finally revealing her pink strapless bra. A devilish grin spreads across my lips when I realize I can unclasp it from the front.

"I want to see you," I demand huskily. I felt her body at the club, but I have to see her; I have to know how beautiful she is everywhere. Her whole body trembles beneath me, and when I glance up, she has her bottom lip tucked between her teeth in an innocent pose. Those blue eyes urge me forward; they beg me to unclasp her bra and feel her sensitive nipples between my fingers.

"Do you want me to touch you, Charley?" I ask as my finger gently slides along the seam of her bra, setting her skin on fire.

She nods coyly and bites down even harder on her lip. With a deft flick, I unclasp the front of her bra, but I leave the lacy cups covering her breasts. I want to tease her. Knowing we can't go all the way tonight makes this moment even more spectacular. With each inhale, her chest rises and the material threatens to fall away and reveal her to me, but it only slides down slightly, revealing the very tip of soft pink nipples. My dick hardens even more as I take in the beautiful sight. I feel like I'm torturing myself beyond control.

"Do you want me to slide these cups away?" I ask, tightening my hold on her wrists.

"Please," she begs softly. I like making her beg; I'll remember that for tomorrow. As I shift my weight, I let go of her wrist and lean back enough to see all of her chest.

"Do not move your arms. Leave them by your head or I'll stop touching you." I doubt I'd actually manage to fulfill that consequence, but I want to keep her just like that—breasts pushed up, provoking my carnal desires.

She nods, losing herself in my dark commands. I knew she'd like it just like I do. I slowly reach down to peel away the remnants of her bra, revealing the most beautiful pair of breasts I've ever seen. They're firm and slightly larger than I'd expect for her small frame, and I know they'll fill my hands perfectly. Her hard, erect nipples tease me, and I can't help but reach out and feel their soft beauty. She arches into my hand as I drag my palm against her pink buds, kneading and twisting them.

"I want to taste these sweet nipples," I demand gruffly.

She moans deep in her throat, and I wonder how long it's been since a man spoke his dangerous thoughts aloud to her.

I cup each of her breasts, licking and sucking her tight buds, spurred on by her cries. I can tell she wants to reach down and touch me, but she leaves her hands above her head like a good girl. I reward her with a teasing nip and then sweet licks. She cries out loudly, conveying a raw mixture of pleasure and pain.

"Do you like that, Angel? When I bite down and make you cry out?"

She nods, crooning under me, preparing herself for my next move. I can feel her wiggling, grinding her sweet spot against me—but she's not getting her release tonight. This is meant to be a sampling. I want us both needy and hot tomorrow.

"You're so receptive, sweet girl. Your breasts are divine, they beg to be touched and worshiped."

I sit up and grasp them hard, hard enough to make her arch her back, giving me even more.

"Do you see how they fill my hands? They were meant for me. They're mine. Say it."

I never stop massaging her breasts as I speak, and I can tell she's so close to losing it I'll have to stop soon, but not until she answers me. I reach down and caress her nipples again, taking them between my teeth gently enough so her soft cries fill every ounce of air in the hotel room.

"Say it," I demand.

"They're yours. God, Jude. Yes."

I pull back suddenly, shifting my weight off her and away from the bed.

"What? What are you doing?" she asks with a soft, needy voice.

"It's been thirty-one minutes. I promised I wouldn't keep you later than that." I take a few deep breaths, knowing I'll have to take a cold shower as soon as I get back to my room—though even that might not help. I don't think any number of cold showers could pull the vision of her lying there, completely submissive for me. I know if I swept my hand beneath her yoga pants I'd feel such sweet wetness, but I can't go there. I tug a hand through my hair and lean forward to pull her to a sitting position. As I kneel down in front of her, I have to force myself to keep my gaze above her neck.

I kiss her forehead, her cheeks, her neck, her collarbone, and then I pull back and study her eyes. They're so sweet and sad—sad because I'm leaving, but I know if we keep going, we'll never stop, and we both have to sleep or she'll kill me in the morning.

"Tomorrow after the shoot, Charley. I promise to finish what we've started." I bend down and kiss her gently before resting my forehead against hers.

"I hate you so much right now."

"That's not what your body is telling me."

"It's traitorous. It can't be trusted when you're around." She narrows her eyes playfully.

I reach forward to whisper in her ear, wanting her to be as ready for tomorrow as I am. "I promise that the moment we're alone, I'll slide a finger into that sweet wetness of yours and find the one single part of you that makes you tick, makes you crumble beneath my touch. I'll tease you until you come apart before me and then I'll do it all over again."

She moans and a shiver of anticipation crashes through her. In a moment of boldness, she reaches out and clasps the sides of my face, bringing me toward her for one more heart-stopping kiss.

• • •

Charley

I uncurl my toes as the tingles fade from every inch of my body. Jude was arrogant to think I couldn't finish what he started. Just the image of his raw passion made it so a few fluid strokes brought me to shuddering ecstasy, but it was merely a temporary salve. I want his touch, his fingers in me. After having thirty minutes of the most sensual touch I've ever felt, every nerve ending feels bereft and naked. How can my body feel completely turned on and utterly stripped?

Rolling waves. That's the first noise that seeps through the fog as I lie spent on the luxurious bed. I watch the ocean through the thin sliding-glass door, listening to the water roll in and out like white noise.

Thoughts drift through me: things I want to tell Jude, things I want to confess. Some are easy, like the fact that I wanted him to stay. I wanted him to sleep with me. Some are far more difficult. Some involve digging up buried skeletons and well-covered scars. I've never wanted to share them with another soul before, but everything about Jude rocks me to my core and I can't help but feel my mask beginning to slip whenever I'm in his presence.

I know there comes a point when the baggage becomes too much and you have to cut your losses and move on, but maybe if I keep my baggage tucked away until we're back in New York, I can pretend this is real life and get to enjoy it while it lasts. I know it will surely end like everything in life does; whether it's today or in twenty years, it ends.

Chapter Fifteen

Charley

"DID I CATCH you on your lunch break?" I ask as soon as the call connects.

"Yes, but I don't have long. Bennett and I have a date with a secluded corner in about ten minutes," Naomi states suggestively. I highly doubt she's kidding.

"You hussy."

"Tell me something I don't know. How's Hawaii? Have you gotten it on with any locals?"

"Half a dozen, but who's counting? But seriously, I don't have long and I need your advice about something."

"You need my advice about *Jude*," she clarifies for me, seeing straight through my bullshit. "If we don't have long, you'd better spill."

"It's creepy how good you are sometimes, but yes."

"Have the models been throwing themselves at him?"

I huff out a breath, thinking of the bevy of girls he has to choose from while we're here.

"Yes, but he doesn't seem to care at all. In fact, yesterday he told me he wasn't interested in any of them. He saved me a seat on the plane and then he brought me dinner last night."

"Of course he did," she answers flatly. "Damn, he's good."

"And then after dinner he stuck around and he made another move on me," I ramble quickly.

"I'm not seeing the problem here."

"I'm not ready for this, Naomi. I didn't want any of this to happen and I still don't think I do. What happens when we go back home?"

"Charley, slow down. What's wrong with having a little fun in Hawaii? Jude doesn't seem like the type to want a long-term thing, so maybe you're both on the same page."

"Yeah, that's true."

"Do you want to have a fling with him in Hawaii?"

I think about her question for a moment even though my gut is screaming *yes*. Her nails click repetitively on her desk and I know she's trying to hint at her impatience with me.

"Yes! Okay? Yes. I do," I respond with angst.

I can practically hear her smile through the phone. "Then do it, and don't worry about what happens after. I've got to go, Bennett just got to my office."

"Okay yeah, I have to go to breakfast. Tell him I said hi, and I'll try to listen to your advice."

• • •

Our photo shoot is taking place right on the beach so the plush Hawaiian landscape will fill the background of each shot. At breakfast I learned that the hotel sent a crew out at the crack of dawn to block off a few yards of beach on either side of the set so visitors would know to stay away. The setup feels very exclusive. Apparently the moment the barriers were placed, paparazzi and various beachgoers started to gather round, clamoring for a good view of the shots. So, if it wasn't enough to model in front of twenty people, I'll now be doing it in front of a couple hundred. Lovely.

They hired ten models total. Half of them are scheduled to shoot before me and half are scheduled for after, so by the time I'm finished with hair and makeup and wrapped in a short pink robe, the shoot is already in full swing. My white bikini is strategically placed over the *important* areas, and my hair is styled in big, beachy curls. They used gold and brown tones for my makeup, so I feel natural and glowing. I just pray the effect will last long enough for me to get a few good shots. Already, I feel my nerves starting to seep in.

"It was really easy. Ryan has a good vision for what he wants from each model, so it didn't take as long as some other shoots I've worked on," Bella assures me as my sandals clap against the concrete steps toward the beach. Bella already finished for the day, so she offered to hangout with me until I have to start. I'm happy for the distraction because after last night, my entire body practically buzzes in anticipation of seeing Jude. I don't have any idea where his head is today since he was already on set by the time I made it down for breakfast. Hopefully nothing has changed since last night because if I concentrate, I can still feel the lingering presence of his lips on my skin and each time I do, it sends a surge of desire through my veins.

"That's awesome," I comment. "He seems like a cool guy. I've worked with some interesting directors over the past two years. I hate when we start the day and no one seems to have a clue how they want the shots to be laid out. It makes the whole process drag," I add, brushing past a bright pink hydrangea plant that seems to be blooming in every direction.

"Yeah, you don't have to worry about that with Ryan and Jude. They're like the dynamic duo."

I laugh. "I like the sound of that."

After two more concrete steps, the palm trees and lush island vegetation open up to reveal a white sand beach. Vibrant blue waters with white-capped waves roll into view as salt dances in the air, no doubt leaving a thin layer of dew atop my fresh makeup. Definitely not a bad day at the office.

Just as soon as paradise is unveiled before us, the moment is interrupted by the snapping lenses and jarring camera flashes of the paparazzi. I groan inwardly at the vultures peering over that thin line of orange tape. Then, as if the entire scene wasn't ludicrous enough, one overly-ambitious photographer spies Bella and me veering out from behind the line of palm trees and leans so far over the rope, his camera flashes into his face as he plummets to the sand in an awkward somersault. I clasp my hand over my mouth while Bella laughs hysterically. In all, the poor man has taken down nearly half the platoon of paparazzi before everyone's righted themselves again.

With a sharp tongue, Ryan huffs over to them and casts half of them away, threatening to call security and the local authorities. Thankfully, their clapping lenses die down somewhat after that. Having Jude's lens trained on me in a few minutes will be *more* than enough.

Bella and I take a seat in collapsible metal chairs near the crew area so we don't interrupt the current shots taking place even more. Bella reaches toward the table for a plate of fruit for us to share just as Ryan's assistant smiles and waves. It's her job to make sure I've arrived on time, and she looks relieved to see me on set a few minutes ahead of schedule. After she's marked that I'm present, I let my eyes drift past her, toward Jude. I completely ignore the plate of pineapple and strawberries Bella shoves in front of my face because I've spied something much more tantalizing.

He's completely focused on his work, unaware of the calamity that just took place around him. He's squatting low in the sand, knees bent, every sexy ounce of muscle balancing deftly on the balls of his feet. The elegant muscles in his back stretch beneath his shirt. He has no clue I've arrived and I like it that way. I feel sneaky watching him work like this.

He moves fluidly as he snaps pictures of the model on set, as if his sole purpose in this life is to capture beauty in the precise moment in which it presents itself. I don't know who the model is, but she has dirty blonde hair and the biggest boobs I've ever seen. I'm not kidding; I think they could potentially have their own time zone. She's poised in the sand with her arms angled behind her head. Jude's shooting her from every angle as her breasts practically spill out of her black string bikini, no doubt pulling every pair of male eyes into their gravitational pull.

"Any chance she's married too?" I laugh bitterly, recalling Bella's giant rock from the day before as I pull my gaze away from the set and fidget on my uncomfortable metal seat. Even though the island's weather is warm and humid, I wrap my arms tightly around my robe trying to quell the unwelcome jealousy leaking from my heart.

"Pfft, no." Bella snorts and shakes her head dramatically. "Veronica is probably the craziest girl I know, but she's hilarious. You'd like her."

I smile, feeling the tinge of jealously wane slightly as I steal a piece of mango from Bella's plate and pop the morsel of sweetness into my mouth without smudging my lipstick. "Sounds like my best friend back home."

Bella sets her finished plate of fruit back on the table in front of us and nods. "Maybe you'll get to meet her later. I think the models might go out after the shoot wraps for the day."

Jude's sexy promises from the night before spring to mind and I don't even have to think about which I'd rather do. "Oh, yeah we'll see. I have no clue how tired I'll be after this."

Bella smiles, not pushing the subject. "No problem. I'll just keep you posted."

Ryan's voice suddenly booms across the beach, catching our attention. "All right, Veronica. You're done! Good job." He claps encouragingly as the model beams and practically follows after him like a puppy. Ryan doesn't notice though; he's already turning toward his assistant, staying focused on the photo shoot. I choose to follow Ryan's movements for the time being, not yet prepared to stare into the pair of sharp blue eyes just behind him.

"Do we have our next model?" Ryan asks, glancing down at his clipboard while his papers flap wildly in the ocean breeze. He has to keep slamming his hand onto the errant sheets of paper, and I can't help a private smile from creeping across my lips.

"Charley?" his assistant asks, waving me over, and I look up and nod with a gentle smile, realizing it's my time to shine whether I feel like it or not.

"All right, Bella." I start to step forward, away from the security of the craft service table. "I'll try and catch up with you after. You're not going to stay, right?" I ask, starting to untie the robe. "You should go enjoy your afternoon."

She smirks, glancing over my shoulder for a moment, no doubt locking onto the sexiest man on the beach. "I think I'll stay just long enough to see Jude's reaction to that suit."

I roll my eyes and then narrow them playfully toward her. "Oh God, thanks for the pep talk."

"Good luck!" she calls as I laugh and shake my head, walking toward Ryan and Jude. Now that she's drawn my attention back to my suit, I decide to leave the robe on for the time being. They'll want to talk to me for a few seconds before we start shooting and I don't feel like having that conversation in my tiny bikini.

As my toes dip into the warm sand, my gaze finally meets Jude's and he smiles wide, stealing my full attention like a camera flash. I'm left blinking toward his brightness before regaining my composure. I offer him a timid smile, taking in the sight of him in a thin vintage cotton shirt and long khaki pants that are rolled up at the bottom, out of the sand. The clothes aren't overtly sexy, but he fills them out so well with his dangerous muscles and trim lines. I can tell he's already acquired a nice tan from standing out in the tropical sun. His blue eyes seem even more striking in contrast to his newly warm complexion, and I can't seem to avert my eyes even as Ryan begins to give instructions about the shoots.

I nod. Yes, yes, blah, blah, blah… Jude is the sexiest thing I've ever seen.

"All right, Charley," Ryan says, clearing his throat

pointedly, and I make an effort to appear as though I'm listening. "I'm not sure how much you saw of Veronica's shots but yours will be completely different. You're on the cover. We need a photo that's going to draw attention and sell magazines. Obviously we won't display any nudity, but we need these shots to ooze sex appeal…" He pauses, scanning down my legs with such studied intent that I follow his gaze to confirm that my legs are indeed not glowing bright neon or on fire. I fidget awkwardly as he continues. "Although I don't think you'll have any problem with that."

Is he flirting with me or is that just the way he usually preps models? His assistant's baffled stare and Jude's dominant pose point to the first option, but I can't focus on that right now. He just wants me to feel confident and sexy, that's all.

"Sounds good." I nod, trying to relax and get into character even though I know Jude is moments away from forcing Ryan's gaze away from my legs *manually*.

His assistant steps forward then and reaches her diminutive hand out. "Let me take your robe for you, Charley," she offers with a polite smile. She's so small, maybe five feet on the dot, and I focus on her as I follow her instructions, feeling the hot sun beat down on my newly exposed skin.

The gold necklace slinks across my flesh as I hand over the robe and turn toward Jude. I can't blame Bella for staying to watch; he's practically smoldering, and his entire demeanor changes as he glances over my skimpy bathing suit. The Brazilian bottom is composed of a triangle piece that covers the most important real estate and then two thin strings that tie on both sides. They sit right on my hips and I keep fingering the fabric to ensure they're tied securely.

The bandeau top is thin, a few measly inches covering my chest with a tight twist in the middle that pulls my boobs up and together. Jude's eyes nearly sear my flesh as they rake down my body and I instantly want to send a thank you card to the designer of this bathing suit, maybe a fruit basket as well.

"Modest, right?" My lips curl into a private smile as I watch him devour me. Anyone within a ten-foot radius could see those blue eyes cloud over in lust. This is more skin than he's ever seen. That combined with the realization that he knows what my breasts look like beneath the swimsuit top makes my cheeks flush and my eyes scan down toward the white sand.

"Very," Jude mocks dryly. My head snaps up just in time to see him start to turn and lead us over to the set.

The other photo shoot I did with him was closed, but since we're outside, on location, all the crew is standing off to the side, either working with lighting and diffusers or running around looking for accessories and swimsuits. I can feel their eyes studying my movements, adding to the growing mass of fans and paparazzi staring from the other side of the barriers. I know they aren't staring because I'm famous, they're merely curious about what all the fuss is about. If I could, I would will them all away. As it is, I'll need to block them out completely or I'll freeze up for every shot.

"Let's start with some poses in the sand," Ryan instructs. "And then we'll move into the water. I think that might be where we get the best shots."

I nod, turning toward the camera and taking a deep breath. I shift around in the sand, getting a feel for the way the bikini highlights certain parts of my figure. I lengthen my neck and then my side and before I know it, Jude's clicking away and the shoot is in full swing. The island breeze blows back my soft curls and the sand feels warm and inviting beneath my feet, but I can't seem to get the crowds out of my head. I'm posing for the camera, but my body feels stiff. Even though I try to keep my gaze over the ocean, I can't seem to move past everyone's judgments. Are they wondering why I was picked over everyone else to be on the cover while I'm standing here like a limp noodle?

"More, Charley! Those arms look dead," Ryan directs, trying to liven me up. His critiques don't help though; they make me even more self-conscious and I have to fight the urge to clam up further. Relax and move.

Another few shots pass and I know I still haven't given them anything that'll sell magazines.

"No, too robotic. Loosen up," Ryan huffs, clearly annoyed.

I smile tightly and shake out my limbs, trying to free my mind, but Ryan's commands don't feel right. They just make me tense up even more. I roll my neck over my shoulders and take another deep breath, willing the island scenery to calm my nerves, but the bright flowers, palm trees, and vibrant water aren't enough to distract me.

"Hey, Charley, look at me." Jude's dark voice croons over the waves, and I comply immediately, sweeping my gaze up to him. Looking at him is like watching my desire unfold. He's dropped the camera away from his eyes and is wearing one of his dimpled smiles across his handsome features. The moment I focus solely on him, my pulse picks up and I start to lose myself in his magnetism. He's all that matters.

"You look beautiful. Look at the camera and move for *me*." His eyes implore me to follow his commands, and suddenly, the rest of the crew fades away and it's just him and me. He steps forward, strengthening our connection until my body softens beneath his gaze.

My limbs start to move as if he has them wrapped around his finger like a puppeteer. The weight of his intoxicating masculinity melts away my fear as I press my arms together down my side. I know the pose will push my breasts together in an alluring gesture for the camera. Then, I slowly slide my hands down my thighs, staring right at Jude as my fingertips graze the skin below my bikini bottom. He nods and I can just barely make out his devilish grin beneath the camera lens. I keep moving, experimenting with different poses, arching my back, stretching my arms above my head, and angling toward the camera. I rise up onto the balls of my feet so my legs stretch out gracefully. My back arches sharply and my butt sticks out as I drag my hands through my hair.

"Much better, Charley!" Ryan yells, but his shallow voice sounds like it's coming through a tunnel. I'm moving for Jude, no one else.

The tropical sun pours over us and a bead of sweat runs down my neck, along the valley of my breasts. Jude pauses, pulls the camera away, and eyes me dangerously. It's the kind of look he'd have before flooring a car down a long dirt road—impulsive and alive.

"Let's move to the water," Jude commands. My cheeks flush under his gaze, and I wonder what he thinks of the photos so far.

As we step closer to the slow-rolling shore, I shake out my hair and let it fall gently around my face.

"Stay facing me," Jude directs, "and walk slowly back into the water, like you're inviting me in with you." I keep my gaze on Jude and do as he says, letting the tropical waters lap up around my feet. With a seductive little wag, I draw him and the camera toward me and he keeps clicking away, stepping closer and closer. Once my ankles hit the water, I drop down onto my knees and part my thighs alluringly, trying to show off the bikini bottom. I'm hardly an inch or two into the water, but it feels so refreshing against my skin. I sigh happily and dig my toes into the sand.

"Good, Angel," he whispers so only I can hear.

I love moving for him, and I blossom under his positive appraisal, wanting to please him even more. I want him to remember this image when he's alone tonight.

Playing off his confidence in me, I twine one hand through my hair and pull my head back gently while my other hand finds the strings on my bikini bottom. I tug down so the bottom exposes another inch of my lower hip. The action should look sexy on camera, like I'm right in the moment of seduction, pulling the tiny string on my bikini and revealing everything—for Jude. He licks his bottom lip and I smile seductively into the lens before pulling another inch down.

"Charley," he warns quietly, but his husky voice turns me on even more.

"Good!" Ryan yells from a few feet away, oblivious to Jude's behavior.

But I don't need Ryan's encouragement anymore. I'm a woman trying to seduce a man and my body knows what to do. I lean back, letting the salty water drench my hair and bathing suit, causing the material to cling my skin even more.

"Stay down like that, Charley," Jude orders, stepping over my ankles and coming to stand above me. His foot hits my leg beneath the water and the touch electrifies my skin.

I follow his instructions, letting my legs fall open a few inches so he can see the thin material between my legs. I reach back and prop my hands into the sand, supporting my upper body. My back twists and I arch up until I see the muscles tighten in his jaw. I love affecting him like this, especially after how he left things last night. I'm exacting my revenge and driving us both insane. My eyes narrow seductively and my lips part, pleading with Jude to push me back into the sand and take me right here.

"Damn, Charley," Ryan huffs.

I want to push the limits; I want to see how far Jude will let me go. It feels like a high-stakes poker game. Who's going to fold first? With one hand still stuck in the sand, I reach up with the other and tug down the middle of my bandeau top ever so gently. I wouldn't have revealed anything, just another millimeter of my skin, but Jude doesn't let me.

"Enough," he snaps, dropping the camera away from his face and revealing his losing hand.

"What! Are you insane?" Ryan huffs with wide eyes.

I drop down into the sand and sit frozen, volleying my eyes between the two men.

"We've got everything," Jude responds sharply.

Ryan's arm shoots out to gesture toward me. "She was completely working the camera!" he protests. Jude doesn't look at him; he's staring down at me with fire behind his blue eyes. He's pissed and he's not even trying to hide it from me.

"Fine, but there better be some damn good photos on that camera," Ryan relents, resting his hands on his hips.

"There are," Jude snaps roughly, glancing at him and then turning back toward me with frigid ferocity. "Can I talk to you for a second before you head in, Charley?"

I nod because my body is already conditioned to respond to this man—not to mention his tone wouldn't have allowed any other response. I haven't even fully processed the situation, and as I glance toward Ryan, his furrowed brows reveal that he's trying to catch up as well.

Sinking my fingers into the sand, I push up to stand on shaky legs. I try to brush some of the sand off the backs of my thighs. Out of the corner of my lashes, I watch Ryan walk away from us to prepare for the next model, but I still can't look at Jude. I keep my eyes focused on the grains of white sand spread across my feet like tiny constellations. He's standing a few inches in front of me. Is he angry with me?

"Charley, look at me," he demands.

My eyes stay focused on a speck of sand stuck to the side of my ankle; at least I know it won't burn me with its gaze.

"Please." His voice is impossible to resist, like licking chocolate off the spoon before you clean the bowl.

With a deep breath, I raise my eyes until I'm glancing at him from underneath my lashes. The moment I find his ocean blue eyes, I cross my arms over my chest, feeling vulnerable in front of him and suddenly wishing I had my robe again. His chuckle is pure sin, reminding me that a moment ago I was revealing every ounce of myself for him, but at least he holds his tongue.

"Is everything okay?" I ask with an unsteady voice, trying to gauge his mood.

He presses his eyelids closed for a moment, and I can tell he's trying to reel in his emotions.

"We'll talk about it later," he answers simply as his eyes flutter open, revealing stormy blue irises.

"Some of the models are getting together after the

shoot…" I trail off, not sure why I'm even announcing those plans to him; maybe so he won't have to feel bad if he wants to cancel on me now?

His jaw clenches. "Is that what you'd like to do?"

"Um, I'd rather go swimming," I offer, toeing the line of honesty.

"You can go swimming with *them*," he answers pointedly, and I can tell he's annoyed.

Damn him. Damn him for always making me reveal my cards when I just want to hide behind the veil of his desires. I like when he demands and orders. Being near him makes me feel vulnerable, like I'm playing on train tracks, but telling him my true feelings is like leaping off a platform toward an oncoming engine.

"I'd like to go to where *you* were exploring yesterday, if you're still up for it." That's the best I can do; I can give him the truth, but I have to give him an out to cover my bases.

He eyes me as if he can see through the cracks in my facade and then unpeels a knowing smile. "I'll come find you after the shoot wraps."

My face lights up, publishing my excitement to the world, but I don't care. "I'll grab some food for us since it'll probably be close to dinner time."

"Sounds good. I'll eat anything you'd like, just make sure you keep that suit on, Charley," he commands, fleetingly sweeping his gaze down my body. His blue eyes gleam in the Hawaiian sun.

"I'll see what I can do," I quip, winking playfully, glad the old Jude finally revealed himself once again.

Chapter Sixteen

Charley

I DIDN'T EXPECT him to ask his two friends to join, but it was too late by then! So I just went with the flow." Victoria's eyes scan across to each of us and then she grins wildly. "Let's just say every girl should experience that once in her life." She waggles her eyebrows and all the girls erupt in laughter.

"Ah! You're insane," Bella laughs next to me.

"Hey, when in Rome." She shrugs playfully and takes a sip of her martini.

"You were in Brazil!" Bella shouts, eliciting another round of laughs.

Bella dragged me down to the hotel bar so I could hangout with the girls while I waited for Jude. He texted me when the shoot wrapped a few minutes ago, but he wanted to head to his room to shower, so I told him he could find me at the bar. After my part of the shoot was over, I cleaned up and threw on a pair of faded jean cutoffs and a slinky blue tank top.

And yes, of course I left the white bikini on.

I wasn't sure where to get our dinner, but when I called the concierge, the hotel offered to bring up a picnic for me. I was nervous about ordering since I have no knowledge of what Jude prefers, but hopefully he'll be too hungry to care. At least the hotel tucked our food into a small cooler, that way I could hide it in my bohemian bag so none of the girls would ask about it.

As soon as I finished packing the cooler up and sliding on my strappy sandals, Bella knocked on my door.

"Have you ever been to Brazil, Charley?" Victoria asks, drawing me back to the present. She tips back her martini until it's bone dry and I watch her bite the olives off the toothpick as I shake my head.

"No, but it's definitely on my bucket list—especially after that story," I joke.

She smiles wide and cheers, "Yes! I bet you'll get to go sooner than you think, especially after your cover. You'll get booked for all sorts of jobs around the world."

I nod, soaking in her words. "I might actually try to lay low for a while."

My declaration causes frantic stirring around the table. "What?" "Why?" "To build your mysterious vibe?" "That's crazy!"

I shake my head, twisting the cocktail napkin in my hand. "Just for personal reasons."

"But there are girls who would *kill* to be in your position, Charley," Victoria presses.

Would they?

I don't know how the conversation became directed at

my career decisions, but I'm starting to wonder if I shouldn't have come with Bella. Thankfully, she notices my discomfort.

"Victoria! Tell us another one of your stories. Maybe about Vespa Boy? Didn't you guys sneak into the Eiffel Tower after it closed?" And just like that, the table is back to laughing and the attention is no longer on me. I recline back in my chair and try to immerse myself in Victoria's story, but a moment later, I feel the energy in the bar change. It's as if every free electron in my body is being drawn to a positive force. I don't even have to turn; I know it's Jude, and my instincts are confirmed when his scent wraps around me like an intoxicating wave. It's fresh and completely male.

Before I can turn to see him, I feel his warm hands engulf my shoulders and a pair of lips press against my shoulder blade. Holy hell. His kiss sends fireworks through me and I know he can feel me tremble beneath his hands. He just kissed me in front of all the girls, and as expected, their eyes are wide with wonder and confusion. Martinis freeze midway to gaping mouths and I know I shouldn't turn around to see how devastatingly handsome he looks. I should just revel in this ignorant bliss, but I can't. I need to see him.

His hands slip from my shoulders as I turn around and take in his heavenly appearance. His dark hair is damp and tousled from his shower, and his new tan and dark stubble make him appear sultry and mysterious. He's got on a white t-shirt you can practically see every muscle through and solid black board shorts. He looks so relaxed, but I know him better than that. He's always in control.

No one speaks for a few moments, and I realize they were all doing exactly what I just did: ogling this dream of a man.

"Sorry, ladies, but I have to steal Charley away for the evening." My heart flutters and I want to record him saying those exact words over and over again.

"Ooooh." All the girls erupt into giggles and sighs. I shoot them a playful glare as I stand to retrieve my bag. It's not heavy, but Jude reaches for it and clasps it tightly in his hand.

"I'll see you guys tomorrow on set." I smile and wave, making eye contact with Bella one last time.

Her smile is practically splitting her face in two, and I know she's getting as much out of this as I am.

Jude

"They're going to have so much to talk about for the rest of the night," Charley comments as I lead her through the hotel. Her tone tells me she's joking, but I know she doesn't like being the center of attention.

"You're right, they'll probably talk about how great I looked *all* night," I tease, knowing my remark fell past charming, landing directly in arrogant asshole territory, but it worked. She smiles and shakes her head, and I get her to forget about them for a moment.

Without thinking, my hand reaches out to find hers. We continue walking and neither of us comments on the gesture, but I notice her glance down for a moment before she squeezes gently.

"So, where are we going?" she asks with subtle

reservation. If I was half as brutish as I think I was at the photo shoot, she's probably wondering if I'm still upset with her.

"Well, since we have the volcano shoot and crew dinner tomorrow, I figured we should swim while we had the chance. I found a good spot yesterday that should be secluded."

"Secluded, hmm?" She purses her lips and hums.

I look at her out of the corner of my eye and smile slyly.

With a gentle tug, she swings our hands back and forth as if we're little kids walking in the park. I can't remember the last time I did something so *innocent* with a girl.

"It feels kind of strange being with you like this," she admits as we step out of the hotel and onto the path toward the beach. It's dusk and the sun will set soon, but for now the evening glow reflects off the water in a breathtaking view.

"Does it?" I ask, even though I feel it too.

"Yeah. Normally there are so many…emotions flaring between us when we first see each other, but this time it feels different."

"Maybe we're just getting comfortable around one another?" I offer with a small smile.

"Yeah, I suppose that's it, but it feels like maybe something more too."

It's such a vague statement, but I won't prod her for anything more; I'm happy she mentioned anything at all. As we walk in silence for a little while, we let our bodies sync into an easy rhythm. We mold our movements together as the ground transitions from concrete to dark wood and then to soft sand beneath our feet. After we stow our shoes next to the resort's entrance to the beach, I adjust my backpack over my shoulder and grip her bag tightly.

When we start walking again, she's the one who reaches out for my hand. The way she gently clasps it makes it feel like she's clamping down directly on my heart, and the sensation makes me wonder how she can possibly affect me so forcefully.

My fingers wind around hers and my thumb runs absentmindedly back and forth across the back of her hand. Another few minutes pass as we move farther from the resort.

"We aren't at the spot yet, but we should probably eat before it gets too dark," I suggest as I drop her hand.

"Everything is in my backpack, but I didn't think about how sandy our food would get." She frowns, running her toes through the sand.

I shake my head and swing my backpack down. "No worries, I brought a blanket."

Her eyes flash up as she grins. "I should have known you would think to bring one."

"Am I that dependable?"

She leans back to eye me up and down skeptically. "I'd say...predictable."

With a thud, I drop the bags onto the sand and eye her devilishly. "I'll remember that, Charley."

"All right, all right. I wouldn't use that word." She pauses, holding her hands up in defeat as I spread out the blanket. "Thoughtful, controlling, and *demanding* all come to mind though."

"Demanding, huh?"

"Oh, yes. *Very* demanding." Her eyebrows perk up slightly.

"You don't sound like you mind," I challenge, sliding down onto the blanket.

She shakes her head. "I don't think I do." She sits down

with her legs tucked under her, but she doesn't meet my eyes again until after she unzips her bag and pulls out a small blue cooler. "I ordered some chicken salad, French bread, cheese, and fruit." Her blue eyes hold a sense of unease. "Does that sound okay?"

Was she nervous I wouldn't like what she picked?

"Sounds awesome. I'm pretty hungry and I like chicken salad."

"Me too, but I bet they didn't make it as good as I can back home," she declares with a grin as we begin to set out the food and make our plates.

"Oh really, Miss Forgets-To-Eat knows how to cook?"

"Hey! When I remember, I'm pretty good at making a few recipes. My chicken salad is really good. I add tarragon, cranberries, and toasted walnuts. It's addicting."

"Sounds like it would be."

The sun keeps sliding down, painting the sky in hues of orange and red as we dive into our meal. The photo shoot wore me out and I know I could have fallen asleep in an instant if I'd stayed in my hotel room, but I didn't want to miss this moment. The tropical air swirls around us, picking up strands of Charley's hair and blowing them past her face. She tips her head up and closes her eyes briefly, accepting the soft caresses.

"Cheers to your first Hawaiian sunset, Charley." I tip my bottled water toward hers, breaking the silence.

"Hopefully there will be many more," she muses before taking another bite and reclining on her hands to take in the view.

"Can I ask when your last relationship was?" I know my question startles her because she sits up and furrows her brow for a moment before catching herself.

"Oh, um, it's been quite a while. Sort of an

embarrassingly long time."

"There's nothing to be embarrassed about. It's not as if I have anything to boast about."

"Well, it's kind of complicated," she starts, and I angle toward her a bit to let her know I'm listening.

"Hudson was my last long-term relationship, although interacting with him now makes me wonder what we even used to talk about. I guess we had more in common back then? Or maybe we've both changed a lot?" She rambles on for a moment, drawing on old memories. "I tried to date a guy my freshman year in college but it didn't work out. My heart wasn't in it and I ended things pretty quick."

She squints her eyes toward the setting sun and takes a deep breath.

"Ever since then, I've just kind of floated around. I've been on a few dates here and there, but nothing past that." She shrugs. "Is that how it was for you?"

Oh, how I wish it was. "Not exactly. I didn't date women when I got back to New York. I never even considered it until..." Too soon. "Anyway, no. I used women and they used me, it was as simple as that. I never offered anything I didn't intend on fulfilling."

I expect her to recoil from my declaration, but when I glance over, she's nodding slowly, methodically. "I honestly thought about doing the same thing," she mutters, and my heart splinters. The idea of a man using her for *anything* makes my blood boil. "I mean, I haven't had sex in a long time." She glances over at me with a sheepish grin. "Like a long, long time. There were moments when I wanted to cave, but I didn't think I'd be good at it. It's not that I would get attached or anything. I'm actually good at remaining unattached; I just didn't think it would be good for my self-esteem."

Her words sound steadied and focused. She's more self-aware than I was at twenty-three, and once again I find myself wondering what kind of life experiences pushed her toward such wisdom. "Why, Charley?" I'm not even sure what I'm asking, but I know I want her to keep talking.

My question jars her one step too far though. Her eyes are a deep, stormy blue one second, and then she blinks and they're crystalline once again. I know I've lost the moment.

"Why were you upset with me at the photo shoot today?" she asks, furrowing her brow. Her question forces me into an ultimatum: either I answer and let her hide away from her demons, or I don't and I push her, maybe past a tipping point. I want to push her, I want to provoke her to reveal her true feelings, but I've learned my lesson before and tonight doesn't feel like the right time. When will there be a right time? Fuck. I push my subconscious aside and inhale deeply, catching a whiff of her vanilla scent teaming with the island breeze. It's a heady mixture and it soothes my unease just enough so I can answer her question in a semi-normal tone.

"I feel slightly ridiculous saying it now," I admit gruffly.

"I'm sure it wasn't ridiculous at the time," she murmurs timidly, and her words undo me. Even if she can't be honest with me, I can't keep my words from spilling out for her.

I haven't talked about my feelings this much since I got back from overseas and was forced to do it three times a week.

"I hated being helpless," I begin with a reluctant sigh. "I hated watching you seduce the camera, seduce Ryan, seduce the future readers of the magazine, and not being able to do a thing about it. In fact, I had to push you further, when in reality, I don't want you seducing anyone or anything other than me." Brutal honesty spills from my mouth and now that I've started, I want to get it all out. "I want everyone to know you belong to me. Ryan was flirting with you on set and I wanted to deck him. I've never cared about a model before—hell, I've barely paid attention to them at all—but you set my world on fire, and now there's no going back to the way it used to be."

I drag a hand across my stubble, hearing her unsteady inhales. Good, at least my words are affecting her. "It was torture watching you tug down that bikini bottom. I don't want anyone fantasizing about you the way I do."

"You fantasize about me?" her soft voice chirps, and without my permission, my face splits into a grin. I turn toward her and unlock my hands so I can inch closer.

"Every minute of every day since I met you, Charley."

She doesn't look away from the ocean. Her teeth tug on her bottom lip and she wrings her hands nervously. "You drive me insane, Jude."

I inch closer, willing her to open up for me. "I like *driving* you, Charley. I don't care if we both go insane, as long as you stop fighting me. Let me in."

"Don't you understand?" she storms. "For the past two weeks I *haven't* been letting you in." She sweeps a hand angrily across the blanket for emphasis. "You've been bulldozing through every wall I've subconsciously built around my life and I hate it. It makes me feel, makes me uncomfortable and even sad at times—but then it feels fucking amazing, like I'm not numb," she says, reaching for my hand and tugging it against her heart. It's beating so fast, like a hummingbird's, and I sit frozen, waiting for her to finish. "You deliver a shock of energy to my heart every time you're around."

I watch a tear slip down her cheek to rest on her pretty pink lips.

"I hate it. I hate it," she repeats until my lips are on hers and I'm muffling her passion with my own. Our kiss is different than anything I've experienced; it's alive and greedy as we attack one another, trying to express conflicting emotions of love and hate. She's trying to use her nails, her biting teeth, and the hard yanks of my hair to prove her hate, but she doesn't realize how transparent her actions are. That's the thing: Charley wants me to run—it'd be easier for her that way—but I'm not giving up. I'll never let her feel numb again.

With quick movements, I tug off my shirt and her clothes, pick her up, and carry her toward the water, all the while keeping our mouths sealed together.

Charley

His words wreck me. Brutal honestly is not something I'm used to dealing with, and he says everything like it's so cut and dried. I can't just accept him into my life; I don't even think that's possible anymore, but he doesn't shy away from the challenge. He's carrying us into the water as I wrap my legs around his firm waist. Even if words aren't feasible at the moment, I'm pouring my emotions into each tug of his hair, each nip of my teeth on his lips, and he's responding like a hunter—quick and feral and hungry.

He carries me like I'm a ragdoll, barely exerting any effort as he drags us deeper into the water. Somewhere in the back of my mind I know the sun's going down and we shouldn't go out too far, but I trust Jude.

Water laps around us as we go deeper and deeper. It inches up my calves and thighs, finally coming to rest at my waist; both of our lower bodies are concealed by glassy water. It seals us together tighter, wrapping us in serene layers of salt, sand, and lust. My mind doesn't even register the temperature, not when I have Jude's warm body pressed against my thighs, overwhelming my equilibrium. Oh god. My hands run down his chest, trying to commit each sinewy line of muscle to memory. It's impossible though. His body is a work of art, one that would take years to memorize.

I tilt my head back, breaking our kiss and capturing a sliver of my sanity again. My eyes scour over him, adding another sense to my exploration of his body. Even his torso is a shade darker than when I saw him playing soccer the other day. I wonder if he took his shirt off after I left the photo shoot.

"What are you doing?" he asks, tightening his hold on the back of my thighs. His fingers are just close enough to the edge of my bikini bottom that my toes curl in response.

"Looking at you," I explain simply, tracing down his broad shoulders to wrap my hands around his hard, muscled arms. My fingers don't even come close to wrapping around his bicep, and I can see his amusement out of the corner of my eye.

"I want to keep you in this moment forever." I smile dreamily, letting my hands caress down his chiseled abs. He's being so patient, letting me touch him like this, though I know it won't last. He'll regain control soon, but for now it feels like he's my own personal paradise and I revel in the thought.

"Your hands are torture, Charley." He breathes huskily, spurring me on even more. The pads of my fingers drag along the sharp v-cut under his abs. I'm barely an inch above his board shorts and I can feel his body reacting to my touch as he subtly grinds against me, separated only by flimsy swimsuits.

Suddenly, his hand reaches down to capture my wrist so he can pull my hand up to his lips. I stare up at him in shock as he slowly, deliberately dips my fingers into his mouth and sucks each one until I'm putty in his hands.

"I want to taste every inch of you, Charley, and tomorrow I will, but for right now, your pretty little fingers will have to do." Fucking hell. I've never had a man say things like that to me before. I realize why he does it though; hearing him declare the yearning to deliver sexy deeds turns me on almost as much as if he were actually performing them.

With predatory movements, he takes my hand from his enticing mouth and drags it down my own body. It's his hand forcing mine, but the combination bewitches my senses as if I'm touching myself while he watches me, commands me. He skips over my bikini top, skimming down my stomach and creating a surge of butterflies in his wake. I know where he's leading our hands but I can't process it; it's too raw, too exposed, and it sends my mind into overdrive. Our hands sink below the water and he presses my fingers along the tiny piece of triangular fabric of my bikini. Oh. My. God. Can I do this? Do I want to stop this? No. Hell no.

In the next moment, every thought dissolves from my mind because *our* hands pull my bikini aside, exposing my sensitive flesh to all of Jude's mischievous deeds.

He drags our fingers lightly over my folds and my head

falls back in ecstasy.

"God, you're so soft, so silky. Do you feel that, Charley?"

His words ricochet through me, dripping with every titillating promise of what he'll do to my body. His hand presses against me—feeling me, marking me, owning me. I'm unraveling beneath him and attempting to keep up is hopeless. I yank my hand away from his and pull him toward me so I can show him what he's doing to me the only way I know how: with my lips. I tug his hair, hard, and press our bodies together. He responds with greedy pets and long, delicious strokes before he finally slides a finger into me, and I'm lost. I'm no longer rooted down to earth.

This is pure bliss.

His finger drives possessively into me as his other hand grips my ass. He's not letting me go anywhere. His hands hold me tightly against him so I have no reprieve from his overwhelming touch. As gravity and the ocean's current push me down, he slides another finger in to join the first. He knows exactly where to stroke, how to curl his fingers and find the spot that seems to be the center of my universe.

"Ju...de..." I moan, keeping my head tilted back as he continues his relentless pursuit of my pleasure with his deft fingers.

He kisses down my neck, nipping and licking a trail down to my collarbone. "My sweet girl, you're so tight around my fingers. I want to sink into you right here. I'd let you ride me and milk out your orgasm again and again."

His words rip me apart until I'm completely exposed to him.

"I... Jude. Don't stop." My voice sounds feral and wild

as I fall closer and closer to the edge.

"Come for me, Charley," he demands, sinking his teeth into the delicate skin between my neck and shoulder.

"Come," he demands again, and my body explodes obediently.

Delicious tingles spread through each limb as my world teeters off axis. Crashing waves of pleasure roll through me again and again, combining with the ocean's gentle tide to coax out every last morsel of my ecstasy.

As the world around me slowly begins to filter through the fog of my waning pleasure, I realize there's a voice shouting at us from shore. I open my eyes to see Jude squinting past me and when I twist my head, I can see a figure standing up on the beach: a man waving his hands, trying to get us to come back to shore.

"What in the world?" Jude asks, letting my legs slide down to the ocean floor. Thankfully my lower body is weightless in the water or my knees would have buckled under the pressure of the last few minutes. I reach down to adjust my bikini bottom, realizing how sensitive my flesh still is. Ugh. If this man hadn't interrupted us, I would have no doubt been well on my way to another orgasm.

"Get up here, you two!" the man yells again, shaking his head admonishingly. Jude takes my hand in his and starts walking us back to shore, but then he pauses.

"Oh, shit," Jude whispers under his breath, drawing my attention.

What?

"Are we in trouble?"

"No, but we're probably on his private property. This isn't where I meant to take you, remember? We just stopped here to eat."

Clarity sinks in and a wave of embarrassment crashes

over me. Surely the man couldn't see anything, and how could we have known? It's not like there's red tape or a fence along the beach. My question is answered, however, as we step closer to shore.

Three signs are stuck into the sand along the beach with bold, bright letters: "Private beach, NO TRESPASSING". How did we miss those earlier?

"You stinking kids think you can just go wherever you want! This is my property and I pay a hell of a lot of money to keep people like you out!"

Jude's hand tightens around mine and for a moment I wonder if he'll say something to make the situation worse. The distinguished-looking man has every right to be frustrated, but he's clearly overreacting. We should just grab our stuff and leave.

Except, he's standing on our blanket and clearly isn't going to budge. The closer we get to our stuff, the angrier the man becomes, waving his hands and huffing dramatically like he's trying to flag down a helicopter. Jude lets go of my hand without a word and starts to gather my bag and his backpack, leaving the blanket where it is.

"I've already called the police," the man slurs, pointing his shaky finger in Jude's face. That's when it clicks: he's completely wasted. What the hell? Jude slides his steely gaze toward me for reassurance and then turns to face the man.

"I understand you're angry, but we honestly didn't know this was a private beach," he answers with a respectful but hard tone. "We're leaving and we'll be sure to check next time."

"Like hell you are!" The man rears back in anger and grabs my arm, jerking me toward him with an angry tug. I stumble over the sand trying to regain my footing; in a flash, my arm is free and Jude has the man by the throat.

I'm thrown back by my own resistance to the force no longer holding me. My awkward seat in the sand offers me an oblique view of the tense scene unfurling before me. Dammit, that guy grabbed me! How did this escalate so quickly?

"If you ever touch her again, you'll be enjoying your *private beach* only after they release you from the hospital," Jude growls, picking the man up off the ground and clutching his neck even tighter. I watch his fingers dig into the man's flesh unrelentingly as we all teeter in the moment. Jude's a dominant force, ready to enact his will as if the inebriated man were nothing more than a dry leaf to be crushed in the palm of his hand. My stomach rolls as I call out for Jude to stop, and somehow my plea must make it through his angry haze because a moment later he's tossing the man down onto the sand. The coward crawls backward like a scared crab. Despite his weary appearance, he still feels the need to yell about the police arriving soon, as if Jude isn't a wild hair away from pounding his flesh into the sand despite my pleas otherwise.

Jude's sardonic laugh echoes through the broken night. He's perfectly aware that the police will care more about the man's drunken shenanigans than the fact that we mistakenly entered a private beach.

I watch Jude gather our belongings again, preparing to leave, but I stand frozen, trying to process the scene. A moment later, when Jude reaches for me, I rear back in fear, not of Jude, exactly, but of the entire situation. Everything happened so fast: one minute I was having a mind-boggling orgasm and the next, a crazy drunk was yanking me around. Suddenly Jude's blue eyes pierce through my haze like an old friend and his soft words melt over me.

"Hey, Charley. It's okay. We're leaving." He caresses my hair gently, and I nod, taking his hand and letting him pull me back toward the hotel.

Chapter Seventeen

Jude

"ARE YOU OKAY?" I ask, keeping her tucked near me as we walk back into the hotel. Neither one of us offered to speak on the journey back. I wanted to make sure I'd calmed down enough that I wouldn't take any of my anger out on her. That guy was completely out of line, and I should have done something more. The asshole won't even have a scratch on him when the police get there. Charley, on the other hand, will be sporting a colorful bruise by tomorrow, no doubt. Poor Angel. I can't believe he thought he could touch her like that and get away with it.

Undoubtedly, the situation shook her nerves, and I'll have to be sure she isn't scared of me because of it. I have a temper—most people do when they come back from wars—but I keep mine in check unless it's provoked for reasons like that.

"Yes," she answers, so quietly I have to consider if I actually heard her or not. She clears her throat and meets my eyes. "I am." Her faint smile barely reaches her cheeks, and the hair framing her face almost acts as a shield against the world.

When we arrive outside her suite, I'm prepared to bend down and kiss her goodnight, knowing she needs space, but then her words catch me off guard.

"Sleep in my room tonight."

Her hands tighten into a ball at her waist and she lets her head fall while she waits for my reply.

I pause, glancing down at her, trying to read the emotions playing behind those delicate features. Her eyebrows are tugged together, her cheeks are flushed, and her lips are still rosy red from our kisses on the beach.

"Just sleep," she adds, and before she says anything more, I slide the key into her door and push it open.

"I'm going to shower and grab some clothes to change into. I'll meet you back over here in a second." In reality, I want to wash away the remnants of my rage before I step closer to her.

"Okay," she murmurs. There's a sweet gleam behind her eyes when she glances up at me.

• • •

Her room is dark by the time I wedge through the door, but a small lamp illuminates my path to her bed. She's lying down, watching the ocean through her window. When I pad closer, she doesn't even turn to look at me. Is she sleeping already?

Bright blonde hair, still damp from her shower, splays

out across her pillow in a golden halo. She's wearing pajama pants and one of those spaghetti-strap tank tops. There's a harsh red thumbprint already forming across the beautiful skin on her arm.

"Charley?" I ask, stepping around the corner of the bed so I can see her face. She's not asleep; she's focused intently on the window, or rather what lies beyond it.

"Charley?" I ask again, and this time she blinks and props her head up on her hand.

"Sorry, I was studying the colors of the ocean." She smiles up at me.

"The colors?" I ask incredulously.

"Yes. I'm trying to commit them to memory so I can paint this scene when I get home," she explains, glancing out to the ocean once again.

I follow her gaze out toward the dark water and try to discern what she's seeing with her artistic eye. Blue is all that comes to mind. Dark blue that turns to black as it fades away from the moonlight. Is that what she wants to remember? It seems easy enough.

"Tell me the colors you see, Charley."

She frowns, trying to understand my request.

"I want to know what you see," I explain.

"Come lay with me and I'll tell you," she replies with a tired smile.

Within a moment, I'm climbing up onto the bed to lie beside her. The blanket is thick and fluffy, successfully concealing Charley's entire body underneath. With a steady hand, I slide underneath to join her and let her back rest against my chest. When I prop myself up on my elbow, I can see past her head and out through the window, just like her.

"I'm ready," I whisper in her ear, wrapping my arm

around her petite frame and tugging her in close.

She doesn't speak right away, but when she does, there's unbridled passion behind every word and I know she's speaking of her life's true love. It's inspiring hearing her expose the very nature of her soul.

"At first you notice the overwhelming amount of blue, right?"

"Yes." I nod.

"But if you let your eyes study each part, truly let your mind explore the complexities of the scene before you, other colors begin to appear and demand that their presence be known as well. For instance, the sky itself isn't merely blue. It's black at its darkest points and then it degrades slowly toward navy and marine blue. Eventually the light from the stars turns the sky a bright turquoise, especially around the moon."

I kiss the back of her neck sweetly. "Tell me more."

Giggling, she leans into me. "The sand closest to the rolling tide is bright gold in the moonlight, but other areas are hidden and shadowed. I'll use deep oranges and browns to darken and shade those areas."

I kiss her gently, encouraging her words.

"And white," she declares proudly. "There's white everywhere. It's used to highlight elements or to mix colors into the perfect hues. There's so much white on a night like this.

"Most people think the elements are formed with one pure shade, but everything's an amalgam of colors mixed in just the right combination. The feeling of the black sky, the emotions it draws out of you as you stare toward the stars...that's what I want to take back to New York with me."

I kiss up to her earlobe. "I like hearing you talk about

your painting. Will you show me the pieces in your apartment when we get home?"

She nods and her hair tickles my cheek. I want to turn her to face me, but I don't want to push her too far. I just want to savor every moment.

"I'm sorry if I scared you earlier," I apologize, nuzzling her neck.

Her warm hand finds my arm beneath the blanket and she runs her fingernails gently back and forth across my skin. It's a subtle act, but it feels intimate, like something a lover would do.

"You didn't. I was really glad you held your temper as long as you did." She sighs. "I can't blame you for getting upset after he grabbed me."

"Does your arm hurt?" I ask, pushing up off the bed to inspect it.

She glances down at the mark, an indecipherable expression marring her serene features. "No. Not really, and I'm thinking the redness will fade by tomorrow morning."

I look down into her wide blue eyes, trying to discern any hidden pain. "Good."

"We should go to sleep, Jude," she smiles, turning her head and laying her cheek back down onto her pillow. I find my spot behind her once again.

"I don't think it'll be possible with you lying so close," I admit, inhaling her sweet vanilla scent.

"I know. My body feels like I've just had three cups of coffee."

She sighs and I know she's being truthful because I can feel her quick pulse against my finger as I spin small circles under her tank top. I should stop and pull my hand away; the movement won't help either one of us get to sleep, but her warm, sexy body is too enticing to ignore.

"We'll have to think of other things," she declares softly.

"Hmm...like what?"

"I don't know. Nuns, babies...something really gross," she laughs.

I smirk even though she can't see it. "None of those seem like good options to me."

"Shhh...we're supposed to be sleeping." She laughs gently, pushing her face into her pillow playfully so her golden hair is all I see.

"Goodnight, Charley," I relent, pulling her in tight and cocooning her against me.

"Night, Jude."

• • •

Charley

Warm breath and soft stubble caress the back of my neck, just behind my ear, and I careen toward the sensations greedily. The action is instinctual, like the hardwiring of my DNA acknowledging its complement strands. Even in my dreamy state, when his lips find my skin with soft nips, a hum sounds from the back of my throat. His persistent touching forces consciousness to begin to filter in. I hold off as long as I can, trying to stay in the brief moment of blissful emptiness where there is only us: Jude and me.

"I have to go, Charley. We have to be ready in thirty

minutes to drive to the shoot."

No.

I groan in protest as the layers of my sleepy haze peel away. "Don't make me. Let's just sleep all day."

"I wish, but it'll be fun once we get there. You've probably never seen an active volcano before."

"Is that supposed to make me want to get up?" I groan, trying to roll toward him, but he's already crawling off the bed to leave.

He chuckles and leans over to kiss me again. "Up, pretty girl. I'll meet you down in the lobby soon."

Chapter Eighteen

Charley

THE DAY PASSES so quickly that as I walk toward the resort's restaurant for dinner, I realize it feels like an entire week of activities were crammed into the last few hours. This morning, after Jude practically pulled me out of our bed, the crew trekked to Hualalai, an active volcano on the western edge of the island. I learned as we were driving to the location that "active" is a relatively loose term in relation to volcanoes. This one hasn't erupted since 1801, so our photo shoot was safe and sound.

All the models dressed in skimpy red and black swimsuits of varying styles. The makeup crew gave us dark, smoky eyes and layered on the mascara until I could hardly lift my eyelid. It was much different than anything I've ever done before, and Jude was right: it ended up being really fun once we got there. We didn't do any solo shots;

instead Ryan directed us in small groups and then we took a few with all ten of us for the large centerfolds of the magazine. They should be artistic and sexy, and I don't think anyone will look at volcanoes the same after they see us in our bikinis.

Luckily, the magazine won't come out for a couple months, which gives me just enough time to forget about the impending fame. Hell, maybe I'll miss the release all together and just pretend it never happened. The only evidence will be the big fat paycheck sitting in my bank upon my return back home.

Since it's our last night in Hawaii, the crew is meeting in the hotel restaurant for dinner. It feels bittersweet to be heading home tomorrow, but I miss being in my own space, away from crazy models and intrusive makeup crews. While I've enjoyed paradise, I can't wait to get back to my normal routine.

Except, there's the question of Jude. I haven't let myself consider how our relationship will change when we get back to New York. I want to transplant every feeling I've had here back home with me, but I can't avoid the truth forever. I'd be naive to think there's any kind of future for us.

"Charley!" Bella calls my name, jarring me from my reverie. I glance up to see her standing with a few of the models just outside the restaurant, waiting for me to catch up. My lips curl into what seems like a genuine smile as I step closer.

"Hey, thanks for waiting," I offer, trying to shake the black cloud that had suddenly darkened my mood. It's strange how quickly that hopeless feeling can weasel its way back into my world. I wring out my hands. Is it from thinking about things ending with Jude? I've been alone for a long time; it's nothing new.

"No problem, but I'm starving, so let's go eat." She links her arm around mine and tugs me forward until we're stepping into the tropical restaurant.

The restaurant itself is gorgeous, but they have the porch screens open so the Hawaiian sunset becomes the focal point of the entire eastern wall. The ocean's waves are audible over the soft island music streaming from the corners of the room.

Modern tiki torches adorn the perimeter walls, offering sultry lighting and leading our path to the porch where the hostess declares that our party will be seated.

The open porch blankets the restaurant in warm humidity, making me glad I opted for a thin dress with delicate criss-crossed straps. My hair is rolled into a messy low bun, but a few strands have already escaped the hair tie. I have to keep coaxing them back as the breeze blows them gently against my cheek.

I know Jude's here already because Ryan asked him to come down earlier for a drink. I was hoping we'd have some time together after the shoot, but we ended up getting back later than we expected. All day I was busy getting plucked and prodded and he was busy snapping photos. We haven't been able to say more than two words to each other since this morning. It's strange how quickly the sinking feeling in my stomach can return. It's like Jude wields the power to relax me, and when he's not around, my stomach coils into the same tight ball it's been for the past four years.

"Are you okay?" Bella asks with a concerned look. I twirl my antique ring around my finger out of habit and try to sound genuine as I lie to her face.

"Yeah. Probably just hungry." Such bullshit. I've only

felt genuine hunger a few times in the past four years and only when I've been with Jude. Isn't that strange? What the hell is wrong with me? I don't even know him. The more I consider it, the angrier I become. What do I think he's going to do? Swoop in and save the day? Erase every memory that keeps me awake at night?

Just then we cross the threshold out onto the porch and the hostess passes each of us a drink menu before excusing herself.

"Hi, girls," Ryan calls as we step down onto the open patio. The restaurant staff has pushed a few tables together so the entire crew can sit together. Gorgeous orchid leis are arranged on the back of each wicker chair and soft candles glow in a line down the long tablescape. Immediately, everyone starts shuffling around, clamoring for spots next to one another, but I hang back, taking in the scene from the top of the stairs.

It takes two breaths before my eyes land on Jude.

He's standing off to the side with one hand wrapped around the neck of a beer and one hand tucked into his jeans' pocket. He has on a white cotton button-down that's half tucked into his jeans and a smooth smile, drawing me closer like a moth to a flame. I step closer with fluid movements and each inch seems to release the coil in my stomach until it dissipates completely. Just like that, he's unraveled every worry I'd built up throughout the day.

He narrows his eyes with intense focus as he watches me approach.

"We match." I smile, glancing from my white dress back to his shirt.

"Should I take it off?" He cocks his brow.

My heart flutters wildly at the thought.

"And send every girl here into heart failure? Let's save

that for dessert...at least."

He grins and then gives my body a onceover. "I like when you wear white." God, when he looks at me like that, I feel as though I have nothing on at all.

"Do I wear it often?"

He squints, takes a sip of his beer, and changes the subject, apparently not willing to elaborate.

"Did you have fun at the shoot?"

"Surprisingly, yes, though I felt like a vampire or something with that black swimsuit and crazy makeup."

He laughs gently. "I could see it. You aren't pale enough though." His gaze lingers on me momentarily before he takes another sip.

My hand runs over my exposed shoulder, feeling the skin that's darkened nicely since we've been under the Hawaiian sun. It'll fade once we get back to New York, but for now I feel tanned and pretty, especially under his gaze.

"You have some freckles on your nose," I point out, and he wrinkles his nose in protest. They're hardly noticeable in comparison with his mysterious eyes, tousled hair, and charisma distracting any girl within a ten-foot radius.

"Do I? Usually I get a few when I'm outside for a long time."

"I like them. You're a manly-man, so the freckles seem...*charming*."

He narrows his eyes and reaches out to wind his hand around the back of my neck, tugging me toward him. His finger skims along the bottom of my hairline and my heart kicks into overdrive.

"I'm not charming," he protests as his fingers glide under my hair, sending a delicious shiver down my spine.

"No?" I ask, pressing my hands against his chest and feeling the play of his hard muscles beneath the thin fabric.

"Not usually."

"Mmm…I'm flattered," I murmur, watching his lips creep closer to mine.

"I'm going to sleep in your bed again tonight, Charley."

"Okay," I say breathily, never looking away from his mouth.

"But we aren't going to sleep," he whispers.

"Oh." My mouth forms a perfect O and then hangs there, frozen.

"So, let's get some dinner in you so we can leave."

Can he feel my pulse riot from his declaration?

"Let's just go now," I plead.

"Charley, Charley." He bends and kisses my neck briefly; my skin aches for more. "You need food, and we should be respectful of the rest of the cast."

I narrow my eyes, mumbling, "To hell with them," under my breath as he drags me over to the table so we can sit down. He chuckles and ignores my hollow threat.

There are still a few people mingling around the porch and chatting, but for the most part, everyone has started to sit and order drinks and food. Jude and I pull out chairs next to Bella. Ryan's already relaxing across from her, nursing some kind of island cocktail with Victoria sitting beside him, hanging on to his every word. I wonder if she likes him or if she just wants to have fun the last night in Hawaii.

"How'd you like your first cover shoot, Charley?" Ryan asks with a bright smile after we take our seats.

Within seconds, I feel Jude's hand skim the back of my thick wicker chair, barely touching my skin but sending a clear message all the same.

"I really enjoyed it actually. I liked your vision today. I haven't seen anything like it before."

He nods, soaking in my approval. "I'm glad you liked it. We wanted the vibe to be different from any shoot we've done in the past. Did you see last years' issue?"

I nibble on my bottom lip and glance quickly to Jude, then back to Ryan. "No, actually. I'm terrible about picking up magazines. Where was it shot?"

His eyebrows shoot up in surprise. "Oh, that's a shame. You should find a copy. We shot in Greenland. Do you remember how pissed the models were the entire weekend, Bella?" he asks, turning his attention to her with a mischievous smile.

"Oh my god, I thought we agreed to forget that weekend all together!" She laughs, turning to me. "They expected us to pose in bikinis in like negative twenty degree weather. We were all threatening to sue."

"Jeez! That's just cruel. I'll take active volcanoes over snow any day."

Jude laughs next to me. "I felt pretty terrible wrapped in a parka when they were all shivering."

"What a tough job you have, Mr. Anderson," I quip, eliciting laughs from Bella and Ryan, but Jude's gaze clouds over in an instant and he turns toward the table to adjust his silverware. Did I insult him? He should be proud; he's a great photographer.

"Hey." I lean in gently, wrapping my hand over his. "Everything okay? I was just kidding."

He nods distractedly, fiddling with his fork. "Yeah."

"Would you guys like to order?" a chipper voice asks behind us, and we all mumble apologies, realizing we haven't even looked at the menus yet.

• • •

"That was amazing! I would have never thought to combine pineapple and pulled pork," I rave as we push the door open to my hotel room and pad across the plush carpet.

"I'm glad you liked it."

"Mmm. I loved it." I toss my purse onto an overstuffed armchair and splay back onto the bed like a sated princess. Jude stands a few feet away with his head cocked to the side and a smirk coating his beautiful lips. "Did you like the food?"

"I think I liked our picnic yesterday better," he hints, all amusement seeping from his feral gaze.

I bite my lip nervously and mention the first thing that comes to mind.

"Do you think there could be something going on between Ryan and Victoria?" I ask, propping myself up on my elbows and staring up into his blue eyes.

His fingers run along his stubble as he mulls over my question. "Maybe. They've worked with each other a lot, but they could just be good friends."

"But they shared a meal *and* he offered to walk her back to her room," I say, wiggling my eyebrows. "There's definitely something going on between them," I declare confidently, like a detective solving a crime.

He nods slowly, accepting the idea. Then his captivating eyes stare into me as he asks, "Is there something going on between *us*?"

For a brief moment, the oxygen leaves my body and I'm left paralyzed.

Yes! shouts my subconscious, but then my lungs inhale and my defenses are already gearing into motion. "Of course…I mean, we shared a meal and you walked me back to my room too," I joke, making light of his serious question.

"Charley..." His tone is dark and deadly.

I want to scream, *"What do you want from me, Jude!?"* He can't ask me questions like that unless he wants to hear answers he won't like.

"Why did you get upset earlier when I joked about your job being easy?" I ask with narrowed eyes. If he wants to make me feel uncomfortable, then I'll do the same and see how much he likes it. We're both hiding demons, but he seems to have forgotten that fact since we've been in paradise. I thought we were having fun and forgetting about everything but us, here and now.

His hands run through his hair forcefully, tugging on the dark strands as he stares out over the ocean.

"It's not a story I've told many people," he offers vaguely, as if that's enough to end the conversation. Like hell it is.

I scoot back over the duvet cover until my body rests against the headboard. I don't say a word; I don't goad him into speaking. Honestly, it'd be easier if he shut off like I do, closing the subject so we can move onto the physical side of our "relationship". That way there wouldn't be any confusion about what our arrangement is. A part of me desperately wants him to open up and reveal his secrets, but I know it'll complicate things. We should just stick to what's on the surface: our chemical attraction. Plain and simple.

He doesn't move and he doesn't look at me. His hands are folded around his chest and his eyes are glued to the ocean beyond my room's window.

But then he starts talking, and my heart slowly crumbles under the weight of his words.

"After college, I went to work for a popular magazine as a war photographer. It's the goal most photojournalism majors aspire to: covering real news in areas of the world that need exposure. I'd interned at the magazine through college and when they offered me the position, I would have been insane to pass it up."

I had no idea he had been a war photographer. He said his current job was easier than the last, but I just assumed it was something else, something light.

"We were stationed in various villages inside Iraq. My assignment was meant to last a month, but they ended up extending it a few times and I stayed for a little over eight months in total. It was the longest eight months of my life." As he speaks, his eyes darken and his jaw clenches tight. "The war we fight over there is different than the wars of the past. Today's conflicts aren't fought on battlefields. Instead of marching troops toward your enemy with rifles at the ready, modern militaries engage in urban fighting. We had to keep our eyes peeled every moment because the enemy could have been anywhere. There was no separation between war and life, only constant paranoia about what could be waiting around the corner."

My hand clasps over my mouth, but I don't make a sound.

"At first, I tried to focus on what I could control: the exposures, saturation, and white balance of my photos. I was taking photos that were meant to shock the western world and was doing a great job at it. I followed marine units, protesters, and civilians step for step through decaying neighborhoods and crowded markets so I could take photos of the combatants and the afflicted. Civilians suffering from food shortages, hospitals overflowing with the sick and injured, and entire villages burning beneath the weight of war."

"Every night as I scrolled through photos, trying to decide which to send to my boss, the tragedies of the day would hit me. I'd push everything away during the day, compartmentalizing the overwhelming suffering, but at night the disguise would slip and I'd start to contemplate the darkness surrounding me." He pauses and takes a heavy breath. "But it wasn't until I met Ali that everything fucking collapsed."

A tear rolls down his cheek and I'm taken aback by all he's had to endure. What could have happened to him?

"Jude...you don't have to keep going."

He wipes the tear away forcefully and continues his story. I think it might be easier for him to say it all at once. If he stops now, I wonder if he'd ever want to bring it up again.

"Ali was a little boy that lived in the village we were stationed in during the end of my assignment. I'd see him every morning, begging for food with the rest of the orphaned boys. We were taught to keep the civilians at a distance, to remain unbiased observers."

"I couldn't begin to understand the culture of that village. Hunger will do crazy things to people, but I didn't know. I had no clue what the consequences would be." The anguish behind his confessions overflows my eyes with sad tears. What could have possibly happened?

"Charley, he was so fucking skinny I could see every bone in his body." Finally Jude looks at me and my heart splits in two. "I couldn't just ignore it. Every day it weighed on my conscience. To be a good war photographer you have to be willing to get as close as possible to the subject without feeling a goddamn thing. What kind of bastard can do that?"

"Jude," I plead through quiet tears. I want to assure him he did the right thing, but I don't want to interrupt him.

"After I'd thought about it for days, one morning I packed an extra protein bar and some bread in my camera bag. I went to the village center to find him like I did every morning. He'd picked up a few words of English and he would ask me my name and if I had a 'family in America'. He asked me that every day, and every day I'd say no and keep walking. That morning, I told him to follow me over to a side alley. I had to pull him away; there were too many people starving—not just these orphans, but the entire village. The UN was trying to send aid, but it wasn't getting to these small villages fast enough."

"I gave him the food and he started crying. He tore into the bread as quickly as he could, but I couldn't stay; I'd already been gone from my crew for too long."

With slow movements, I crawl off the bed and wrap my arms around him, not knowing what else to do. I want to reach in and take away every ounce of sadness, wipe him completely clean. He doesn't deserve to feel any of this.

"I should have fucking stayed. I'll regret leaving him with that food for the rest of my life." His sob breaks through the room, and I feel his heart beating wildly against my ear.

"Jude, you fed him. He was so hungry and you gave him food."

I feel his head shake above me. "They found him. A group of teenagers found him with the food, and they tried to steal it. The other orphaned boys saw it happening. They said he wouldn't give it up and they beat him. They *killed* him to get that fucking protein bar. Because I couldn't just do my job and stay the fuck away, Ali died."

"No! Jude!" I pull back to look into his eyes, but his

gaze is focused on the bed just over my head. "If you didn't feed him, he would have died anyway. You did the right thing, Jude." I know my words fall on deaf ears. It's like I'm looking at him through a one-way mirror; he's so far away from me, but I can see every emotion etched across his beautifully sad features. He hasn't forgiven himself and nothing I say will get through to him now.

"It doesn't matter, Charley. Even if there was no Ali, the war changes everyone. I watched soldiers, coworkers, and civilians get injured or die *every day*. It wears you down. Having to constantly be on watch turns your body into a bundle of nerves. They diagnosed me with post-traumatic stress disorder when I got back and I went to therapy for a while, but even therapists can't quite grapple with the trauma. Soldiers have a mission: to eliminate the enemy. They have their own set of difficulties, and I can't image what it would feel like to kill someone, but the lines are blurred for journalists and photographers. We *have* to get close, too close to the tragedies. The closer we get, the better our photos, and the more fucked up we become."

He shakes out of my tight grasp and steps away to take a few calming breaths. "Now I've just come to live with the night terrors. They've lessened over the years, and the more I fill my life with meaningless photography jobs, the less I have to think about what happened over there."

"That's why you never dated."

He shrugs. "It wasn't a conscious decision. It fell into place. Girls were a means to an end. I'd learned how to compartmentalize every demon when I was in Iraq and it seemed easier to keep everyone at bay."

"I'm glad you let Bennett in."

He nods and I see his features starting to relax. "Bennett has been my friend since we were kids. He knew me before

232

I went overseas and he could see how much it changed me. I've talked about it with my family briefly as well. Other than that, I've just learned to live with it."

"Jude. I'm so sorry." Those are the only words I can say. Everything else that springs to mind seems cliché and trite.

"There's nothing to be sorry about. I'm alive and I truly enjoy most parts of my life. Ali is dead and that knowledge will forever haunt me."

We sit in a long period of silence, the kind of silence that wraps around your body and freezes you in place as you try to process the intricacies of the world we live in.

I tuck my head under his chin and wrap my arms around his chest. "Thank you for telling me."

"I'm glad I did. I want us to be honest with each other, Charley."

I close my eyes, inhaling his scent and pretending I didn't hear his last sentence.

"Let's go to bed, Jude."

"No," he demands, his grip tightening around my waist. "I don't want to go to bed. I want to be with you. I want to feel you moving under me. After everything that's happened, you make me feel alive, like the last four years don't have to be what the rest of my life looks like."

It's too much. I can give him an inch, but he's demanding a mile. His words wind around my soul and each syllable tugs the rope tighter and tighter until I'm sure I'll shatter.

"Let's just be here, Jude. That's all I can give you right now. Just be here with me for tonight," I plead, hearing the desperation in my voice.

I have to be honest with him about that. I need him to know my limits before we do anything we can't take back.

I expected him to argue against my request, but the hunger building behind his gaze highlights the transition taking place between us, the shift from a deep conversation toward the concession to our passionate desire. It sparks between us like the brewing of a storm and I step back instinctively, trying to separate myself from the consuming downpour.

My movements are futile though.

Jude reaches down with his hands, sliding them from my lower back, down to the sides of my hips. He slowly bunches the bottom of my dress in his palms. His eyes are focused and demanding, never straying from my gaze as he pulls my dress up and over my lacy underwear.

"Take it off." He tugs on my dress, forcing my obedience with his heady touch.

My tongue reaches out to wet my lips as my shaky hands find the hem of my dress. I pull it off in one quick flourish and then let it drop from my fingers without a glance toward the silky white material.

I'm standing before him in a matching lace bra and panties. My strappy heels are still adorning my ankles, but as Jude's eyes take in every inch of me, he doesn't seem to mind their presence.

He steps closer, dipping low to connect his supple mouth with my neck while his hands drift up my arms. He nips and licks, trailing his mouth down the front of my chest while his hands reach from my bare shoulders down my neck to cup my breasts.

My soft cry awakens my desire even more.

I wasn't expecting his touch. He grasps me with such possession that I dip toward him, letting him take his fill of me. For tonight, I'll be his, and I'll pretend he's mine. It feels so right and I want all of him, every inch of him against me, taking me and pretending to love me.

His fingers find the back of my bra, flicking it open and letting it fall between us. I fumble for the buttons of his shirt, needing, wanting to feel our skin crashing together. I curse trying to unbutton as fast as I can then he tugs the last few buttons off. When his shirt slides down his arms, I push myself toward him, feeling his hard chest press against my sensitive nipples and igniting my soul.

Each movement passes faster than the last and soon the lines blur between which of us is controlling my body. My legs wrap around his torso and he hoists me up and shoves me back against the hotel's wall. The armoire next to us rattles loudly from our wild tango and I giggle before his mouth finds mine. He sucks me in, kissing me hard, almost bruising my lips, and I meet him kiss for kiss, trying to eradicate the space between us. His breath is minty and consumes my senses, drawing my attention to the lust building in my core.

Fuck.

Nothing seems to be enough. I need more. I scratch my nails down his back, making him groan huskily as he forces me up against the wall harder.

"Fuck, Charley," he drawls out as his hips roll into mine, grinding our bodies together.

His mouth captures my nipple and I cry out loudly, not caring if everyone in the hotel can hear us. I just want to give him everything, all of me. His teeth tease my tight bud as his hand finds my other breast, kneading it in his hands and unraveling the ribbons of lust throughout my body.

"Tonight, I'm going to do anything I want with you. You're mine."

"I…Jude."

"Are you on birth control?"

God, I don't even care! "Yes." I breathe. "The pill."

"Good."

He spins me around so fast I tighten my hands around his shoulders for fear I'll lose my grip around his waist. He bends down, placing me on the bed with my legs bent up and open wide for him. Subconsciously, I move to readjust and hide myself, but his hands clamp down on my inner thighs, pushing me back open for him.

"Don't hide from me, not tonight. This sweet spot is all mine and I plan on tasting it until I get my fill."

My body clenches in anticipation. It's been so long, years, since anyone has done this to me, and my adrenaline spikes, wanting his lips on me so badly I can't wait another second.

"Please, Jude."

"Shh, baby. I'll give you everything you need." His wicked voice holds so much promise that I have to bite down hard on my lip to tamp down my overwhelming desire. I just need him. My body hums, alive and waiting for him to fill me. I watch him unbuckle his pants and slide them down his hips, revealing his tight black boxer briefs. The bulge hidden beneath fills me with a new wave of wetness, but I can't ignore the brief moment of fear.

There's no time to worry because he's already bending down on his knees and tugging my body to the end of the bed so my skin glides along the silky duvet cover. My eyes flutter closed as ecstasy starts to overwhelm my entire world. I feel like I'm on the seat of a roller coaster, rounding the top of the curve, waiting to plummet down.

Then suddenly Jude's warm breath falls on the sensitive flesh around my panties and there's no more silence. Soft moans break through my throat as his finger trails along the edge, so close to where I need him to be.

Cold air suddenly douses my flesh as he drags my panties to the side, completely exposing every inch of me. He doesn't touch me. Instead, I watch him gaze at my flesh with heated desire. It's such an intimate feeling, having him study me, and my curiosities are answered the moment he starts to murmur soft words.

"You're so beautiful, Charley. Pink and wet just for me." My head presses back into the duvet cover as I arch away from his searing words. This can't be real. He fulfills every desire within me—possessing me, controlling me, loving me. His deft fingers open up my delicate folds and I almost lose it, my body almost shattering beneath his touch.

Each touch of his is willful and calculated. He takes his time, examining me and kissing all the delicate flesh surrounding my center. Then without warning, his warm breath caresses my clit, and a moment later his tongue finds the same spot. I buck my hips beneath him, but his strong hands pin my legs to the bed, forcing me to feel his relentless torture. It's impossible to lie still as he kisses me, lapping me up gently. I'm crooning in a lust-filled haze as his tongue dips deep into my folds, over and over again. Waves of pleasure follow every lap of his tongue.

He sucks my clit into his mouth, stimulating every single nerve in my body, but it's not enough. I know because when his finger slides into me, my pleasure heightens tenfold and fireworks explode behind my eyelids.

"Yes," I cry, wanting him to know how much his touch affects me.

His long, deft finger slides in and out, coated in my wetness.

"I'm going to watch you come while I finger you, Charley," he declares with such arrogance and confidence, I know my body will comply with his every whim.

He slides a second finger in, stretching me, and then his mouth swirls around my clit, bringing me closer and closer.

"Do you feel how tight you are? How much my fingers stretch you? I want to feel you around my cock, Charley."

My hips meet his fingers, pushing him deeper, needing more.

"I want you inside me," I murmur, knowing we both need the same thing.

He doesn't listen though. His fingers speed up, fucking me hard, and my body kicks into overdrive.

"Come for me, Charley."

His tongue finds my clit again, sucking it into his mouth, matching the quick thrusts of his fingers. The combination completely breaks me and my orgasm comes so fast as I scream out his name. I love the way his name sounds, breaking through my throat like a wild plea. The ripples of pleasure extend to every part of my body, leaving no cell untouched.

My eyes blink open as Jude shoves his boxer briefs down and rips off my shoes and panties, leaving us both completely bare. There's so much more to feel and all too soon. My body cries out for his touch.

He starts to crawl over me, onto the bed, cocooning me beneath his hard muscles. His smoldering blue eyes glare down at me as he groans, "I love making you come, Charley, making that sweet little pussy of yours ripple around me."

"Take me," I plead, drowning in his enticing scent and touch.

He grabs my hips and shoves me up higher on the bed so we can both fit. I pant beneath him, waiting for his next move.

"I've been tested and I always use protection. I want to

feel every inch of you. Charley, do you trust me?"

Absolutely.

"Yes, Jude."

Suddenly he pulls my legs apart and settles his hard erection against my folds, running it up and down, coating it with my slickness.

"Please." I wiggle my hips, trying to press him into the exact spot where I need him. He never stops stroking himself against me as I speak, and my words come out harsh and jagged. Any hope of trying to quell my exposed desire is forgotten when his mouth crushes against mine, claiming me, branding me as his for the night.

I open up to him willingly, pressing my legs hard against the bed so every inch of him crushes against my skin. He stretches my lips and with one hard thrust, his dick slides into me. I cry out, trying to adjust to the overwhelming sensations. It's been so long since I've had sex and the last time was so different. I wasn't expecting the pain, but in a flash it's gone, flooded over by desire and red-hot need.

"Oh, my angel. You feel like heaven. We were made for each other," he coos into my ear as he thrusts into me slowly, torturously drawing his cock in and out of me. Shivers erupt down my body as he drags himself against my most sensitive spot.

Our bodies respond together, moving in a rhythm that builds, each thrust harder than the last, until finally he's fucking me with absolute ownership. He fills me completely, digging his fingers into the sensitive flesh of my inner thigh and pinning me under him. I like it. It's scary how much I like this—him controlling me, forcing me to feel every inch of him inside me. His movements are so controlled, and his desire for me spills out between us, coating me in sweet seduction. God I need him so bad. I want him forever; tonight isn't enough.

He rocks against me harder, pushing me into the bed forcefully. Meeting his demands, I reach up to twist my hands through his hair, yanking his head down to me. Our lips touch, and then like magic, our mouths open and our bodies meld together completely. I taste myself on his tongue, sweet and sexy, such a divine combination that sends my mind reeling.

His tongue, his kiss, his taste all make me want to beg for more.

With a quick shove, he pushes himself up onto his knees so he can see his dick sliding in and out. The new angle forces him even deeper inside me and his hard thrusts jolt my entire body to life. His hands wrap around my breasts, engulfing them with his sweet touch as he rams into me harder and harder. Our sweaty bodies press together in frantic, primal need.

"I want to feel you come around me," he commands roughly, plunging deeper with quick, mastered movements. His deep groans meet my soft cries as every single inhibition melts away and my body cries for release.

"Jude! That feels so good," I cry out.

"You like that, Angel? Feel me. Feel me stretching your tight pussy."

My body obeys and once again I find myself careening toward complete bliss. I tighten around his dick and come undone, screaming his name with such unabashed pleasure I'm sure he can see straight through me. He milks every drop out of me, pushing the pleasure to last longer and longer until my consciousness completely fades for a moment and I'm left with only the sensations he gives me—hard, raw passion pounding into me as his own orgasm meets mine. He groans loudly, filling me with his sweetness and caressing every inch of my core until I'm left completely satiated.

So much so that I may never open my eyes again.

Jude

She's everything. The way she screamed my name as we came together will forever be burned in my memory as the most erotic and beautiful sound I've ever heard. My hand strokes her cheek as we lie paralyzed, trying to float back to reality. Her bright blue eyes stay focused on me, but as she blinks, her eyelids start to linger closed longer and longer. I know she'll soon slink away from the conscious world all together.

I hop up off the bed and quickly clean myself off before grabbing a washcloth for Charley. I don't want her to get up; I don't want this moment, or this night, to end. When I crawl back into bed, she smiles up at me with a lazy grin and stretches out to envelope me in her arms. I accept willingly, dragging the washcloth over her sensitive sex and cleaning up the remnants of our lovemaking.

Were we making love?

I push the thought aside. It isn't the time for monumental decisions. Tonight was more than anything I could've hoped for, and that is enough for right now.

After I set the washcloth on the side table, I relax against her and she wraps herself around me like ivy winding up a tree.

"Mmm…thank you…for everything," she hums before pressing a chaste kiss to my chest.

I capture one of her hands in mine and bring it to my lips, kissing her palm and trying to show her every unspoken word hanging on the tip of my tongue.

"I don't think anything will ever compare to that," she muses, letting her eyelids flutter closed against my chest. I lie awake watching her for a few minutes, getting carried away with the idea of falling asleep with her like this every night. Her body feels so small and warm against mine, but the way she's wrapped around me makes me feel needed, desired.

"Goodnight, Charley," I whisper wistfully, even though she's already drifted off to sleep. I stroke her pale blonde hair away from her face, revealing every inch of her delicate beauty.

"I wish I could keep you," I murmur into the dark void.

Chapter Nineteen

Charley

"YOU DIDN'T HAVE to escort me home to my apartment, Jude," I point out as the taxi passes sprawling urban blocks on its way back from the airport. Our plane landed just after six PM, but the sun was already down and the Manhattan chill seeped in the moment we left the airport. City lights flash around us, blocking the moon and stars. I zip up my tight leather jacket, trying to adjust to the drastic changes in temperature. Just this morning, we were lazing on the beach in our swimsuits, managing to fit in one more quick swim before leaving the island. Now, I'm wrapped in three layers of warm clothing.

Jude raises his brow and offers me a silly smirk. "And cut this vacation short sooner?" His tone makes my statement sound utterly ridiculous.

I can't help but laugh as I gesture toward the window.

"We're in the back of a cab, in New York City, a block from my apartment. I think that means the vacation is officially over."

He shakes his head knowingly, narrowing his intense gaze right onto me. "Charley, until we are outside your apartment door, this vacation is still happening." Then he dips his head back against the seat and plasters on an easy smile. "Now relax and enjoy the island breeze."

I laugh at his playfulness, loving these little exchanges of ours. It's been too long since I've had easy conversations like this with anyone other than Naomi. "I think that's smog," I offer cheekily.

He pries one eye open and tips his head toward me. "Ha ha. Who taught you to be such a smartass, my dear?"

"It's *au naturel*, built in with my WASPy DNA." I smile wryly.

"Mmm, we'll have to get some more Brooklyn in you."

"Is that where your apartment is?" I ask, suddenly curious to know how he lives. "It's strange that I haven't seen it yet."

"Yeah. It's just across the river. We'll have dinner there tomorrow." Of course there's no invitation because it's not necessary. I'd cancel any plans I had to go to his place for dinner.

"Sounds good."

"There's an outdoor market a few blocks from my place. We can go there to pick up ingredients."

"Oh!" My eyes light up with excitement. "Maybe we can make one of my recipes. It's been forever since I've had an actual kitchen to cook in."

"I'd like that." He reaches out, puts his hand over mine, and we ride the last few minutes in silence.

I'm scrolling through my rolodex of recipes in my head,

purposely ignoring the nagging sensation in the back of my mind. I know it's there, trying to remind me that we're home and that this thing with Jude has to change. We either have to take a step forward or a step back—but maybe not. Maybe we can just be in this perfect state of happiness without the world pushing in from all sides, threatening to crumble our budding relationship before it even has time to grow.

"Jeez. Who ordered the limo?" Jude asks as we pull onto my street.

My heart instantly sinks. There's no way.

Surely it can't be her.

"Shit," I mumble under my breath as we get closer. I recognize the distinguished-looking driver positioned outside of the limo: David. He's worked for my mother for twenty years and he's like a loyal sidekick, staying with her through both marriages, always in the background but consistently present.

My tongue drags along my top row of teeth as my instincts kick into overdrive. Jude cannot talk to her. My two worlds can't collide like this. It's too soon. I haven't had nearly enough time with Jude.

"Charley?" he asks, placing his hand on the back of my neck, gently massaging. "Is everything okay?"

"Um, yes. It's just…" Crap. Nothing. Absolutely nothing comes to mind, and I don't want to lie to him. There are so many lies building on one another; this cannot be another.

In a blur of events, the cab driver stops and Jude pays him then hops out to grab our luggage. I slink out of the cab and try to hurry Jude along so he can get back into the cab before the dragon rears her ugly, coifed head.

"Clarissa, darling!" Her voice screeches through the air

like nails on a chalkboard. I haven't seen her in four years, and this is how she decides to greet me, as if we do lunch three times a week.

I don't turn toward her. My eyes stay glued on Jude as he pulls my bags out of the taxi and rests them on the sidewalk. The moment she says my name—my old name—Jude's head pops up and he looks past me. I know he connects the dots. Unless she's stopped getting plastic surgery since I've been gone, we probably only look ten years apart in age.

"Darling, aren't you going to greet your mother?" She pronounces every word slowly with her Upper West Side hoity-toity accent.

Jude's gaze volleys from her to me and then back again, trying to keep up.

Fuck.

With a disgruntled sigh, I swipe a hand over my face and turn toward her. This situation is happening whether I want it to or not.

"Hello," I clip out, taking in her appearance. There isn't a single strand of hair out of place on her beautiful blonde head. She has on tailored silk slacks, kitten heels, and a printed shirt that looks straight off the runway. Her makeup is flawless, concealing all her inner ugliness from the rest of the world.

"Did you just get back from a trip?" she asks as her eyes scan down to my luggage, probably disgusted I'm not using the monogrammed Louis Vuitton set she bought me when I turned sixteen. Sorry mother dearest, I sold that a long time ago.

"We were in Hawaii for a shoot," Jude answers simply. Can he feel the tension pulsing around us?

For the first time since we've arrived, her eyes fall on

Jude. Her expression never falters; she doesn't smile or frown, simply stares toward him with a look of disinterest. "Oh, excuse Clarissa's manners. I'm Mrs. Temple, and you are?"

"Jude," he says, extending his hand to empty air. She doesn't even look down at it, and she definitely doesn't step forward to grasp it. I step closer to him, instinctively wanting to shield him from the vile woman that created me.

"How are you associated with this *photo shoot*, Jude?" she asks as his hand falls back down to his side.

"I'm a photographer," he answers confidently with his head held high, not intimidated by her coldness in the least.

She glares toward me and looks like she's just had a hefty whiff of sour milk. "Oh sweetie, a photographer, really? What has gotten into you lately? This isn't how we raised you. When will you put this silly modeling behind you? How do you think I look when the ladies at the club ask about you posing for smut magazines in a bikini! Really, Clarissa, I expected better—"

"Mom!" I yell, before taking a deep breath. Don't let her affect you, I remind myself.

"What are you doing here?" I bite out as calmly as I can, which is to say not calm at all.

A slow, wicked smile spreads across her lips and the expression sends a chill through me. "Oh, I've come over to help with the wedding planning, dear."

You've got to be kidding me.

"You're insane! What do—"

"I'm going to go…" Jude murmurs, interrupting my question and taking a step back toward the taxi.

"No!" I exclaim. This entire fucking situation is wrong, but he's the only part of this that I want, that I *need* right now.

My mother clears her throat behind us before offering me advice in her prim tone. "It's best not to lead the poor boy on. Does he know about your engagement?"

The entire world slows as her words filter through the air. I turn toward Jude just as his eyebrows push together in disbelief. Then, like rolling thunder, the expression takes over each of his features. His blue eyes glaze over in shock, his jaw clenches, and his hands tug through his beautifully dark hair, tousling it even further. Then suddenly, he's turning on his heels, clenching his hands into tight fists, and walking off.

"Jude! Stop!" I run after him, but he climbs into the taxi without a single glance back. He slams the door closed, blocking me out. I don't know what to do, so I bang on the window, trying to get him to stop. I bang so hard my palm starts to sting, but he shakes his head, keeps his focus out through the front window, and tells the driver to leave.

"Jude!" I scream through the night air as I watch his taxi drive away. How did this happen? How the hell did he just steal my heart? I thought I was protecting it, so why do I feel like my entire fucking soul was just ground into the pavement underneath the weight of that cab's tires?

"Mom! You're delusional!" I scream, turning to face her and pacing forward with determined strides. "I broke off that 'engagement' four years ago. Why would you say something like that?! Are you actually insane or are you just trying to ruin what little of my life I have left?"

My hands hang in the air for a moment before I drag them down the sides of my face, trying to make sense of this woman in front of me. She glances down at her manicured fingers, not a hint of emotion marring her gorgeously evil features. "I guess one gets behind on the current events of a daughter's life when she refuses to speak with them."

Are her words meant to affect me? I don't even know how it's possible to hate her even more than I already do, but seeing Jude drive away adds one more notch to her growing list of vile deeds.

I force a slow inhale and exhale, and when I finally speak, my voice is eerily calm. "Mom, I need you to leave me alone. I'm not ready to be around you, and I don't know if I ever will be. I'd rather not have a family at all than deal with a mother like you."

I start to turn to collect my luggage, mistakenly thinking the exchange had hit its peak, but then my mother glances up and I gaze at her icy blue eyes reflected back into mine. I don't know what I expected to see, but cold annoyance wasn't it. "You always had a flair for the dramatic, *Clarissa*. It was embarrassing when you were growing up, but now it's just pathetic. No one likes a depressed girl, not even that photographer."

With that bomb, she turns on her nude kitten heels and slides back into her limousine, leaving me like she has my entire life: ten times worse than the way she found me.

Chapter twenty

Jude

IT'S BEEN FOUR years since I've felt like my life was out of control, four years since I worked for the magazine. The moment I came back from my assignment overseas, I molded my life so I could exist and be happy. I worked, I played soccer, and I picked up fast women. I never once felt like I was lacking anything, so why the hell does it feel that way now?

I pick up my pace, practically sprinting down the blistery city streets. The wind is working against me, pushing my body and adding extra resistance. I use it to work through my anger. I press on harder, whipping around the sidewalk and into Central Park. It's too early for anyone to be here. Even in New York, not many people want to get up and run at five AM, especially in the fall. Cold air whips through my black fleece jacket, reminding me of the changing seasons. Does Charley like fall? If I had to guess, she would probably prefer fall and winter to springtime. She just seems like she'd rather curl up by a fire with her paintings instead of dancing in a flowery meadow—although who would actually do that anyway?

She's called me a dozen times in the past few days, but I haven't answered. She's even left a few voicemails, and although I should, I couldn't force myself to delete them. It seems too final, not to mention I know I'll be desperate in a few days. I'll need those voicemails for proof that she really did care…at least on some level.

• • •

As I round the corner back to my apartment, her little blonde head comes into view. It almost looks like a mirage at first because a perfect angel waiting for me at my doorstep seems too good to be true, but there she is with her hands propping her chin up and the sleeves of her knitted sweater pulled over her knuckles. She looks like a scared animal, but I can't pretend she's that innocent. I can't pretend she hasn't been lying to me, or hell, maybe just lying to herself.

"What are you doing here?" I ask as I approach the weathered stoop that leads into the refurbished warehouse that is my apartment building.

When she hears my voice, her eyes widen and her head snaps to look in my direction.

"We need to talk." Her blue eyes plead for me to listen.

"Do we?" I ask, crossing my arms.

She bites her bottom lip and glances away for a moment, down toward the bottom of the stoop. I'd be blind if I didn't notice her lip quivering or her blue eyes starting to cloud with sadness.

"Yes, Jude. Please," she finally begs.

"How'd you find out where I live?" I ask in a clipped tone.

"Bennett gave me your address."

"Huh." I raise my eyebrows sardonically. "Good to know where his loyalties lie…"

"Jude," she protests, not wanting to drag Bennett down with her. "Can I just speak to you for a few minutes? If you're still upset with me after, I'll understand completely, but I can't let you believe anything my mother said was true."

I squeeze my eyes closed, taking a deep inhale, and then I sigh and brush past her. The industrial door to our complex slides open after I tap out the combination key, and without looking back, I start heading to my apartment. If she's that desperate to talk, she'll follow me.

Our footsteps echo across the smooth concrete floor and I almost turn around and cave. It's torture trying to fight the connection we have but giving in now won't do either of us any good.

I enter my apartment and appreciate the wide, open layout and floor-to-ceiling windows; I feel like I need some space to breathe. The second my apartment door closes and we have privacy, Charley starts speaking so quickly I can barely make out each syllable. Does she think I'm going to kick her out mid sentence?

"My mother was lying when she said I'm engaged. Well, I was engaged, or technically 'betrothed' to Hudson when we were in school, but that was just our parents trying to control everything. We never took it seriously, but my mom really thought I'd go through with it. She thought we'd go off to the same college, he would officially propose, and then we'd live happily ever after. I have no clue why she brought that up today. It's a blatant lie, Jude!"

"Charley, stop!"

My stomach is twisted into a tight knot and I can't listen to another word she says. Everything she spouts seems to complicate things even more.

"Obviously I know your mom is full of shit, but that's not what made me leave. It's the overwhelming secrecy that weighs you down. You won't let me in. I would've known your mother was lying right away if you had told me anything about her at all."

I take a deep breath, but I still have so much left to say.

"What happened to your family? Why do you avoid speaking about them?" I pause, glancing up to see if she'll answer; when she doesn't, I keep asking questions just to prove how much she's been hiding from me. "How did your father die?" I grip the side of my black granite countertop. "Is your real name Clarissa? You told me Charley wasn't a nickname, so is it your middle name? At times I feel like I know nothing about you and it scares the shit out of me. I've shown you every demon in my closet, and yet you keep yourself hidden away from the world like a porcelain doll."

"Jude…" she murmurs, but my name hangs in the air. She still doesn't answer my questions.

Silence fills my apartment and my heart starts to sink all over again.

"I don't want to be with someone who can't be honest with themselves, Charley. I don't expect you to trust me with everything right away, but I walk on eggshells around you. That's not what relationships should be like."

There. I said it.

My hands relax enough for blood to start flowing back into my white knuckles once again, but it takes a few minutes before I can look up at her. When I finally lift my head, her eyes are distant and focused a few feet above me. Her features are relaxed—soft eyes, tan pore-less skin, rosy cheeks—but I know there's a war raging behind that facade.

She doesn't protest or even offer a rebuttal. She doesn't have a sudden epiphany and tell me every sad memory from her past. Charley nods her head slowly, just once. Then she turns and walks out of my apartment and out of my life.

Chapter Twenty-One

Charley

I CAN'T RUN away fast enough. I knew I was playing with fire, but I couldn't stop. I should have stayed away from the very beginning, but I didn't because I'm selfish and depressed and I wanted someone to heal me.

I wanted him to be enough to take away the blackness, but he's wasn't, and so for his sake, I walk away.

My mother said it best: "*No one wants a depressed girl.*" I'm flawed at best, and Jude needs someone strong and happy. He's already had too much sadness in his life.

I have to fix myself—not in hopes of getting Jude back, but in hopes of living a life worthy of his love.

So, it's time to finally face the past.

Jude

I almost fool myself into thinking the last few weeks didn't even take place. After all, it's not like I have to avoid our favorite restaurant or that one park bench where we'd sip our coffee on Sunday mornings.

Nope. Charley and I never got to find our favorite places; she made clean work of that.

So I go about my life as normal, returning to the routine and pretending the status quo is good enough. It's strange how the brain works, though. Charley shouldn't weave her way into my mind since our lives were never completely intertwined...yet I find myself constantly wondering what the answers would be to the questions I would have gotten to ask if we had actually worked out.

What does she look like when she loses herself in a painting?

Does she listen to music while she works?

What recipe would she have made for me at my apartment if we hadn't been interrupted by her mom?

• • •

Charley

I scroll through the search results, rereading archived articles again and again. When it happened, I clipped every newspaper and printed out every online publication I could find on the subject. I kept everything in a neat folder with no label and no description of what lay hidden inside, but it's been four years since I ripped everything up.

When I read about him back then, the wounds were fresh and I could hardly process the written words in my mind without sliding back into the dark void. Now, the articles seem less severe and I can process them with a hardened perspective. Certain words still jump out at me—criminal, father, life imprisonment—but I hold my breath as I read each one and push forward, past the pain.

A hard knock on my apartment door jars me from the middle of an article.

"Charley!" Naomi yells from the other side. She's been by every day this week, but I can't talk to her right now. She's my best friend, and I hate ignoring her, but if I let her in, she'll do what she always does—make me forget. Right now, I need to keep up my momentum or I'll never dig up my demons.

"Charley! Please, let me in. This is ridiculous." Her anguished tone pierces through the oak door, but I can't let her in.

It would be too easy to fall back into old habits if I did. My nails run across my bottom lip anxiously as I try to decide what the best option is. I know I'm doing the right thing, but I shouldn't ignore her either. I don't want her to have to worry. With a resolved sigh, I shove my computer off my lap and pad across my apartment toward the door. My socked feet thump softly on the wood floor and I know she's probably relieved to hear movement, to know I'm at least alive.

With both of my palms pressed against the oak surface, I lean in and console her. "Naomi, I'm fine. I just need some privacy for a few days. Don't worry about me. I love you, and I'll text you when I can."

"Charley, that's not good enough."

"Please." My voice cracks with the plea, and I pray she doesn't keep fighting me. There's so much weighing me down; I just need her to understand.

"I'll give you a week, but not a day more."

In spite of everything, the edges of my lips curl at her loyal persistence. One day, I know I'll be just as good a friend as she's been to me these past few years.

• • •

Jude

Bennett stalks into the living room and slams a six pack of beer onto the coffee table. I barely flinch. I've had the TV on for the past few hours even if the noise hasn't actually been registering. Bennett raises his eyebrows as he steps over an empty pizza box that's a few days old.

"I see you've been taking good care of the place," he mocks, taking a seat in the overstuffed armchair adjacent to the couch.

"Fuck off," I snap back, although most of my words are lost in the cushions pressed against my mouth.

"That bad, huh?" he asks, popping the top of his beer.

"You don't want to know." I push my upper body up off the leather couch cushions and reach for one of the beers.

"How are things with Naomi?" I ask, not because I want to hear it, but because Bennett should be able to talk to me even if I'm a mess.

"Pretty good. We made it official while you guys were in Hawaii."

"Wow. That was fast."

"Not really. We aren't twenty-one anymore. It's pretty easy to tell if things can work."

He leaves out the other part where it's also easy to tell if things won't work.

"I like her," I offer, finally meeting his eye.

"Thanks," he mutters with a skeptical glance.

We sit in silence for a while after that, letting the football game on my flat screen take over our conversation. My mind's not really focused on anything. The game filters through my ears, but I don't listen. The beer slides down my throat, but I don't taste it.

"Dude, what the hell is up with you? I haven't seen you like this since you got back from overseas."

I don't answer because I don't know what to say to that other than the raw truth, which I haven't even been willing to admit to myself until this very moment.

"I didn't account for Charley."

Fuck, saying it out loud, putting the feelings out into the oblivion somehow makes it even worse, but my vocal cords don't stop. "I wasn't prepared for her to wreck my life. You know that night at the club when Natasha came to meet me again? I could've slept with her, but I walked away and just left her hanging."

"Why the hell did you do that?"

"Because Charley and Naomi were at the club. I saw them on the dance floor," I divulge, finally sharing that snippet of information with someone.

"What? They were there that night?" He leans forward in his chair, intrigued.

"Yup."

"You never told me." He frowns, trying to piece together the new information.

I nod, staring into the dark ale, not willing to meet his eye.

"Did you talk to her that night?"

"No, but the moment I saw her on the dance floor, I knew I wanted her. I had to have her. And instead of listening to logic and reason, I went for her." I tip back the beer, drinking half the bottle in one long drag.

"How long has it been since you guys have talked?" he asks with a frown.

"Two weeks."

He nods slowly, taking a sip of his beer, and then another.

Finally, he leans his head toward me and cocks a brow. "Well, chump, what are you going to do about it?"

I shake my head. "Nothing. Charley has her own shit to work through. I can't force her to want to be with me."

"So you knew better than to fall for her and then you did anyway?"

"Looks like it." I scrub a hand across my overgrown facial hair.

He chuckles regretfully. "Damn, I'll drink to that."

• • •

Charley

I decide to try to work everything out without therapy. It

didn't work for me last time and I already know they'll want to put me on drugs. We live in the era of ever-present and ever-available uppers and downers, but I don't want either. I know I can fix myself. I know the root of my problem; I just never thought it was possible to overcome my past until I met Jude.

He taught me how to experience life through my senses, never holding back, never pushing feelings away. He didn't let me hide; he told me I had to be honest with myself. Hearing him say so was the biggest wakeup call I've had in four years.

For the first time since my father's death, I lie alone in my room letting my mind wander. Will the memories even come? My head rests back on my pillow and my eyes study the white paint chipping above my head. For a little while I think of nothing at all, just white noise. Have I pushed them away for so long they've disappeared completely?

But then, like a faint echo, I remember my father's deep laughter. The sound is faint and fades in and out like the reception with a bad antenna.

He was always laughing.

Before I realize my movements, I slip off my bed and pull a large blank canvas from the armoire beside my bed. My bucket of paints tumbles out after it, but I let them spill out onto the ground, not caring about the mess. I grab the colors I need, mixing them on my palette and letting the reverberating remnants of his laughter push me forward. As I let the memories overtake me, I begin to paint my father as I remembered him.

His image is hazier now, but the important aspects are still there. His strong jaw and angled cheekbones were always so prominent. Then I think of his dark gray eyes, starkly different from mine and my mother's.

To the untrained eye, his facial features and expensive power suits appeared stern and unyielding, but I knew better. He showered me with love, much to the dismay of my mother. He was everything to me growing up. Every girl has a special love for her father and mine only grew with age. I never confided in my mother, but my father was an excellent listener, even about silly things like friends and drama at school.

He worked late and often took long business trips, especially as I got older, but we talked every day. Even if he got home at midnight, he'd wake me up just to tell me he loved me, then more often than not, we'd end up staying up late, talking and laughing.

Which is why his suicide blindsided me.

My hand freezes mid stroke. God, I haven't let myself actually think that word since his death. *Suicide.* My father killed himself and I saw him do it.

The thin palette slips from my fingers and then my brush tumbles through the air after it. Paint scatters across the hardwood floor, splashing my bare feet and my yoga pants, coating the unfinished canvas and the woven rug next to my door. My eyes lose focus as dark rings impinge on my vision. I pinch my eyes closed, trying to find a grip on reality while simultaneously remembering why I have to let myself slip away from it.

The memories are so hard to process; I'm afraid they'll finally splinter my soul in two and leave me a hollow shell, even more so than I am now.

Tears stream down my cheeks as I clamor over the art supplies to find the half empty bottle of tequila Naomi left here the night we went to the bar, the night I stripped for Jude.

I steal it off the bookshelf, twist the cap off, and step

back to look at the half painted portrait of my father staring back at me. The blue and orange hues cast shadows across his features, but his gray canvassed eyes stare back at me, pulling all my buried sadness to the surface.

Fuck you. I take a long drag of the tequila and relish the pain as it burns down my throat, setting my mouth ablaze. Fuck you for killing yourself. Another shot slips down, coating my stomach with sweet warmth. Fuck you for leaving me. One more long gulp of the hard liquor, and then I drag my finger across the wet paint, smearing his features into a blurry mess of mismatched hues. Fuck you for not stopping, even as I begged.

Jude

My phone's buzzing reverberates through the silent room and I reach over to grab it from the nightstand without looking at the caller ID.

"Hello." My pulse rises as I wait for her voice to filter through. Charley hasn't called since she walked out of my apartment three weeks ago and my heart leaps at the chance that it could be her on the other end of the line.

"Jude! Thank god you answered." A female voice sighs into the phone, but it's not Charley.

Naomi?

"Naomi? What's up?" I glance down at the screen to see it's only half past nine at night. I've been working, hitting the gym, and passing out early every day this week.

"It's about Charley."

What? I have to fight to keep my calm.

"What about her?"

"Listen, I know you don't owe her anything...but I think something is wrong and I felt like you should know."

My teeth grind together as I stare up at the ceiling. What am I meant to do here? She left; of course there's something wrong.

"Tell me," I demand with a gruff tone.

"She hasn't even told me everything, but, Jude, she's worth fighting for. She keeps everything so private, but I've never seen her like this. I can usually get through to her on the low days, but the past two weeks have been complete torture. She's been ignoring my calls and won't let me in when I go to her apartment."

Naomi pauses and I hear her soft sniffles in the background. The next time she speaks, her words are muffled through quiet sobs.

"She has the most beautiful soul, but Jude, it's tormented. She's had such a hard life, the kind of life that looks perfect on paper, the kind of life no one ever questions—but you have to keep pushing, Jude. I don't know what to do."

"She walked away from me, Naomi," I point out, trying to remind myself of that fact as well.

"I know." She says the words, but her voice doesn't sound so convinced.

"I begged her to open up and she left. Why would she want to see me now?"

"You get to her more than anyone else I've seen. Hell, I had to pry my way in over the years, but in a few weeks you seemed to peel away every layer."

"I don't want her to suffer anymore," I admit, feeling my steely resolve melting away.

"I don't know what to do," she cries into the phone.

"I'll go by in the morning. I've only been keeping my distance because I thought it would help her."

"Thank you, Jude."

• • •

It's Saturday morning, which means Charley should be running her route in Central Park. I could hardly sleep last night because I wanted to call her, but I didn't think she would have answered. So instead, I decided to wake up early, throw on my running gear, and find her on the trail to talk to her in person.

The temperature has dropped a few degrees in the past week so everyone is running in thick jackets and hats. I inspect each person that jogs by, but there's no real way to tell anyone apart. Every time a blonde woman runs by, I convince myself it's her, and every time, my heart falls once I realize the features don't match up.

I stand in the center of the park where most of the trails intersect, turning in a circle and waiting for her. Cold wind whips by, making my eyes water as runners swerve around me. Some of them curse at me for blocking their path, while others clearly see the desperation playing across my features and offer me sympathetic nods.

I'm not sure what will happen when I see her. I wish I had a poetic apology or a simple way to make everything better between us, but right now I just need to see her. I want to find her on the trail and sweep her away, back into our own little world. Maybe once the sun is shining on my angel, the words will come naturally.

But after hours pass, my confidence dwindles. I must

jog the entire park three times before I finally decide I'm not meant to find her. Either I missed her running by, or she didn't come out to the trail at all. It's possible our paths didn't cross, but it doesn't feel right. My gut tells me she's not here.

Why not? It's Saturday morning.

Various reasons start flitting through my head, sending a panic racing through me. Without another thought, I jog toward the perimeter of the park and hail a cab.

"Greenwich Village," I shout at the driver as I jump into the back seat and toss forward a hundred dollar bill so he'll take the quickest route. My eyes scour the streets as my thumb taps against my thigh incessantly. I'm trying to calm my nerves, but nothing helps. I keep picturing scenarios that send a shock of sadness through me. Hope for the best, plan for the worst.

Charley, please let me in. I plead to the universe as the cab driver rounds the city streets.

Was I a fool to push her away? Was she beginning to open up to me? I couldn't tell. I felt like I'd given her everything, but she wasn't ready. I can't save her and she can't save me. We can't be bandages for one another...but I never thought of her as bandage. If anything, being around her felt like ripping a band-aid off: fast, sharp, exhilarating, painful, and alive.

She's so sad, but I made her smile. I forced her to live. And now what? Did I push her too far?

Fuck.

The moment the cab pulls up to her apartment, I throw open the door and jump out. By the grace of god—or whatever other deity I'd prayed to on the way over—one of her housemates happens to be walking out right as I pull up. I yell at him to hold the door and jog down the hall to her room.

One piece of solid red oak stands between Charley and me. I bang on that barrier until the entire house—and maybe the entire street—can hear me.

"Charley! Let me in," I yell through the crack in the door hinge, but there's no movement from within.

"You don't have to deal with everything on your own. I want to be with you—whatever part of you you'll give me!" My voice echoes through the old house, hopefully reaching the one person who needs to hear it the most.

I bang louder, hearing the wood splinter in the doorframe. Am I insane enough to break it down? God, what if she's just not fucking home?

No. Naomi said she's been worse than usual. She's in there.

"Charley!" I yell once more before deciding I have to go to Mrs. Jenkins. If she truly cares about Charley, she'll come check on her.

I bolt up the stairs, but I guess my pounding didn't go completely unnoticed because the old woman is already coming out of her second floor apartment.

"What is it, young man?" she huffs indignantly.

"I need to get into Charley's apartment. I think there might be something wrong."

She tisks, shaking her head. "I don't make it a regular habit of breaking into my tenants' apartments when they aren't expecting me."

Dammit, woman!

"You know Charley. You know how she gets. If she doesn't want to see me, you can lock the door behind me and I'll never come back, but I think there's something wrong."

It takes some convincing, and I'm pretty sure she thinks

I'm Charley's estranged boyfriend, but who am I kidding? I'm actually not far from it.

"Young man, you seem respectable enough, so I'll do this because I really like Charley, but I pray that poor girl isn't just taking a shower or napping—or, god forbid, you're some kind of stalker."

I open my mouth to assure her, but she's already heading down the stairs and I don't care at this point. I don't care if standing in Central Park for four hours waiting for her to run by makes me crazy. I just can't let another person in my life slip through my fingers and become one more regret.

My mouth goes dry as Mrs. Jenkins slides her key into the lock. I can't swallow or breathe; I can't process anything as that door slides open. My eyes cast down to the doormat that looks like an abstract painting threw up on it then up toward the empty bottle of tequila that has wedged itself behind the door. It clinks across the floor as Mrs. Jenkins pushes the door completely open and my heart breaks.

She's lying there in a heap on the ground. Her face is ghostly pale and tears glisten across her cheeks as they stream down in a constant wave. She's alive, but completely immobile. Her blue eyes are cloudy and focused out toward the wall above the door. I rush in, pulling off my jacket and leaning down to feel her pulse. It's there, she's breathing, but her expression is dead and she doesn't seem to realize we've broken into her apartment.

Paint is spilled everywhere and canvases spread out across the room; there must be half a dozen lying around her. They're all covered in the same dark image painted from different angles. A man hanging himself, depicted with such agonizing clarity that a cry breaks through me. He's mirrored over and over again across her apartment floor with dark black brushstrokes. His cheekbones and light blond hair are perfect replicas of Charley's, and in a moment, I'm lying next to her on the ground, caressing her cheek and trying to coax her out of her darkened days.

"Charley."

Nothing. Not even a blink in my direction.

"Should I call an ambulance?" Mrs. Jenkins asks with a shaky voice.

"I don't know," I answer before turning my attention back to the fragile creature in front of me. "Charley. You have to talk, baby. Are you hurt?" I try to ask gently, but I need to know if she's injured herself.

I reach down to grab her wrists and then search the rest of her; there's nothing that looks injured. My eyes flit around the room; there aren't any pills or drugs. It doesn't seem like she's done anything but paint like crazy and drink the rest of the tequila.

I crawl closer to her, cupping her cold cheek in my hand. Her skin feels like ice beneath my fingers. Has she not had the heater on? How long has she been like this?

"I'm going to take you to the ER unless you start talking, Charley. I don't know if you're okay or not. You don't have to be scared. Tell me, baby."

Her head shifts a fraction to the left and she blinks her eyes, but when she speaks, her tone is flat and empty. "I'm fine…not even drunk…anymore."

It's hardly anything, but I sigh and feel the initial shock begin to wane ever so slightly.

"Do you want him here, Charley?" Mrs. Jenkins asks, still standing in the doorframe.

Charley doesn't move or speak for several long

seconds, and I start to panic that she wants me gone.

"Yes," she finally gets out, barely louder than a whisper, but the old woman nods in acceptance.

"I'm going to go make some tea and get you something to eat," Mrs. Jenkins calls as she starts to close to door. I glance up to watch her leave, and I notice that finally her eyes hold a morsel of kindness for me. She seems to realize I want the best for Charley. I know she's letting us have some privacy now that she trusts my reasons for being here.

Once she's gone, I lie down on the ground and face Charley. The hard, cold wood greets my body with its unyielding mass. My clothes dip into the paint scattered across the room, and I'm so close to her now, mere inches. We don't touch and I don't try to speak again. I just want to be here with her. We could lie here all day if that's what she needs.

My eyes roam across her features. Her cheekbones look more prominent than they were two weeks ago and I know she's lost weight. My poor Charley. Her long lashes flutter closed every now and then, pushing more tears to fall from her pale blue eyes. Her lips are a dark red, such a contrast to the rest of her pale features. Has she been chewing on them while she cries?

"I've never been to his grave," she says out of the blue. Her eyes don't meet mine, but her words hang in the air between us. Is she talking about her father?

I nod once, slowly. She doesn't need my questions or input right now; she just needs me to listen. She's been trying to fight for so long, but it's time for her to let go.

"I didn't go to his funeral either," she admits with a soul-crushing wail that echoes through the small room.

"I hated him," she screams.

I don't move a muscle.

"I hate him!" she cries, lashing out and hitting her hand against my chest. In a flash of limbs, our bodies collide. I tug her into my lap and her hands clench my shirt into tight fists. She thrashes against me and cries out, letting the tears wreck through her. She has so much pain stowed away. I know how it feels to implode from within. She pushes against me, slaps my arms, my chest, my cheek. Her pounding feels like beautiful caresses though; it means she's opening up and letting her demons see the light of day. She's finally facing the past.

"He left me!" she cries once more before collapsing into silent sobs.

We sit there rocking back and forth for hours.

Chapter twenty-two

Charley

JUDE DIDN'T LEAVE me once last night. I didn't think he would come; I didn't let myself truly wish for his presence until he was pounding on the door outside. When his loud yells broke through the silence in my apartment, the tears started pouring down all over again. He came back, he ignored my stubbornness, and he wasn't going to give up where so many others had before him.

After he made sure I wasn't physically injured, he just lay there with me, never pressuring me to talk. Mrs. Jenkins brought me tea and soup, and Jude fed me bite by bite. I fell asleep with him on the floor, but I stirred when he carried me up onto my bed and wrapped himself around me. I let myself soak in everything about him: his intoxicating aroma, his soft words wishing the darkness away, his strong arms wrapped around me telling me he'd never let me go.

I've never slept so peacefully than cradled in his arms on that tiny twin bed.

He left ten minutes ago and I've used those few minutes to assess the complete mess that is my apartment. Hopefully all the acrylic paint will come off the wood floor or I'll owe Mrs. Jenkins a fortune.

I thought I wouldn't be able to look at the canvases in the light of day, as though the dark secret was better kept in the night, but I don't glaze over them. I lay in bed, flicking my eyes from one to the next, taking them in from the distorted angles of my horizontal position. They're truly haunting, but so magnificent. I don't have any idea what I'll do with them.

Suddenly my door crashes open. "Up and at 'em!" Jude commands, storming into my room just like he stormed into my life: fast and uninvited.

I jump back against my pillow. "What? Why?" I ask as he strides across the room and places two bagels and two small coffees on the nightstand by my bed.

"Up. Get dressed," he demands, leaning down and kissing my hair. His hand strokes down my cheek and I glance up into his earnest blue eyes. He's the one I always dreamed of...a dream I can't possibly possess.

"Jude...I don't know. I think I just want to res—"

"Charley. I will drag you out of this room or you will come willingly; it's up to you." He grips the sides of his waist in a predatory stance. His broad shoulders tug on the dark green shirt he's paired with gray pants. His brow is raised in a cool arch, as though he welcomes the challenge of dragging me out of bed.

I groan and crawl out of my warm blankets to throw on some clothes.

"There's a bagel here for you. Sesame or blueberry?"

"Who eats sesame bagels?" I glare over my shoulder teasingly as I tug on my jeans.

"A lot of people." He smiles, leaning down to kiss me with strong, tender lips. I arch my neck to kiss him back. It's such a natural feeling to open up to him and I'm tired of fighting it.

"Blueberry, please." I smile wistfully.

I'm absolutely ravenous now that he's here.

"I picked up some cream cheese as well," he offers with a contented sigh.

We're not out of the storm—more like we're in the calm eye of a hurricane. Jude and I didn't have a heartfelt discussion about how much we've missed each other; it's written all over our actions. When I wrapped around him with every inch of my body last night, I gave him every apology I could muster. I don't know where we'll go from here, but we're in it together. That much is clear.

After I've put on a sweater dress, cashmere scarf, and warm boots, he pushes me out of the apartment and locks the door behind me.

There, on the ground beside my door, are the first clues to where Jude is taking me. My breathing shallows.

Jude

I picked up a New York Times and some red roses from the shop across the street, and I left them all outside her apartment lest she catch on too soon. I don't know how she'll react when I tell her we're going to her father's grave, but I know no matter what, I'll try to persuade her to let me take her. There's no way to know how it'll affect her, but it's clear she's built a wall of guilt around her heart over the past four years. Hopefully today she'll begin to break away some of it, enough to start letting love in.

The moment her eyes fall on the items outside her door, her posture straightens and her coffee pauses midway to her mouth. Her eyebrows furrow in thought and then her eyes slowly scan up from the newspaper toward me.

"Do you know the address of the cemetery, Charley?" I ask calmly, trying to gauge her reaction. Her tongue dips along the edge of her bottom lip as she examines me, trying to read between the lines.

"Yes," she offers simply. The plastic wrapper around her bagel crinkles as she moves to tuck it under her arm. With her spare hand, she reaches down to grab the fresh roses. Their fragrance wafts through the air and the ends of her mouth curl up gently when she gets a whiff.

"Here, let me get your coffee so you can get the newspaper too," I offer, already reaching for her drink.

We don't say a word on the cab ride over, but her shaking hand squeezes mine every now and then, reassuring me of my decision. She scans the road outside as the autumn leaves swirl like tiny tornadoes across the asphalt. Her head swivels as her gaze locks onto the people we pass on the sidewalk. She follows their movements until they're out of sight, as if their small cameos in her life are worth the effort. I don't think that will ever change; I think Charley will always be tucked between two worlds, daydreaming and thoughtfully watching life move around her. Her gut instinct isn't to participate, but then again, for the past four years, mine wasn't either.

As we pass through the elaborate wrought iron gates of

the cemetery, I suddenly wish I had brought her in spring—autumn hasn't been kind to the cemetery grounds. The grass is dying and most of the leaves are falling off the trees, leaving them haunting and bare. It's quite a bleak sight and since we're early, no other visitors have arrived. The cemetery is quiet and completely empty, as though even the resting memories haven't awoken yet.

"I know where the plot is. I've looked online a few times. They have a map of all the different sections, but I've never actually made it this far," she mutters as the taxi begins to slow to a stop next to the first section of graves.

"It's okay." I squeeze her hand. "We'll find it."

With one last timid smile, we hop out of the cab. I've got a pack of tissues in my back pocket and make a silent plea that I'm doing the right thing for her. I hold the newspaper, she clutches the red roses, and we link our spare hands, stepping into the desolate landscape in search of Charley's peace.

Tombstones pop up every now and then. Gold and crimson leaves cover most of them, but we don't bend to unbury any until we arrive in the section where she knows her father is buried. There, we start meticulously cleaning each stone, reading the name and moving on.

"Do you think he'd have a statue or anything?" I ask, trying to narrow down our search.

"No. He wouldn't have wanted that," she declares, scanning the bleak horizon for any tombstones that stand out.

I nod and continue searching, inspecting each tombstone we pass. Names and dates are etched in marble, commemorating the lost lives beneath us. Most of them are much older than the timeframe we're looking for, and then it hits me: I don't even know her father's name. I've just been looking for a 2009 year of death.

"Charley, what was your father's…" I begin to ask, but then I look up and see her slowly slide to the ground in front of a glistening slab of marble.

Beneath a giant oak tree, on the border of the cemetery, is a solitary tombstone: her father's. The oak's branches wind over our heads and a few of the heavier limbs bend gradually toward the ground. It hasn't lost its leaves like many of the other trees in the cemetery, and the blanket of foliage funnels the light into intricate shadows, cocooning us in a sliver of natural paradise.

Her trembling hand reaches out to brush away debris, and the movement catches my attention, drawing me toward her. I keep my distance at first, wanting her to process everything without my presence, but when her hand cups her mouth and she reclines back onto her heels in silent study, I step closer, hoping my slow steps won't disturb her.

When I'm a few feet away, I can finally discern the words written on the marble. The epitaph is much less elaborate than I was expecting, simply his name and years of life.

Charles Lock III
1957-2009

"His death made every single headline," she begins softly. "My senior year of high school, it came to light that his company was participating in countless criminal acts: accounting fraud, insider trading, embezzlement. He got caught up in the riches, in providing for his family and having it all. He started out as mid-level management, and I remember noticing that he was under more and more pressure. His stress and irritability only worsened with each new promotion, but he never lost his temper with me. I'd hear snippets of hushed phone conversations that would turn into brutal yelling matches between him and the rest of the board."

"Everything he did—or *approved* of, at least—cost a lot of families their livelihood. I had to change my name when I went to college, but I didn't want to leave him behind." Her voice descends into a soft murmur by the end of her sentence. She pauses to rebuild her courage.

"I loved him so much," she continues. "He was the only real family I had, and I wanted to keep a part of him. So, I changed my name from Clarissa Lock to Charley Whitlock, and for the most part, people from my old life have left me alone."

She pauses, tilting her head to the side and reaching out to run her pointer finger along the sunken script. Her finger carries away a layer of dirt that had settled over *Charles*, cleansing his name and her soul all at once.

"The media tore him to shreds, and I listened to every single word, hoping their image of him would tarnish mine, but nothing they said could take away the memories he gave me. He was the most loving father I could have ever asked for. I don't know why he took his own life instead of going to prison, but I have to believe it was because he was sick...

"I walked in as he was about to kick the chair away. He hung himself in our garage. I was going in to grab my sneakers."

Her eyes glance up to me as she clutches her hands on top of each knee, gripping them as if her life depends on it.

"I had run in the rain the morning before and my sneakers were muddy, so I'd left them in the garage to dry out. I can still picture it in my mind as clear as this gravestone in front of me. He didn't stop when I walked in; he was already too far gone. He'd made up his mind a long time ago and nothing I said could have changed it.

"When we locked eyes as he toed the edge of that chair, he had a tortured expression across his features. He knew how much it would hurt me to witness him take his own life. By that point, I was the only thing he had left to live for...which is why I've never been able to comprehend how he still kicked the chair away.

"But now I realize that for him, it was the only outcome he could reconcile, the only option that truly set me free from his mistakes. He didn't want me to watch him get dragged through the mud, rotting away in prison for the rest of his life. He didn't want me to spend my weekends and holidays in the visitation room of a federal penitentiary."

She pauses, allowing a few shallow inhales to pass. For a moment I think she might not continue, but then her brows furrow in frustration.

"For the past four years I've clutched my mother's guilt like a lifeline. She was already planning her next marriage to his best friend, Brad Temple, before the charges against my dad were even investigated. She broke his heart. She didn't give a shit about him or his arrest. He busted his ass and broke the law to provide the kind of lifestyle she demanded, and in return, she left him without a second glance." I cringe at the hatred in her tone as she continues. "I've wished every day that I found her hanging there instead of him, but I know that wish will get me nowhere. It's been eating away at me for the past four years."

Her heels collapse and she sinks down to sit on the soles of her feet as her hands splay open. The red roses roll out of her grip and scatter against the bottom of her father's gravestone. They're the only color against a bleak gray backdrop.

"I have to forgive him…and forgive *her*, or I'll rot away, just like they are. For four years I've let my wounds putrefy…" Her words spill forth as her eyes cast up toward the heart of the tree. The golden leaves rustle in the wind and I let their song comfort her rather than trying to stumble over some shitty condolence. She looks utterly spent, but the tears and the breakdown don't come.

I stand a few feet away, studying her intently. Small particles of dust swirl around her, visible only in the beams of light that break through the tree's canopy. The scene makes her truly look like a fallen angel, never meant for this world.

"Will you tell me more about him?" I ask, stepping forward and taking a seat next to her. My gut tells me she's kept him tucked away in her mind for the past four years. If it were me, I'd be brimming with untold memories.

Her eyes don't meet mine, but she falls back onto her butt and wraps her hands around her knees, staring wistfully toward his grave. "He was really silly when it was just us. To the rest of the world, he was a strict businessman, but around me he had the best sense of humor. His laugh was the first thing I let myself remember. It was so deep and passionate. He didn't hold anything back. If he was going to laugh, he wanted the entire world to laugh with him."

I smile, thinking of her infectious laugh. "You have that effect as well when you let yourself laugh."

Her eyes narrow and she rocks her body gently on top of the ground.

"I got most of my identity from him. You hear about children getting their features from one parent and their personality from the other, but not me. I'm the spitting image of my father in every way."

We sit at that cemetery the entire day. There must have been other visitors, but we didn't see or hear them. We stay in the private shade of that oak tree as I listen to Charley talk about her father. Her words are like the trickling of a faucet, slow and steady. She has so many memories to unravel and her eyes light up each time she remembers another happy time.

"The country club had a father-daughter dance each year." Her mouth curls into a sly smile as the memory overtakes her. "My mother insisted we attend, and every year my father and I would dress up in obnoxious matching outfits, take pictures at home…and then skip the whole thing entirely. We'd go see a movie or just sit in his car and share hamburgers and a milkshake. I don't know which one of us wanted to avoid the dance more, but it was clear that we were in it together." She fiddles with the stem of a rose, twisting it between her fingers and then placing it down in front of his grave once again.

"Did your mother ever find out?" I ask with a crooked smile, wishing I had been fortunate enough to meet her father, to shake his hand and thank him for being the love of his daughter's life when she needed him the most.

"The fifth year we skipped, one of her friends finally mentioned that she didn't see us 'in attendance'. My mother was livid and wouldn't stop huffing around the house. We tried to take it seriously—we didn't want to make her more upset—but we just couldn't stop laughing at the absurdity of the whole thing. You know when your whole body turns into a tight coil of laughs and the moment you glance at your accomplice, you laugh even more? That's how it was for weeks. God, we made her so mad."

Charley

The day turns to night and we finally pull ourselves up from the dry cemetery grass. It's strange that the world continued around us, that dusk still fell even though we stood still in that moment of profound relief.

By the time we reach the cemetery's gates, we still haven't called a cab.

"Can we just walk?" I ask, glancing up with a newfound contentment behind my gaze.

Jude's bright blue eyes flicker down to me. "We can, but it's a little over four miles. Is that okay?"

"Sounds perfect." I sigh and reach to lace my fingers with his.

We don't say a single word during that walk home. After speaking for so many hours, my thoughts are finally calm and silent. Cold wind whips my hair and rich autumn smells fill the air as we pass the coffee shop he took me to on our first date. His hand squeezes mine in silent recognition, and I tilt my body against him as we keep walking, wrapped around one another.

The farther we walk from the cemetery, the livelier the city blocks become. Bright lights flicker through windows and groups of teenagers huddle in front of stoops, their voices clamoring over one another to be heard. Each step away from his grave offers one more bit of peace, like I'm a snake shedding the skin that had weighed me down since his death. I'll never agree with my father's decision, but I can't wrestle with the past forever. My pace picks up as my lungs fill with deep, hopeful breaths. I can't go back now, and that knowledge spurs me forward, away from my darkest days.

Chapter twenty-three

Four Months Later
Charley

I HAVEN'T HAD a low day since we went to the cemetery. My life won't consist of cupcakes and sunshine, but the gray fog tinting everything with its murky haze has finally lifted. For the first time in four years, I don't feel like I'm breathing through corrupted lungs.

Revealing the truth was one of the hardest things I've ever done, but once I started, the words slipped out with an easy cadence, as if each syllable carried my broken heart away with them.

Jude and I have been inseparable ever since. The bond we forged that day in the cemetery can't be broken, and I'll be eternally grateful that he pushed me to take the next step. I have no doubt I would have eventually found my way to the light myself, but when I'm around Jude, my life glows brighter, and he led me there much quicker than if I had tried to find it on my own.

We're walking to meet Bennett and Naomi for brunch like we do most Sunday mornings. The air still holds a bit of a chill even though spring is starting to invade the city. I've never been a "spring" kind of girl, but this year, for once, my life seems to parallel the changing seasons. Jude's hand wraps around mine in a secure grip and I slide my gaze over to take him in. He's dressed down in worn jeans and a long sleeved t-shirt rolled up to his forearms. That short, sexy stubble is ever present, toughening his already gorgeous appearance. His soft blue eyes catch me staring and I smile wide, proud of being caught ogling the man I get to call mine.

"Can I help you, Ms. Whitlock?" he asks with a dubious smirk.

"Oh, I'm merely observing," I offer innocently. With a knowing smile, I turn back to the street, exuding confidence and ease. I wish we could sneak away somewhere before breakfast. Normally Jude wakes me up early enough that we can make love before starting the day, but we both overslept, leaving me desirous and greedy.

He narrows one of his eyes skeptically. "Mhm, yeah. Your eyes say differently."

My hip bumps into him teasingly. "Enlighten me."

He rubs his chiseled jaw. "They have a little heat behind them, like you want to cut this breakfast short."

I toss my head back and laugh because he's absolutely right. "You're lucky I let you leave the apartment at all."

"Mrs. Jenkins thinks I'm your sex slave," he teases with a wicked grin.

"What?! Yeah, right. She's half in love with you herself," I point out with raised brows.

He shrugs nonchalantly. "She didn't like me at first."

"Well, you brought me home drunk," I joke.

"That's not the way I remember it...but sure thing, Angel." He tugs me into his side, wrapping his arm around my waist.

I'd stay in this little cocoon all day if I could. "She's been hounding me about being home more," I admit as I recall our conversation from earlier this week. Most nights Jude and I stay together, but since his apartment has a king-sized bed, we usually end up staying there.

I feel his head nod above me. "Should I invite her to my apartment with us?"

I laugh. "She'd probably enjoy it."

"We'd get some of her awesome coffee cake," he points out, as if actually contemplating the silly idea.

"Sounds like a win-win."

Suddenly, his body stops propelling us forward and he tugs me back beneath the awning of a nearby shop.

"What is it?" I ask. The shop hasn't opened yet and the security bars clink together behind us as I stare up toward him. His expression is completely indiscernible, but I quell the nerves beginning to spread through me.

He tugs a hand through his unruly hair and I fight the urge to twirl my finger through the strands in his wake. "Charley, before we get there, I need to talk to you about something."

"Wow. That sounds ominous," I quip, trying to lighten the mood, but my eyebrows still bunch together in concern. "What's up?"

He takes a deep breath and wraps his arms around my waist, connecting our lower bodies. His hand starts rubbing small circles on my back as he speaks. "You know how the magazine called me last month to offer me a freelance position?"

"Yes…" I answer hesitantly, no longer able to push the uneasiness aside. He's *leaving*. When they called, I knew he would have to leave, but I didn't think it would be so soon.

He squeezes me closer, his charming gaze never faltering. "They talked to me about another opportunity, and I want to get your opinion about it."

"You can't l-leave," I stutter, already preparing for the worst-case scenario. Way to play it cool, Charley.

"Charley, pause." His leans down to kiss me softly, but he pulls away before I can fully lose myself in the taste of him. "You haven't even heard everything yet."

I take a deep breath. "Okay. I'm listening."

"They want me to do a three-month assignment overseas. I'll be traveling through various countries, but I said I would only go if I could bring along an *assistant* of sorts."

My eyes go wide. Please bring me. Please say you want me to come. "What? Who are you taking with you?"

He glances down from my eyes toward my lips, and then a cheeky grin breaks across his face. "I'm *only* going if you come with me. It's nonnegotiable."

"But I—" I begin to protest, for no other reason than it seems too good to be true.

"Am painting," he finishes for me. "You have enough saved from your photo shoots and you told me you wanted to take the next year off. What if you traveled with me? You could paint along the way. We could ship your canvases home as we go."

I absorb his words. It's too good to be true. How is this my life?

He bends down, kissing the skin beneath my ear and

making me break out in a bloom of goose bumps. "All I know is I'm not going without you."

Holy hell.

"Where would we go first?" I ask, buying myself more time to process everything.

"We'd fly into Rome." He kisses me gently. His minty breath captures me under his spell and I feel my toes curl inside my boots.

"Then?"

"Greece." He gives me a peck. "Turkey," he says, adding another kiss. "Syria, Egypt, then around to Morocco, Spain, and France."

A shiver runs down my spine as his mouth possesses me, and I know my voice sounds shaky as I ask, "Is your assignment just around the Mediterranean?"

"Yes. I'll be shooting for a piece they're writing about urbanization on the coast of the Mediterranean Sea. While I'm there I'll have small assignments along the way, but we'll be traveling at our own pace. After I get the photos I need at each location, we can explore until we're ready to move on to the—"

I cut him off midway through his sentence as I leap up into his arms. My mind was made up the moment he said he was leaving the country, but I had to let it sink in. My arms wrap around his neck and my feet dangle a foot or so off the ground as he holds me like a ragdoll. "Yes. Absolutely yes. When do we leave?"

"You'll come with me?"

"Yes!"

His dimpled grin melts my heart and his blue eyes dance with excitement. "I haven't confirmed with them, but it would be within the next few weeks. We can arrange everything with your apartment before then."

This is happening. We're going abroad together.

"I'm so excited." Then a sudden realization sinks in. "Why did you need to tell me before we met up with Bennett and Naomi?"

His smile widens. "I want them to meet us in one of the destinations and I'm planning to bring it up at breakfast. The magazine just confirmed everything yesterday, and I couldn't work up the nerve to ask you until just now."

"Because you thought I'd say no?"

His gaze penetrates mine with easy confidence. "Oh, no," he answers confidently. "If you had said no, I would have just invited Mrs. Jenkins." He waggles his eyebrows playfully.

"Jude!" I swat his arm, hitting solid muscle, and he drops me back onto my feet then takes off down the street with his hand outstretched for me to latch on to. The early morning sun encases him like a golden backdrop and I have to hold my hands over my eyes like a visor to make out his silhouette.

"C'mon! We're gonna be late for breakfast, slowpoke," he yells back to me, but I don't budge. I stand there, telling myself to remember this moment always, knowing my life will never be the same.

The smile that forms on my lips nearly splits my cheeks in half as I try to contain every emotion short-circuiting through me. I was so used to the gloom, the loneliness, the pain, the fog, but this is the exact opposite.

This is blissful oblivion.

Behind His Lens

46828058R00174

Printed in Poland
by Amazon Fulfillment
Poland Sp. z o.o., Wrocław